Frank Preston Stearns

Modern English Prose Writers

Frank Preston Stearns

Modern English Prose Writers

ISBN/EAN: 9783337386412

Printed in Europe, USA, Canada, Australia, Japan

Cover: Foto ©Andreas Hilbeck / pixelio.de

More available books at **www.hansebooks.com**

MODERN ENGLISH PROSE WRITERS

WITH THE

COMPLIMENTS OF THE AUTHOR

———

G. P. PUTNAM'S SONS
NEW YORK & LONDON
The Knickerbocker Press
1897

The Knickerbocker Press, New York

The Knickerbocker Press, New York

PREFACE

IT is time to take a review of the century. Periods of history are not usually confined within even and symmetrical dates, but the present era clearly began with the appointment of Napoleon as sole consul in the year 1800. How much longer it will last no wise person will predict, but the present decade seems so quiet and uneventful, that it reminds one of those periods of uncertain weather which precede the gathering of a storm. It has been an era of scientific discoveries, commercial enterprise, and mechanical inventions. The century has also witnessed terrific political convulsions; and it has given birth to a literature distinguished for its originality, its delicacy, and boldness of expression. A review of what has been accomplished since the year 1800, could not be condensed into one volume, or perhaps into twenty. Every department of art, science, and literature, as well as politics, economics, etc., would have to be represented. The results of science and economics can be abbreviated: not so with literature and art. Here a full statement is essential to a just understanding of the subject. Criticism itself is literature, and amenable to the laws of prose composition. The object of the present volume is to give a thorough account of the most eminent and influential prose-writers who have flourished in England during this epoch. Biographies of most of them are already before the public; and what we are concerned with here is the character and quality of the work they performed.

CONTENTS.

MODERN ENGLISH PROSE WRITERS

It is a pleasure to stand upon the shore, and to see ships tossed
upon the sea; a pleasure to stand in the window of a castle, and see
a battle and the adventures thereof below : but no pleasure is comparable to the standing upon the vantage ground of Truth (a hill not to
be commanded, and where the air is always clear and serene), and to
see the errors, and wanderings, and mists, and tempests, in the
vale below.

LORD BACON.

The foolish think as they will : the wise will as they think.

WASSON.

Modern English Prose Writers

INTRODUCTION

IT is generally recognized that English literature in the eighteenth century was by no means equal to that of the French, either in its artistic quality, or its influence on civilization; and still less favorably does it appear when compared with the somewhat later German literature. In the nineteenth century, however, it has again retaken its position as foremost among all nations; abounding in a good number of the finest poets, and in excellent prose-writers, too numerous to be easily counted. In critical and historical work, the Germans still continue to lead the world, and I notice that most of the foot-notes in Hallam's *Middle Ages* refer to French authorities; but in Germany, Heine has proved the only poet comparable to Byron or Tennyson, and France has not produced a novelist equal to Thackeray or George Eliot. The next place ought properly to be assigned to American literature, which if it had received equal encouragement might have pushed the mother country to a pretty close race.

The distinguishing character of the best literature of the present century both in England and America, has been freedom and variety of style, almost bordering on eccentricity. If we look through the best English writers of the eighteenth century, we find differences of style, it is true, but nothing like the difference between Tennyson and Browning, between Carlyle and Froude, or between Emerson and Lowell. And this, on the whole, is to be considered an advantage; indicating a larger liberality of thought, and independence of judgment. The greatest painters are those who have the most decided peculiarities of style. Small hills all look alike, but every mountain peak has an outline of its own. A Titian was never mistaken for a Raphael, nor a Correggio for a Van Dyck. A characteristic style is only possible through character; and as soon as literature becomes conventional and impersonal its best qualities of authorship have departed from it. It requires rare courage to write in a style like Browning's or Emerson's. It requires courage enough to publish any book with the consciousness of what Mr. Snigidibs is likely to say about it; but to publish a book to which critics of every class are likely to be opposed, may be compared to the French cavalry charge at Sedan.

Among so many excellent prose-writers, how are we to distinguish those who are of superior and enduring value ? Matthew Arnold made a classification between Aristotle as a great philosopher, and Cicero as a great writer. Plato was both. The distinction lies between those who are artists in their particular line, and those who are not. Lord Bacon holds the first rank among English philosophical writers, but his *Essays* and his *History of Henry VII.* are also fine literature. John S. Mill and Herbert Spencer are celebrated for their philosophical works, and they also wrote very good English, but we can hardly call it literature. By the same rule we dispose of a good number of historians. Greene's *History* is a useful condensation, but its very condensation prevents it from having a value as art. The historical researches of Mr. Freeman will always be valuable, but he lacks style as a writer, and has injured his work by the adoption of impracticable political theories. Professor Seelye's *History of Prussia* during the dictatorship of Von Stein is a valuable book though somewhat verbose, but his *Life of Napoleon* can only be designated as an obstinate effort to distort and even falsify history. If we take Von Holst, who has written the best history of American politics, as a standard to measure by, we find only three—Macaulay, Carlyle, and Froude —who equal or surpass him.

Darwin, Huxley, and Tyndall are admirable writers of scientific prose, and something more than that. They have almost created a literature of science—if that were possible,—and Tyndall, especially, has gleams of true imagination. The consideration of their work, however, belongs properly to scientific records, and not to the present treatise.

Of novelists there has been a prodigious number, whose productions range all the way from trash to the very highest merit. Lord Lytton, Charles

Kingsley, Charles Reade, Miss Sheppard, Charlotte Brontë, Disraeli, Wilkie Collins, Anthony Trollope, Jane Austen, George MacDonald, Miss Muloch, have all written interesting books; and there may be others. *The Caxtons* may pass, perhaps, for a classic, though more like Lucan than Horace. *Jane Eyre* offers an example of womanly devotion as rare in English literature (at least since Shakespeare's time) as the *Alcestes* of Euripides. *Christie Johnstone*, which was greatly admired by Emerson, though it has some of the faults of Macaulay's essays, is a bright, spirited story. *John Halifax* was the first, and is, I believe, the best of Miss Mulock's stories, and certainly worth reading. Collins and Trollope are keen, sensible writers, and furnish us with pleasant pictures of English home life. *Charles Auchester* stands by itself, and illustrates the power which fine music has to mould the lives of men and women. *Counterparts* is even a more remarkable story; the only instance in English fiction where human nature is treated independently, as it is in *Wilhelm Meister*, of all arbitrary rules. Disraeli's novels are strongly artificial, and their art is made subservient to political purposes. They have a kind of nickel-plated character, but they are also very bright, and his exposition of the methods by which modern Catholicism makes converts will go into the archives of religious history.*

* A well-known American lady, who was converted in Rome more than twenty years ago, wrote, while her mind was still doubtful, a number of letters on religious tenets to her former pastor in New York City. These letters never reached him, while those to other friends in America were duly received.

Disraeli's writing is not art, but an exercise of ingenuity.

If, however, we compare any of the foregoing with Scott, Dickens, Thackeray, or George Eliot, we find them not only at a disadvantage in their knowledge of human nature, but also suffering from some other deficiency which causes them to fall short of true greatness. Charles Reade has a brusque, feverish, and at times sensational method of expressing himself. Miss Muloch frequently becomes common, and fails to explain, sufficiently, those transitions from one event to another, by which the movement of a story is preserved. Miss Sheppard lacked practical experience; and Miss Austen, according to her own confession, wrote on an ivory tablet with a diamond pen,—that is, she is perfect in a narrow sphere. It is not easy to find fault with Collins and Trollope, and I suppose critics would place them next to Dickens. They are exempt, it is true, from some of Dickens's faults, but, at the same time, they never rise above a certain level. They have not Dickens's deep sympathy with the poor and oppressed; nor do they feel Thackeray's finer sympathy for noble natures, in their struggles and trials with the more brutal sort of humanity. There is a fault in Kingsley's writing known to musicians as *bravura*. *Hypatia* is a brilliant historical novel, but German critics have called him to account for his unwarrantable injustice to Hypatia herself.

Harriet Martineau was a vigorous writer and her book on Egypt has even a kind of scenic grandeur; but her philanthropic writings are too strongly prejudiced.   They served their purpose and may now be dismissed.

In the literature of art, Ruskin stands alone. Eastlake, Walter Pater, and Mr. Crowe are more trustworthy critics, but they do not possess a tithe of Ruskin's insight and eloquence.

John H. Newman and Francis W. Newman remind one of the story of the two friends who had started to go around the world in different directions, trusting that they would meet on the opposite side of the globe.   Where one member of a family develops some special trait of character, and makes a point of cultivating it, it often happens that some other member is affected in precisely the opposite manner.   These two brothers, whose elevated lives have been the admiration of their countrymen during the present century, would seem to have differed chiefly in independence of character.

Francis Newman had a mind of his own.   He was a devoted student, a thorough investigator, and formed opinions for himself on all subjects, religious, political, and social.   He neither lacked courage in uttering his views, nor consistency in maintaining them.   It is likely that he missed in this way the influence he might have possessed over his own people; for men are obliged to act in masses, if their action is to be of any effect.   His writing is clear, cool-headed, analytical, and penetrating,—by no means brilliant or impressive.

J. H. Newman was more of an artist than his brother, and far more sympathetic.   He was often an eloquent speaker, his writing has a more distinguished style, and he was consequently more popular; but he lacked independence of character. He commenced his public career as a faithful vassal of the Church of England, and closed it as an humble servant of the Church of Rome. To trace the course of this mental and moral transition, would be a valuable study, but this is not the place for it. What we have to show here is, that the man was not only inconsistent in the beginning and the end of his life; that his life was not only illogical and contradictory as a whole, but also was inconsistent in detail; and that despite his superior nature and rare talent,—in spite of his long-continued public activity, and the eloquent memorials he has left of it,—Cardinal Newman's work belongs to the past, and does not form an ingredient in the solid stock of English literature.

It is inevitable that a young writer should be aggressive, and attempt to win his spurs by attacking the supposed abuses of his time. It is the conflict between the old and the new; but the manner in which he does this is often significant of his future usefulness. The question is, whether he shivers his lance like Wendell Phillips against a true national evil, or like Don Quixote tilts against a wind mill. The following extract will give some apprehension of the way in which J. H. Newman attempted it.

"We must deal with the Church of Rome as we would toward a friend who is visited by derangement; in great affliction, with all affectionate tender thoughts, with tearful regret and a broken heart, but still with a steady eye and a firm hand. For in truth she is a Church beside herself, abounding in noble gifts and rightful titles, but unable to use them religiously ; crafty, obstinate, wilful, malicious, cruel, unnatural, as madmen are. Or rather, she may be said to resemble a demoniac ; possessed with principles, thought, and tendencies, not her own, in outward form and in outward powers what God made her, but ruled within by an inexorable spirit, who is sovereign in his management over her, and most subtle and most successful in the use of her gifts. Then she is her real self only in name, and, till God vouchsafe to restore her, we must treat her as if she were that evil one which governs her.

Such intemperate poetizing is excusable in times of great public agitation, but the Catholic Church never assumed a more modest and unaggressive attitude in Great Britain than between 1830 and 1840, when this address was delivered. We have only to look around us, in our own families, to perceive the good which Catholicism accomplishes. It serves as a light and a path to the uneducated now, as it served them during the dark ages, when the Church of St. Peter was the only hope of civilization. In country districts, it is true, the poorer classes can generally find gospel comfort, but in the cities Catholicism is their only refuge. At least in American cities it is so.

Twenty years later we find Cardinal Newman lecturing on education from the Catholic point of view. In true course he treats of Abelard, who may fairly be called the founder of modern education. Gladstone speaks of him as a transcendent genius; and it was the impetus which he gave to the University of Paris that placed it in a position before all others. He introduced *reason* into mediæval life; he was to the twelfth century, what Luther and Melanchthon were to the sixteenth. France has not yet produced a greater man.

Cardinal Newman does not recognize the whole of Abelard's actuality, but he sees a large portion of it, and he tells us himself how men thronged from all countries to listen to him and be instructed by him,—how the crowd followed him from Paris into the provinces, and built tabernacles for him to lecture in. Yet he considers Abelard's life a failure, on account of the Héloise incident and some heretical ideas which he propounded. Cardinal Newman concludes as follows:

" In reviewing his career, the career of so great an intellect so miserably thrown away, we are reminded of the famous words of the dying scholar and jurist, which are a lesson to us all '*Heu, vitam perdidi, operose nihil agendo*'—A happier lot be ours!"

This last invocation does not appear to have been granted. What this heresy was, would be a most interesting item to us, but the Cardinal prudently refrains from making it known. It could not have been serious, for Abelard was never punished for it. In like manner the Héloise incident ought to be regarded in much the same light as Goethe's marriage; but even if we regard it, as it was considered by his co-temporaries, the evil it occasioned was but an ounce in the scale compared with the weight of good which he accomplished. Cardinal Newman's conclusion is sophistical and pusillanimous.

There are numerous beautiful passages in his writing,—fine idyllic descriptions of life and character,—but their æsthetic quality does not compensate for the lack of those traits which would give it enduring value. The self-contradictory nature of the man constantly reappears, and mars the tissue of his thought. With all his brilliant rhetoric, his English is not always of the purest, being too colloquial, in many places, for the gravity of his subject. In one of his essays I noticed a sentence more than a page in length, and before I reached the end of it I had forgotten the beginning. People do not write in that manner for any honest purpose.

Justin McCarthy is of opinion, that the influence of Francis Newman, though not so widely extended, was really more potent than that of his brother. The present age is one in which people care much more for reason than they do for sentiment; an orator impresses them for the time being, but it is the cool-headed logician who finally carries the day. Froude, Thackeray, Tennyson, Browning, and even Matthew Arnold (though he would have resented the obligation), as well as many other public leaders, were all indebted to him for their first mental impetus. He was the chief of the party of Disestablishment; and it certainly seems a national injustice that whole cities and counties of men, as in Ireland and Wales, should be obliged to pay taxes for a creed which they do not profess. His favorite argument was, to point to the United States of America, where, as he said, all the religious sects exist as in Great Britain, but they are self-supporting, and in no respect dependent on the patronage of the civil authority. It were well if we could consider in this connection Webster's well-deserved eulogy in the Girard Will case on the character of the American clergy, and the efficiency of our system of religious worship. A German writer, however, complains that American ministers of the gospel are too much under the influence of prominent parishioners. This, no doubt, is true in certain cases; but men like Channing, Beecher, Manning and Phillips Brooks have certainly enjoyed all the freedom they could wish for in the pulpit.

It is doubtful if either of the Newmans was capable of perceiving more than one side of a question; an unfortunate deficiency where great social and political problems are concerned. Francis Newman thinks that the Reformation arose through the development of nationalities, and the spirit of patriotism in England and Germany. He should rather have said, that nationalities gave the Reformation a basis and a sustaining force. His suggestion is a valuable one; but we know that it was the irreligious spirit, and selfish levity of the higher Roman prelates, which led directly to the revolt in Germany. Good Catholics have admitted that their Church was at that time in a sadly demoralized condition.

Buckle ought, perhaps, to be considered with English historians, but judged by the character of his work he belongs with Cardinal Newman. Physical causes are too narrow a basis to build a philosophy of history upon; and the writer who attempts to prove that in history " all is order, symmetry, and law, and that the movements of nations are solely determined by their antecedents " has a most difficult task before him.   It was the difficulty of this undertaking, as some suppose, that killed Mr. Buckle.   It is impossible to escape the personal element in history; and though the laws of cause and effect are in constant operation, the value of an individual will, in certain cases, cannot be overestimated.   What would Prussia have been without Frederick, or the United States without Washington and Hamilton ? Let us suppose Bismarck to have been on the throne of France in 1870, and Louis Napoleon or some such person Chancellor of Prussia.   Would history have been the same under such conditions ?   The true historian does not find symmetry in history, but quite the reverse.   The most glorious of human achievements have often an unfinished character.

If there is any author to whom I do injustice, by the neglect of an elaborate criticism and express valuation of his merits, it is De Quincey.   It is long since I have heard his name mentioned in literary conclaves, but Stopford Brooke says of him: " Thomas De Quincey was, among the miscellaneous writers of his time, the greatest master of English prose.   De Quincey's style has so peculiar a quality that it stands alone.   The sentences are built up like passages in a fugue, and there is nothing in

English literature which can be compared in involved melody to the prose of the *Confessions of an English Opium Eater.* One man alone in our own day is as great a master of English prose—John Ruskin." This is pretty near the truth. De Quincey's sentences are so laced together that, like a yacht in racing canvas, he caught all the popular breezes of his own time. There is a keenness and flexibility to his style, which is more French than English, and suggests that the prefix to his name may have brought with it a genuine Gallic quality. If Thackeray's satire may be compared to the acid of a lemon, we might say that the pleasant flavor of De Quincey is not unlike the juice of a lime. I am informed that a new edition of his writings has lately been published, and I trust it will be appreciated, and that he will long continue to be read.

At the same time there is not much more to be said of him. His writings have a varied character, and do not form a complete whole. His account of Coleridge, like Boswell's life of Johnson, is more valuable now than Coleridge's own prose; but he did not, like Boswell, make a complete statement of the man. De Quincey did not accomplish a work which can be called intrinsically great. He was not, like Macaulay, a writer of great virtues and great faults; nor did he come, like Carlyle, with a great lesson to mankind; nor, like Froude, could he see clearly into the labyrinth of political affairs. He is essentially a writer for private life,—for the fireside, and the quiet, winter evening. He does not belong to the great outside world.

Much the same may be said of Charles Lamb. He is a humorist, but not a Cervantes. If there is an English prose-writer of whom it would be difficult to decide whether he belonged within or without the pale of English classics, Lamb would be the one. He was a domestic person, and his mild, gentle temperament constrained him to a limited acquaintance, and an equally limited knowledge of the world. A neighbor of mine, for whom I have most sincere respect as a man of character and ability, once delivered a lecture on Charles Lamb as a humorist, and perhaps, if I could read it now, I might have more to say. It may be my own idiosyncrasy, but a book like Crabbe Robinson's *Diary* is much more interesting to me than the essays in *Elia.*

If any one writer has been included in the present volume, who ought properly to be omitted, it is Matthew Arnold. Doubtless there are some who will think he does not deserve the distinction of being placed with Thackeray and Ruskin, at least for what he has published in prose. His writings are scattered, and no collection of them has yet been made: the books he has published are few in number. Yet I believe Matthew Arnold succeeded where the Newmans failed. He was too fastidious to be always a just critic, but he possessed the rare faculty of looking at a subject in which he was interested from different points of view. He surpassed Francis Newman in breadth, and Cardinal Newman in sincerity. He was a power in his day, and it was not the power of his own personality, but of the truth that he uttered. He made mistakes, but he atoned for them. He did not draw from the English lakes, but from the great ocean. His mind was of the cosmopolitan order; and the qualities which gave his writing value, during his life, will continue to make it vital and influential in time to come.

De Quincey and Charles Lamb require no explanation. They are excellent writers, but not profound, and show for just what they are. It is otherwise with Carlyle, Ruskin, and Matthew Arnold, who sank their plummets deep in the past, and drew their resources not from their own country alone, but from many others.

Walter Savage Landor bears nearly the same relation to Matthew Arnold that Charles Reade does to George Eliot. As Joubert says of Madame De Staël, he had more vehemence than truth, and more heat than light. His *Pericles and Aspasia* is interesting, but in rather a fanciful manner; for it has neither the dignity of history nor the charm of imaginative work. Lowell says that he was " emphatically a *man*," and we may judge from this, that he had plenty of courage and self-confidence, but the rashness of his judgment appears in his estimation of Napoleon III.—" a much greater person than the first Napoleon."

HISTORICAL INTRODUCTION

IN the archives of literature there is nothing so rare as a great historian. You can almost count them on your fingers. How many glorious poets there were among the Greeks; and who are their historians? Only Herodotus, Thucydides, and, perhaps, Plutarch can be classed among writers of the first rank. In the Latin tongue we have Livy, Tacitus, and Cæsar's *Commentaries*. Tacitus says, " The affairs of the republic have been written by many and good historians "; but few of these have been preserved to us, and even the names of the others are unknown. Sallust and Josephus are celebrated because they have no rivals.

Macchiavelli was a great writer; but his *History of Florence*, though invaluable, is rather dry reading, and not what it might have been. The same may be said of Hume's *History of England*, which is written in a grand style but not based on original investigations. It has been stated with some justice that the best history of England previous to the Reformation is to be found in Shakespeare's plays. Bacon wrote his history of Henry VII. as if to fill the gap between Richard III. and Henry VIII. Except Thucydides, no other writer of equal genius has paid much attention to history. It would seem as if he had written it under too much constraint, so that the undercurrent of English political life which we would most like to know, is not to be found in it.

Gibbon was the first of historians to treat his subject in a modern style, and there are those who consider him the first in rank.   He not only wrote from documentary evidence, but brought to his subject a mental method trained by intellectual culture, and ripened by philosophical study.   A history like Motley's *Rise of the Dutch Republic*, which is based merely upon popular opinion, can never satisfy thinking men as an explanation of the course of human affairs. Unfortunately, Gibbon's philosophy was not profound enough, nor his insight quite clear enough, for the work he undertook; and the subject still remains the most mysterious, difficult, and important to which the human mind can apply itself. Besides this, Gibbon's style, though vigorous and impressive, is not one of the best, and his love of rhetoric sometimes launched him into statements which will not stand a fair-minded inquiry. I remember especially his saying that the " long reign of Justinian was disgraced by war, pestilence, and famine." Now the wars of Justinian, his destruction of the Vandal kingdom in Africa and the Gothic kingdom in Italy, were much to the advantage of civilization; and as for the pestilence which devastated Asia Minor during his reign, Justinian can no more be held responsible for it than he could for an earthquake. The real disgrace of his reign was his unjust treatment of Belisarius.

Voltaire is a great historian of the artistic order; though he never troubled himself over-carefully with regard to his facts. Thiers also knew how to poetize, and it is doubtful if he can be considered really great. Where he and Napoleon both describe the same circumstances, the superiority of the latter, even as a writer, is plainly apparent. Neither is Guizot a writer of the best quality. Sismondi, Michelet, and others have made invaluable researches on which Hallam largely depended for his account of the Middle Ages.

In Germany there are many and excellent historians, who are noted for their thoroughness, breadth of statement, and intellectual veracity. Foremost among them is Mommsen, who may fairly be called great. Von Ranke is also justly celebrated; and Dr. Von Holst, who has given to the world the most satisfactory account of the foundation of our government and our political conflict over the slavery question, comes very close to both. The best histories of Greece, of Rome, of the Reformation, and of the French Revolution are to be sought for in the German language, though many of them are now translated into English. German historians, however, are almost invariably university professors, and their writings lack that pleasant flavor of practical activity which belongs to men of the world.

Among all these, Thucydides still holds the first place. He has been called the most impartial of historians, the most graphic, the most original, etc.; but his true excellence consists mainly in this, that he was a man of genius. That distinguishes him from Herodotus, Xenophon, Sallust, and nearly all modern historians.   It has been said of Mozart's *Don Giovanni* that the first notes of the orchestra lift the hearers above themselves, and so sustain them until the green curtain falls again.   So it is with Shakespeare, and Homer, except in the catalogue of ships, and Thucydides,—in whose first paragraph we feel the strong hand, and are willing to follow him wherever he may lead us.   Like a great artist, he disposes the light and shade of his narrative, and fills in the lines of life between with firmness and truth.   We all know what Demosthenes owed to him; but statesmen and orators still go to him for inspiration and instruction, and the plenitude of his wisdom has not yet become the common property of mankind.

The possession of genius implies imagination; and persons who have that gift are not often attracted to history.   They either become drawn into the vortex of practical affairs, or more frequently escape into the ideal region of art, poetry, and fiction. Pegasus does not like being harnessed to a diligence. The examination and comparison of public records, old documents, speeches, and opinions in different languages may be compared to travelling in a hot sun on a dusty road.   This was literally what Herodotus and Thucydides were obliged to do. They had few documents to consult, but they obtained their information from various individuals in different places, and not without dangers and difficulty.   Schiller twice attempted to become an historian, but the occupation was not suited to him, and his collection of materials for an account of the

Thirty Years' War served instead for the magnificent drama of *Wallenstein.*

Carlyle thought that not until geniuses of the highest order give their undivided attention to history will mankind be benefited by the lesson which it has for us, and which lies concealed in it. It is to be hoped that a writer will yet arise who shall be as great an historian as Michel Angelo was an artist. Without history, the human race would be as it was originally, like one lost in a wilderness. At present we grope our way into the unknown, trusting to profit by the mistakes of our ancestors, but without any very clear foresight of the pitfalls and dangers which lie before us.

MACAULAY

AFTER the confusion produced by the general overturn of 1793, and the wars consequent on it in both Europe and America, two men of exceptional ability appeared in either continent whose mission it was to bring back the minds of men to a clear understanding of orderly and constitutional government. There was urgent need of this, for the severe strain of continual warfare had produced a twofold effect: of despotic concentration in the conduct of public affairs among the higher classes of society, and a tendency to insurrection and disorderly conduct among the lower. The battle of Waterloo had nearly extinguished the germs of constitutional government on the continent of Europe, and though it still survived in England, there was danger that, through the immense prestige of the Duke of Wellington, with his military notions, and with the help of the rotten-borough system, parliament would become as subservient to the monarchy as it had been during the Henrys and Edwards, or as the Roman senate was during the reign of Augustus. In America, the arrogant usurpations of Jackson, which were supported by a majority of the people, showed a decided tendency to imperialism, as well as disrespect for constitutional form and sound legal procedure. These two evils tended to exaggerate and intensify each other; and it was evident to far-sighted minds that society would before long become divided against itself, and civil war must ensue. This came to pass in Europe *directly*, in 1848, and in America *indirectly* in 1861. England was the only civilized country that escaped, and this was due chiefly to the just temperance of Lord Grey and other leaders of the Whig party.

The two men referred to are Webster and Macaulay, who, with some decided differences of character, were on the whole very much alike. They were even alike in their geographical extraction. Webster came from the granite ridges of New Hampshire, with an intellect keen as mountain air, and making his way with the force of a mountain torrent. As quick-witted as he was untiring, of enormous force physically and mentally, he yet possessed an artistic nature, and surpassed other men not only by his natural vigor but by the graceful form of his discourse. Macaulay also came from the north and is supposed to have descended from the sea-roving Norsemen who formed a colony among the Scottish isles in the tenth or eleventh century. He had a remarkable faculty for acquiring and reproducing knowledge; and easily won the first places at the university, in London society, and in political life. They were both possessed with such remarkable advantages that among other men they were like what ordinary men are among boys; and the only credit they deserved for their success was that of not wasting their opportunities.

Webster was the abler of the two, and more distinctively a genius. He was not only a better orator than Macaulay, but a more elegant writer, and might have been a greater historian if he had turned his activity in that direction. He is rather copious, as is the nature of orators, but the classic purity of his sentences (for the most part) appears to advantage beside Macaulay's often too highly stimulated rhetoric. Otherwise their mental methods were very similar. They excelled other writers of their time in logic, and in the skill with which they presented their subject. They themselves not only could see clearly into a confused and complicated matter, but could disentangle its various elements and cause others to perceive it as clearly as themselves. This is the true basis of both oratory and history. They were not constructive thinkers, but discursive. They had a wonderful faculty of exposition, and their longest sentences have a clear ring.

Webster's interest in practical affairs never abated until his death. He always continued to hope for the accomplishment of great designs. Macaulay, however, seems to have been dissatisfied with his success in politics, and wisely retired from public life to the contemplation of history and literature. He thus failed of obtaining such influence as Webster wielded in his own time, but was compensated for it by a more enduring influence on posterity. What they both lacked was the poetic element, or we might say, perhaps, the dramatic.

Their form of statement is linear, with a tendency to become monotonous. Neither do we respect their characters as men so much as we admire their abilities. They were fond of show, of ceremonial dinners, and an exaggerated mode of life. We do not think of them as we do of Washington and Canning. Especially we ought to reprobate Macaulay's fondness for scandal, and his readiness to circulate idle calumnies.

Schiller composed an ingenious philosophic poem called the " Three Words of Error," and in it he says that no man will be wise—

> " So long as he dreams of an earthly place
>   Where the good are peacefully dwelling ;
>   For the good a merciless fight must wage,
>   The demon of darkness in quelling."

It is in this continuous conflict that human nature finds its true evolution. Muscles require exercise so that the body may be healthy, and how are they to obtain it without some object of resistance? The intellect requires resistance and even contention quite as much, and so does the moral sense. A mechanical morality is no virtue at all, and it is fortunate for the human race that there are differences of opinion and of religious belief; even if these lead to domestic quarrels and to those national quarrels which are called wars.

It is this struggle of the individual externally and internally which has formed the perpetual theme of poetry and fiction; and it is a similar struggle in the whole community which makes the proper subject of history. The dramatic poet may represent historical events as reflected in the minds of prominent public actors, but it belongs to the historian to deal directly with those grand phenomena, to analyze their character, discover the causes of their origin, and represent their influence on the fortunes not only of individuals but of nations and races.

Gibbon was a better historian than Hume, for he made a thorough investigation of such materials as he could obtain for his subject ; but Macaulay was the first English writer who gave to history a decisively modern character. Gibbon could consult no authentic documents for his work, and Hume apparently made no attempt to do so; but even the mendacious despatch of a foreign ambassador is of more real value to a subsequent investigator, than the unsupported statement of a cotemporary who pretends to construct history himself. Macaulay, like Thucydides (whom he venerated above all others), did not attempt to cover too large a space of time, but confined himself to a definite period of English history, which forms an epoch by itself and seems to be almost complete in itself. It was a period particularly interesting to Macaulay, for it signalized the triumph of constitutional government and liberal theology in England, and the escape from the intolerant belief and antiquated political methods of the middle ages. For this work he made the most thorough preparation, and it was one well calculated for popularity, since there is no other portion of their history of which Englishmen are more proud, although it was not, on the whole, an era of prosperity and chronicles no great national actions. It is commonly referred to as the " glorious revolution of 1688."

Macaulay paid slight attention to form, except in the construction of sentences. He went straight forward like an ocean steamer with barely a pause for his reader to take breath in. He wrote some of the longest chapters on record. The first chapter of his history is one hundred and sixty pages in length, and contains a review of English civilization from the time of the Druids until the restoration of the Stuarts. His second chapter, in which he gave a sketchy account of the reign of Charles II., is a hundred pages in length. George Eliot remarks in her diary that the worst writing Macaulay ever perpetrated was " the introduction to his introduction "; though it could not have been more faulty than some of his earlier essays. His first chapter is not based on original study, but merely contains his reflections on early English history taken from the Anglo-Saxon chronicle and such other books as were convenient to his hand. The first half of it may be easily omitted, but the latter portion is interesting from his clear analysis of the disagreement between Charles I. and the Long Parliament, and also for his eloquent tribute to Cromwell, concerning whom he held an opinion in close agreement with Carlyle's. In the second chapter he gives an account of the course of events through which the change of government took place after Cromwell's death, and this is one of the most interesting passages in the whole work—very remarkable for its clearness and accuracy of statement.

Macaulay came too early to reap the advantage, which all the world has since derived, from German thought and literature. He never was broadened and deepened by what Taine calls the " grand ideas of Hegel and Goethe." Nothing could have astonished him so much as to have been informed that in the latter half of the nineteenth century a knowledge of the German language would be considered as indispensable to a liberal education as Greek or Latin. There was a prejudice at that time in English fashionable society against everything German, except the wines and scenery of the Rhine land, and Macaulay was not quite the man to surmount such an obstacle; but he had the true spirit of a scholar, and would gladly have welcomed a valid extension of the range of human knowledge. Hegel's philosophic examination of the Oriental religions would have greatly interested him, for he would himself have brought to the subject the experience and reflections of a long sojourn in India. The central position of Germany is an advantage to the Germans,—just as a man stationed in the centre of a hall can perceive the objects in it more clearly and comprehend their relative positions better than one that is standing in a corner.

The limitation rather than the fault of Macaulay's history, as it has been of less important English writers, is that he treats the history of his country as if it was separate from and nearly independent of the rest of Europe. We have seen how, within the last thirty years successive British ministries have been overthrown by the influence of foreign events. The success of republicanism in America, proved by the war for the Union, carried Gladstone into power, and the Franco-German war carried him out again. Every one of Napoleon's great victories upset a ministry at Westminster; and the care-worn Pitt is supposed to have been used up by the battle of Austerlitz.   In the seventeenth century the relations between England and the other great countries were not so close nor the tension so severe, but the policy of France or Holland often had a disturbing effect on domestic affairs of the United Kingdom; and in addition there were always more subtile powers at work affecting the habits and thoughts of men insensibly throughout the civilized world.

To go back to the original disagreement between Charles I. and his Parliament, which was the egg whence three distinct revolutions were hatched, we find that Macaulay attributes the occasion of the difficulty to the peculiar character of the king himself.   He sums it up in a celebrated period as follows:

"Faithlessness was the chief cause of his disasters, and is the chief stain on his memory.   There is reason to believe he was perfidious, not only from constitution and from habit, but on principle.   He seems to have learned from theologians whom he most esteemed that between him and his subjects there could be nothing of the nature of a mutual contract, that he could not, even if he would, divest himself of his despotic authority, and that in every promise which he made there was an implied reservation that such promise might be broken in case of necessity, and that of necessity he was the sole judge."

As a piece of vivid character-drawing, this is worthy of Fielding or Molière; but what ground has Macaulay for supposing it to be the true diagnosis of Charles the First's character. He gives no testimony from cotemporary witnesses to support so daring a statement; and how can we judge of the motives of a man so exceptionally placed at so remote a time ? No doubt there were plenty of office-hunters, and other disappointed personages about the Court who considered the king faithless enough. Did he, however, prove treacherous to those who served him and supported him through changes of party and fortune? There is, in fact, another method of viewing the subject, from which we derive quite a different result.

In the tragedy of *Hamlet* there are two remarks thrown in casually which bear peculiar testimony to the political groundwork of Shakespeare's time. In the grave-digging scene Hamlet says to Horatio, " I have noted it for some time past, the toe of the peasant treads so near the heel of the courtier it galls his kibe." The other is the well-known epigram, " There is a divinity doth hedge a king."

The first may be looked on as a prediction of modern democracy. The English made a rapid advance in civilization during the long, peaceful reign of Elizabeth; " and the wild beasts " of whom Cellini speaks, became measurably converted into Sidneys and Raleighs. Macaulay also notices, in his essay on Burleigh, the resolute and independent spirit of Elizabeth's last Parliament. There is also reason for believing that the true offence of Lord Bacon, for which he was calumniated and dismissed, was the unpopularity of a minister who asserted too much for the royal prerogative. This was one element in the coming struggle for political power, and the all-observing Shakespeare was the man to take notice of it.

The theory of a divine right of kings originated in the compact between Charlemagne and the pope, but it did not become a political dogma until the reign of Charles V.—or rather Charles II. of Spain. A king's authority was supposed to become divine by religious consecration, but for that very reason it remained subordinate to the head of the church. When, however, respect for church government declined, and Rome was captured by the army of Charles II., the veneration which common people must feel for some definite object was transferred to royalty, and royalty was not slow to take advantage of this.

This explains the absolutism of Philip II., Ferdinand the Catholic, and Louis XIV. It extended itself over all Europe, excepting the extreme northern countries, and caused immense mischief. Charles I. must have of course been conscious of it through the foreign ambassadors at court, with whom a king always feels more nearly on terms of equality than with any of his own subjects. Thus the general tendency of European politics must have made a strong impression on Charles while the majority of Englishmen would only know of it by hearsay. The independent spirit of Parliament would at the same time intensify the king's feeling of a right to absolute authority. Charles was a masculine counterpart of Mary Queen of Scots, and his career was almost an exact repetition of hers.

From this point of view, therefore, the conduct of Charles does not appear faithless, any more than the extension of its authority by Parliament during the last century was faithless. Authority itself is an historical fact, and does not emanate from any one branch of government or even from the people themselves. At any particular time Charles could justify himself by the example of other European powers. He could have claimed that the aggressive spirit of Parliament was a sufficient reason for his asserting more firmly the dignity of his position. The purchasing power of gold and silver had greatly diminished since the reign of Elizabeth, and Charles could have complained (and I believe he did) that the appropriations made by Parliament were not sufficient to maintain the royal household in a royal and dignified manner. He was supported in this opinion by a strong court party, and by a majority of the nobility, who risked their lives for him on many a battle-field, and looked on him in retrospect as a glorious martyr. He may have been perfectly honest in his belief that a king could be superior to all law and limitation.

The divine right of kings has been tried in the balance of time, and has kicked the beam in all the nations of western Europe. It has ended in mis-

government, corruption, incapacity, and revolution.
Macaulay is therefore justified in condemning
Charles, whether he acted from selfish insincerity or
narrow-minded principle.   Why, however, as one of
his critics has suggested, should Macaulay have tolerated in Cromwell a more extended usurpation of
power than Charles ever attempted?* This certainly
seems inconsistent, and is a point we should like to
have explained.   Cromwell's tyranny was certainly
justified by the result, for the ill effects of his *régime*
died with him, and the good he did lived afterward.
Most people now feel that Cromwell was justified by
the purity of his intentions and the excellence of his
judgment.   He did not claim that he was acting
from any divine right, but rather from the necessity
of establishing a divine order in affairs, for his work
was not yet finished when death came upon him,
and the question is whether he would ever have
perceived that a military despotism was unsuited to
an intelligent and progressive people.   He evidently
did not perceive that a government of natural superiority could only survive during the life of its
founder.   He designed to have it continued under
his son, who had neither the experience nor capacity
for the conduct of great affairs.   It is even a problem
how long the English people would have endured it
under Cromwell himself.

Macaulay's description of Charles II. is one of
the finest pieces of intellectual analysis extant, but it
is open to the same form of criticism as his judgment
of Charles I.   In estimating the character of Charles

* Hon. A. S. G. Canning.

II., he makes no allowance for the difficulties which beset him both before and after he came to the throne, and the effect these must have had on his moral nature. A monarch could hardly have been more free and independent than Charles I. was before his struggle commenced with the Long Parliament. He had no wars, no foreign complications, no domestic insurrections, no dangerous rivals to contend with. Perhaps it was this perfect independence which lured him to destruction. Charles II. was either wiser than his father, or he learned wisdom from his father's fate. He suited himself to the vicissitudes of his life with an almost feminine tact and amiability. He was certainly the best of the Stuarts, and he does not seem to me to have received the credit he deserved. The good will with which he put an end to the persecution of the Quakers in New England is something in his favor; and whether his toleration of different forms of religion arose from indifference or breadth of mind, it has at least a semblance of virtue rare enough in those times. Too light-hearted to feel very seriously on religious questions, he was obliged to become a Catholic in order to maintain himself at the intolerant court of Louis XIV., and afterward concluded like Henry IV. that a change of religion was not too high a price to pay for a throne,—with a mental reservation thrown in, perhaps. The dissolute manners of court life, which he is supposed to have introduced into England, were nothing more than the fashions of Versailles, in which he had grown up and been educated. At least he remained there long enough to assimilate the French mode of life, and is not more to be blamed for doing so than a man is for possessing hereditary tendencies which are too strong for his self-control.   If he introduced into England a fashion of lax conjugal morality, he also brought with it a French sense of elegance and refinement in social life such as had hitherto been unknown.   There are certain men intended by nature to represent the social side of life, and they are quite as useful in their way as those intensely practical persons who stand like exclamation points in the drawing-room.

That Charles II. was extravagant, fond of luxury, gorgeous dresses, and grand entertainments; that he rewarded in a princely manner many persons who had no higher claim to gratitude than making his life pleasant for him; and that he was comparatively indifferent to public affairs, may have been true enough.   We may blame him for this, but we ought not to blame him severely.   A king who enjoyed his throne in England for fifteen years without committing any deeds which we now consider cowardly, brutal, or atrocious, may possibly be pardoned for some smaller transgressions.   Charles had a fine æsthetic sense which elevated him above the vulgar pleasure-seeker.   He liked fine pictures and beautiful women.   To place him on the same level with Louis XV., as Macaulay does, is a sin and a shame. Fortunately, we have Macaulay's own contradiction for the statement,—a clear contradiction not only in terms but in fact.   On the fourteenth page of Chapter II. he says:

" From such a school it might have been expected that a young man who wanted neither abilities nor amiable qualities would have come forth a great and good king. Charles came forth from that school with social habits, with polite and engaging manners, and with some talent for lively conversation, addicted beyond measure to sensual indulgence, fond of sauntering and of frivolous amusements, incapable of self-denial and of exertion, without faith in human virtue or in human attachment, without desire of renown, and without sensibility to reproach."

Again, at the opening of Chapter IV., he makes the following statement :

" The death of King Charles the Second took the nation by surprise. His frame was naturally strong, and did not appear to have suffered from excess. He had always been mindful of his health even in his pleasures ; and his habits were such as promise a long life and a robust age. Indolent as he was on all occasions which required tension of the mind, he was active and persevering in bodily exercise."

Now a man cannot be addicted beyond measure to sensual indulgence, and yet have such habits as might promise a long life and a robust old age. His comparatively early death would seem to corroborate the first statement; but there are other ways of accounting for that, beside youthful irregularities. The Stuarts were not more vigorous physically than mentally, and I do not remember that any of the kings of Scotland survived to above sixty years. The reign of Charles II. was full of anxiety, plots, and political complications.   He may not have been so indifferent to public business as Macaulay supposes; especially where it concerned the security of his throne and person.   It appears to have been a disorder of the brain that brought him to his end.

If he was something of a cynic, like Frederick of Prussia, the fact is not to be wondered at.   The execution of his father, who was at least kind and affectionate to his children, must have made a terrible impression on him; and from his point of view Charles could only attribute this to the malevolence of mankind.   He was in all respects the antipodes of Cromwell, and represented perfectly the national reaction against the Puritan *régime.*   If we cannot admire him as we do grim old Oliver, it is not because he was not without virtues of his own.   Those pretty and amusing creatures called King Charles spaniels always seemed rather appropriate to him.

That the restored Stuarts should have been maintained and subsidized by the French court was a disgrace to England, and if it had been known at the time would have aroused the liveliest indignation. The ostensible object of Louis XIV. in doing this was to give aid and comfort to the Catholic religion, but it really served as a retainer to keep the English government quiet, while he pursued his plans of conquest in Belgium and on the Rhine.   These were the ancient boundaries of Gaul, and Louis, like Napoleon, considered that a sufficient justification for his design.   The subsidy would have had small effect, however, if it had not been for the aggressive enterprise of the Dutch.   The civil disturbances in

Great Britain were a glorious opportunity for the Netherlands, and the latter soon divided with the Portuguese most of the commerce of Europe. That war should ensue between the English and Dutch was a matter of course. Cromwell defeated and suppressed them for a time; but after his death they became bolder and more rapacious than ever. During the latter half of the seventeenth century, the Netherlands were the first naval power in Europe, and their war-ships scoured the seas of both English and Spaniards.

So long as this state of affairs continued, the French subsidy could do no harm, for the national feeling in England was favorable to France in comparison with Holland. There was in truth a fair reason why Charles should have accepted it; and again we are obliged to quote Macaulay's words against his own conclusions.

" The Commons alone could legally grant him money. They could not be prevented from putting their own price to his grants. The price which they put on their grants was this, that they should be allowed to interfere with every one of the king's prerogatives, to wring from him his consent to laws which he disliked, to break up cabinets, to dictate the course of foreign policy, and even to direct the administration of war."

Only Joseph Bonaparte, when he was King of Spain without a partisan in the country, might have envied the position of Charles II. of England, who was distrusted by his own people (even the Catholics); who could not obtain funds to support his own establishment, much less to maintain an army or navy; who was compelled to remain under obligations to one foreign government and to endure repeated humiliations from another, for which he was blamed by those who remained responsible for it. Many private persons have sunk under the burden of a similar situation. If Charles soon showed a distaste for public business, and took refuge from the cares of state in gay company and frivolous amusements, who need be surprised at it ?

This may not be after all the true interpretation of Charles II., but it is probable and worth considering.

At length there came a time when the subsidy would not avail. The successes of Louis XIV. not only began to threaten the independence of the Netherlands but to alarm the English at the increasing power of France. It had been a time-honored principle of British policy, that the possession of Belgium by their ancient enemy would be dangerous to British independence. In consequence, the popular administration of John De Witt was overthrown in Holland, and the Prince of Orange, the most clear-headed statesman of his time, came to the front, and by a master-stroke of genius united Great Britain and the Netherlands under his own leadership. This, quite as much as the persecutions of the Independents in the bloody assizes of Judge Jeffreys, was the cause of King James's expulsion from the government. There are certain changes in politics which resemble chemical reactions; and the battle of Boyne River was a consequence of the marriage of his daughter, which James II. had not thought of.

Macaulay is always a Whig, and the proportion of English history which he wrote shows the Whigs to their best advantage, and the Tories at their worst. The names Whig and Tory originated during the reign of Charles II. and are among the rare instances in language where words can be traced to their source; and yet nobody knows how they originated. The Whigs were always the party of progress in Great Britain, and deserve credit beside for their moderation, patriotism, and practical sense. That they should have been always in the right, and the Tories always in the wrong, was not, however, in the nature of things. The party still exists in Scotland and Ireland, but is nearly extinct in England, as it has been long since in America. The present English Liberal party has an altogether different character.

Macaulay resembles Walter Scott in this, that his good people are decidedly good, and his bad characters very bad. He also discourses of others who are more like ordinary human nature, but the leading parts in his drama are representative of either a virtue or a vice, not unworthy of Scott in graphic delineation. His portrait of Charles II. as an indifferent and indolent pleasure-seeker, despising human nature, and equally regardless of praise or censure, because he had no faith in the sincerity of either, is supplemented by a characterization of James II. as an obstinate, self-conceited bigot, who is unwilling

to listen to the advice of sensible men because he
wishes to have the credit of governing his own kingdom without assistance from others.

Then he introduces with fine dramatic effect the
Prince of Orange: the hero-statesman, resplendent
as the morning sun.   He comes in like the apparition of Lohengrin in the opera,—a champion sent
by Providence to redress the wrongs of suffering
England.   Never was there a more brilliant historical contrast, and Macaulay has not failed to make
good use of it.

This is the most interesting portion of his work,
and does him very great credit.   His portrait of
William III. is presumably an ideal,—Macaulay's
ideal of the true executive; but since at this date
we cannot ascertain what the real William actually
was, it is all the more valuable on that account.   It
has been studied for fifty years both in England and
America, and must have contributed much, like
Webster's speeches, to form the style and character
of our best public men.   Although Macaulay could
not appreciate the finer domestic virtues, and was
even lacking in some of those qualities which constitute a gentleman, the virtue of public life and high-
minded patriotism were all the more valuable to
him.   He cannot find any real fault with his hero.
He admits that the absent-minded indifference of
William's manners gave a general offence at the
English court, and that in a single instance he was
unfaithful to his amiable queen; but he glides over
these matters as skilfully as would a lawyer in court
when he is obliged to touch on points unfavorable to

his client. Mary also is represented to be a pattern of all social virtues, although she was the daughter of James and must have inherited some of the Stuart peculiarities; but they are known in the English household rhyme as " good William and Mary," and we will not gainsay their right to the title.

It is rare good fortune when the best man comes to the top of affairs, either in a monarchy or any other form of government. Even Emerson, whose democratic sentiment was unquestionable, said that if we could once get the best man in the presidential chair we should be only too glad to turn everything over to him. It is well stated by Macaulay that William's stern features were ennobled and softened by the general rejoicing on his entry to London. William was not unlike Cromwell, and the characters of both were largely moulded by the times in which they lived; although this is rather the exception than the rule among great men. Both knew when it was necessary to be severe and absolute, and they both showed the noblest strength of character by their moderation in success. William was wiser than Cromwell in this, that he anticipated his own fate, and knew how to provide for the future; a matter which private individuals often find difficult enough, but in William's case, with only a weak Anne of Denmark and an unscrupulous Duke of Marlborough to depend on, it might be looked on as a most slender thread of fortune.

Men of less experienced judgment would have attempted some other alternative, but William of Orange always saw his objects at shooting distance, and, as Macaulay remarks, " No statesman of modern times has conceived greater designs, or carried them out in a more determined manner." He was more powerful after his death than during his life. He baffled the ambition of Louis XIV. and prevented the Stuart family from ever returning to England.

The revolution of 1688 resembled the change from Buchanan to Lincoln. William found all the minor government offices, which were not filled with rebel sympathizers, occupied by incapable parasites. They could not all be removed at once, neither could the king interfere beyond a certain point in the different departments of his ministry. It was like clearing out the Augean stables. Everywhere, even among the highest officials, there was prejudice against him as a Dutchman; yet in the course of eight months, even with his delicate health he succeeded in inspiring such energy and efficiency throughout the government service as had not been known since Oliver's time. Sinecures were abolished, parasites and incapables suppressed, while men of character and integrity were again brought to the front. Most remarkable of all William succeeded in persuading English troops to serve under Dutch commanders.

It was William's fine policy to give the armies under his control a mixed composition by importing Dutch troops to England, and transporting English troops to the Netherlands. The regiment of Highlanders whose loyalty was most subject to suspicion was the first ordered to embark. They mutinied, and started for Scotland, carrying their cannon along with them. If they had been Englishmen they would have obtained many recruits from the counties to which they belonged, but being Scotchmen, nobody in England gave them aid or comfort. The king sent Dutch Ginkell after them with what was considered a sufficient force. The Highlanders took up a position in a morass, whose only approach was commanded by their cannon; but Ginkell soon proved that he was master of the situation. His cavalry swam the morass where the water was deepest, and the Highlanders, finding themselves defeated before the fight had begun, surrendered without a shot, and were taken back to London like a gang of convicts. They were all guilty of treason, and it is to be feared that in the reign of William I. they would all have suffered for it; but William III., judging that they were sufficiently cowed and humiliated already, pardoned them all, and the regiment went over to Holland in a docile and submissive manner.

This may be remarked as a rare instance of judicious clemency; for it does not always pay to be merciful, as even Cæsar discovered at the base of Pompey's statue.

Still more creditable was William's treatment of the church question as exemplified by the appointment of Burnet as Bishop of Salisbury; and Macaulay's clear, impartial account of this affair, and his remarks on Burnet's character and work are much better than the parliamentary eloquence in which he so often indulges. The following statement deserves a special commendation.

" Though, as respected doctrine, Burnet by no means belonged to the extreme section of the Latitudinarian party, he was popularly regarded as the personification of the Latitudinarian spirit.   This distinction he owed to the prominent place which he held in literature and politics, to the readiness of his tongue and of his pen, and above all to the frankness and boldness of his nature, frankness which could keep no secret, and boldness which flinched from no danger."

William of Orange was really a Lutheran; but so liberal in his views that he might almost be called unsectarian.   Therefore the appointment of Burnet was considered an attempt to enforce his own liberalism on the High Church of England.   Next to the obstinacy of a priest, there is nothing like the tenacity of higher prelates in regard to the least important articles of their faith, for concerning these there is always the most contention.   The Archbishop of Canterbury absolutely refused to consecrate Burnet; but the king was equally firm, and the archbishop having at length wound himself up in a net of his own casuistry, was finally obliged to yield.

William might not have accomplished what he did if there had not been a united England behind him. In Cromwell's time, the lines were sharply drawn. The nation was, so to speak, full of fight; but the most bitter animosities entirely wear themselves out and a reactionary feeling takes place in favor of our former enemies.   England had at last, after a hundred and fifty years, learned the lesson of religious toleration, and both sides were willing to accept such a fair-minded arbiter as William proved himself.

Even more to his advantage was the policy of his ancient enemy the king of France. Louis XIV. was an able administrator, in fact one of the ablest, but he lacked foresight, without which there is no fine statesmanship. His aggressive Catholicism, for which Madame de Maintenon has been largely held responsible, stirred up against himself the class of people in England who would have considered his conquests in Belgium with the least dissatisfaction, and those conquests startled the English nobility and gentry into a sense of the danger which menaced the Protestant religion. The ten million dollars or more which Louis had expended on the Stuart family might as well have been thrown into the British Channel. He succeeded in enlarging the boundaries of France, but he impoverished the country and made a hollow shell of it.

Westminster and the adjacent neighborhood was Macaulay's native heath, and when he escapes to a distance from it his narrative loses force. The account of William's Irish campaign is not altogether satisfactory. Macaulay does not appear to have had a very clear conception of the course of events in that expedition. He does not give us a scientific statement of the positions of the two armies previous to the battle of Boyne River, or of the manner in which the victory was finally won. Both armies appear to have been equally heterogeneous in character, and to have behaved in an equally disorderly and irregular manner. According to Macaulay, the Irish volunteers fled at the first fire; yet in spite of this the English were only saved from defeat by the courage of William, and the heroism of Schomberg. William was obliged to expose himself as no commanding officer should do except in the most urgent necessity.   He was grazed by a cannon shot on his right shoulder.

There is no false patriotism, however, or national self-conceit, about Macaulay.   If he sometimes indulges in parliamentary rhetoric, he never troubles us with a Fourth of July oration.   In this respect at least he rises above either praise or censure; for it is no trifling virtue.   Nothing so perverts the sense of a whole people, or debilitates national character, like the habit of perpetual self-laudation.   It is worse than either whiskey or opium.   If it is bad for the individual, how can it possibly be good for the multitude ?   Demagogues make use of it to bring about their selfish ends in opposition to the public good; and even real statesmen descend to it as a last resort in times of emergency.   In spite of the mischief it has done, no people, taken collectively, has ever yet learned to recognize the evil and guard against it.   Writers and speakers of the highest order have always preferred to point out those qualities in other nations and races which it would be well to imitate, rather than to celebrate the virtues of their own. We should consider what Shakespeare says of Englishmen in the *Merchant of Venice*, and recollect that they were our ancestors as well.

Here Macaulay takes his stand on firm ground. He was proud of being an Englishman, but he never dwells on the fact; and evidently wishes to do full justice to all nations and races, even to the savages.

If he does not always succeed in this, yet his good intentions are commendable. He believed that the nineteenth century was an improvement on previous ages that had gone before it on the whole; but he desired his countrymen to remember that they did not make themselves what they were, but were indebted for it mainly to their ancestors, and it depended upon them whether or no their descendants should be equally civilized. "You should consider the past," he said, "as well as the future." He never quite escaped from his fine, classical scholarship, and valued Greek and Roman literature too highly perhaps; but it was a fault in the right direction. There were no living orators or philosophers like the Greeks; and the militia of Athens and Sparta was probably the best that has ever been known. Those who fought at Marathon and Salamis were as good soldiers as Wellington's Peninsula veterans. He takes particular pains to point out that the cowardice of the Irish infantry at Boyne River is not characteristic of their race, which has often proved a courage equal to any, but clearly resulted from the bad discipline and irregular methods of King James's army. The Danish contingent, he thinks, were the troops that the Irish were most afraid of.

Germany was to Macaulay an unknown territory, but he greatly admires the art and intellect of the Italians, as well as the ingenuity and social elegance of the French. William was by no means to blame, he says, for preferring his faithful Dutch officers to unknown and untried Englishmen whom he had only too much reason to distrust. Again he says, "Among the English councillors such fidelity was rare. It is painful, but it is no more than just, to acknowledge that he had but too good reason for thinking meanly of our national character. That character, indeed, was essentially what it has always been. Veracity, uprightness, and manly boldness were then, as now, qualities eminently English. But those qualities, though widely diffused among the great body of the people, were seldom to be found in the class with which William was best acquainted." There are passages of similar import in some of his essays.

Macaulay says, in one of his earlier magazine articles, that the historian should not take too much pains to be accurate, lest his writing become dry, and he should thus lose the interest of his readers. This is vicious doctrine certainly, and by no means warranted by experience; for a writer who collects the largest quantity of fresh information will always be the most interesting,—even if he does not express himself with elegance. Many instances of this might be mentioned, but it is only necessary to state here that Macaulay's history is constructed on a better principle. To make a work of such extent absolutely faultless would be an impossibility, but even reading it in a most unfriendly manner is enough to convince one that Macaulay's desire to tell the truth is superior to his love of fine writing. In fact his performance is better than his promise. The rank and file of the material he collected testify to the fulness of his preparation. They are so great that only a man of rare capacity could assimilate them, and it cannot be denied that he has made a skilful disposition of them. His intellectual brightness is such that it carries us onward through the most prosaic affairs, and we read until the setting sun apprises us how swiftly the time has passed.

Macaulay has been called to account for various errors which are not so much mis-statements of facts as mis-representations of character. John Paget has questioned the justice of his estimate of William Penn. Hon. Mr. Canning and Mr. Morrison have made a general critical review of his writings, not without finding some flaws to quarrel over; and old Hugh Miller, the geologist, attacked him in vigorous Scotch fashion for his evil report of the Highlanders' mode of living. Considering the magnitude of the work, however, these complaints of Macaulay's critics are not highly important, nor do they make a strong impression. They are such exceptions as prove that Macaulay's *History of England* is a substantial and veracious book.

Wasson says in his essay on Whittier that Quakerism and Puritanism are the two richest soils of historical times; and William Penn was the representative Quaker, both in his virtues and his peculiarities. He was a great man more than four thousand years too soon. Human nature requires a certain amount of self-satisfaction, and the right form of this is to be found in an elevated self-respect. Quakerism, in trying to repress it altogether, only succeeds in diverting it into unusual channels. The true nature of a man breaks through his artificial nature under excitement, or when he is placed in a peculiar position. The self-complacent obsequiousness of Penn at the court of James II., of which Macaulay complains, would be the natural reaction of a character developed in private, and untried by the discipline of public affairs. The tendency of Quakerism is to extract the natural manliness from a character, and replace it by an almost fanatical regard for principle.

Whether this were true of Penn or not, Macaulay works up the case and exaggerates it to a sensational degree. His antipathy to Penn evidently arose from other causes, and is as much a mystery as King James's partiality for the Quakers, who were the only Protestant sect that he treated with liberality. Mr. Canning suggests that this may have been because they were disliked, and persecuted socially, by the other Protestants.

The description of life among the Highlanders is a repulsive exaggeration of the pen,—almost splenetic in violence. It would do shabby justice to the wigwam of the American Indian.

The Essays.

Macaulay's essays are lively and entertaining, but their literary merit has been overestimated. They are really the chips and *debris* of his history, and though there are brilliant passages among them, they are for the most part carelessly written. The best that can be said of some of them, is that they are more interesting than the books which Macaulay pretended to review. In others, serious subjects are treated in a wanton and superficial manner. They are rather dangerous reading for young people, or indeed for any who cannot discriminate readily between the true and false in literature. He has a bad habit of cumulative repetition, and deals too frequently in sharp antitheses. His style of argument in reply to what he calls Sadler's Refutation is in the most domineering parliamentary vein. We feel less compunction in exposing the errors in Macaulay's writing, for he was always most unmerciful in his criticism of others.

The best of his essays are those which relate to English history; as might be expected. Of these the most interesting is the lengthy review, or abstract, of Lord Mahon's *War of the Succession in Spain*, which is properly an afterpiece to his own history, although it appears to have been written before it. It contains an account of the Earl of Peterborough in Macaulay's handsomest style. The essays on the Earl of Chatham and William Pitt are also valuable, as coming from an experienced politician. That Macaulay should have been impartially just to Napoleon was not to be anticipated, although he may have desired it; and his animadversion against Chatham, as an example of a man of genius who was also self-conceited, should be considered with some hesitation. It is doubtful if Macaulay had a clear conception of the nature of self-conceit. Nothing could be more conceited than the remark credited to him in regard to some pamphleteer who made a violent attack on him. " The man intended murder, but has committed suicide."

Macaulay wonders why it is, that we leave the stage-coach and ride outside in the rain, in order to escape from the egotistic revelations of a fellow-passenger, and at the same time admire an equal amount of personal confession in Petrarch's sonnets, of which he has no very good opinion himself. He appears to have been ignorant that the true nature of a sonnet should be a refined subjectivity; and he might have learned from Schiller that the spirit in which a man says or does anything is the main matter,—that egotism does not necessarily consist in the use of the first pronoun, and that the self-communings of a noble mind, expressed poetically, are among the most costly treasures of literature. Macaulay's literary criticism is bright and interesting, but as we perceive herein not always trustworthy. If he had been well grounded in the proper knowledge of a critic he would not have exposed himself in so vulnerable a manner. His remarks on English comedy, and on the comedies of Macchiavelli, are well worth reading. So also is much that he wrote about Milton, a poet for whom he had a creditable admiration.

His reckless essay on Frederick the Great was a most unfortunate blunder, for it has prejudiced the larger portion of the German people against him as an historian. This may perhaps result in causing the French to consider him with more favor; but it has been the Germans heretofore who have appreciated English literature, and the French who have contemned it. Grimm has exposed the undignified character of the essay on Frederick in a single scathing paragraph; for to do this it was only necessary to quote the opening sentences of Macaulay's essay, which was based on an unfinished life of Frederick by the poet Campbell, of which Macaulay says, " It professes, indeed, to be no more than a compilation; but it is an exceedingly amusing compilation, and we shall be glad to have more of it." Any German writer, who might have perpetrated such a piece of charlatanism in Macaulay's time, would have been hooted out of the literary arena at very short notice; but the time is not yet past in England or America when a man with a handle to his name can obtain publication for any quantity of trash.

His account of Frederick contains many errors which any good German scholar would certainly have avoided. Campbell's biography which has since been relegated to the dust archives, and is no longer heard of, was no doubt equally inaccurate. Macaulay was not aware that the ill treatment of Frederick by his father was caused by an Austrian intrigue, and that he made war on Austria partially in retaliation for this. Macaulay seems to delight in representing men of the highest ability as being also the most unprincipled; and no doctrine could be more cynical or injurious to the minds of youthful readers.

In this connection it is our unpleasant duty to reflect on Macaulay's readiness to circulate scandal, which is indeed the worst side of him. , Æschylus says that there is no escape from calumny; and the stronger opposition men excite, the more liable they are to suffer from it. During the siege of Paris in

1870, French newspapers published most atrocious charges against Bismarck, not one of which had the smallest foundation in fact. You would suppose that he was a second Louis XV. In like manner, Macaulay has repeated and supported with his authority a vile newspaper slander on Frederick the Great, for which no evidence or justification has ever been discovered. In describing the character of the Duke of Orleans, grandson of Louis XIV., he says that, like Charles II., he cared more for his female relatives than for any other persons about him, and it was suspected in both cases that this interest was not entirely innocent. Could suspicion be more atrocious ?

In fact Macaulay was very much like Voltaire. Both were bright, witty, and good historians; but also possessed of a rather low standard of morality, with a tendency to cynicism. Voltaire was cynical with respect to religion; Macaulay with respect to human nature, and this is the more dangerous poison of the two. If he had known human nature better he would have been aware, that it was because the near relatives of Charles and the Duke of Orleans were innocent and virtuous that they were so influential. A libertine is scarcely more to be despised than he is to be pitied, for his only moments of genuine happiness are those in which he can escape from the fetters he has forged for himself.

Of similar character is his essay on Lord Bacon, which was ably analyzed by Wasson in the *Christian Examiner* many years ago. A magazine article, however, does not make so lasting an impression as a book; though its circulation may be wider for the time being. The reviews of Dumont's *Mirabeau* and Nares's *Burleigh* must have been written without collateral information on those subjects.

It is with relief therefore that we turn to Macaulay's controversy with John Stuart Mill, and the question of representative government. Without taking sides either with or against him in this matter, we are pleased to admire the clear logic and forcible language with which he supports his position. The following statement can be recommended to those who deal in *a priori* theories of government.

"How, then, are we to arrive at just conclusions on a subject so important to the happiness of mankind? Surely by that method which, in every experimental science to which it has been applied, has signally increased the power and knowledge of our species,—by that method for which our new philosophers would substitute quibbles scarcely worthy of the barbarous respondents and opponents of the middle ages,—by the method of Induction ;—by observing the present state of the world, —by assiduously studying the history of past ages,—by sifting the evidence of facts,—by carefully combining and contrasting those which are authentic, by generalizing with judgment and diffidence,—by perpetually bringing the theory which we have constructed to the test of new facts,—by correcting, or altogether abandoning it, according as those new facts prove it to be partially or fundamentally unsound. Proceeding thus,—patiently, diligently, candidly,—we may hope to form a system as far inferior in pretension to that which we have been examining and as far superior to it in real utility as the prescriptions of a great physician, varying with every stage of every malady and with the constitution of every patient, to the pill of the advertising quack which is to cure all human beings, in all climates, of all diseases.

"This is the noble Science of Politics, which is equally removed from the barren theories of the Utilitarian sophists, and from the petty craft, so often mistaken for statesmanship by minds grown narrow in habits of intrigue, jobbing, and official etiquette;—which of all sciences most tends to expand and invigorate the mind,—which draws nutriment and ornament from every part of philosophy and literature, and dispenses in return nutriment and ornament to all."

This passage is worthy of Alexander Hamilton, and no higher praise could possibly be given it.

CARLYLE

SO he might have said, " Grand, rough old Thomas Carlyle "; who was a kind of Luther to his generation of Anglo-Saxons, breaking through old traditions and venerable, musty stupidities to a new reformation, moral and intellectual,— such as was greatly needed in the time he lived. Of intellectual life in England in Carlyle's early manhood there was very little. Philosophy, which is always the corner-stone of mental activity was nearly dead, or at best dragging out an invalid existence. Of sentimental poetry there was perhaps too much; but of sensible, refreshing, and invigorating prose, little enough. The arts of painting and sculpture, which have never flourished extensively in Great Britain, had not been at so low an ebb for centuries. The taste in architecture was never so conventional, insipid, and meaningless. Byron and Wordsworth had introduced a few fresh ideas, but only a few, and those were neither resented nor accepted by the British public. There was no fresh thought, either in the form of German spiritual belief, or keen ironical French disbelief. Great Britain shut up for twenty years from the continent by the wars of Napoleon, had learned little of the great changes there. Madame De Staël had indeed brought by way of Russia, as a sort of feminine perfume to her intellectual attire, a rumor that certain wise men in Germany knew things not heretofore spoken of or taught in the schools; but it was only a small circle of social acquaintances who paid any attention to this.

The invention of new machines, and especially the application of steam as a new motor, engrossed the minds of men with the prospect of rapidly increasing the material possessions. In accordance with this, the doctrine had grown up that utility was the chief good of all things, including man himself, and that ideas were only of value so far as they proved conducive to this end. The times were materialistic, and the long conflict with France had dulled the sensibility of men, as protracted wars always do, and rendered them almost impervious to fresh impressions. It is most dangerous either for individuals or a civilized people when their mental habits become wholly stereotyped, and their course of life mechanical; and while this lasts no progress is possible.

Almost with the beginning of the century the child was born in the cottage of a stone-mason at Ecclefechan, whose determination it was to break through this hard shell of traditionalism, and let in the light and fresh air again, as into a building which has grown damp and musty from being long closed and bolted. The simple pictures he gives us in the reminiscences of his boyhood, and his family, are as distinct and interesting as wood-cuts. Half the honor of the man belongs to his parents; and so also the dishonor, if the children prove unworthy of their place in life. "Ah, my honored, peasant father," he said, "where among the so-called great of this world have I ever found the like of thee?" Of his mother, also, he had small cause to complain, though his respect for his father was evidently above that of others. At home he was happy, but at school the boys quickly discovered that he belonged to a different species from their own, and united against him as the small birds do against an owl. There is nothing in life more difficult to endure than this school-boy persecution, for it is the first taste of the world's injustice.

As he grew older, the strength of his character earned the respect of his fellow-students, and then the trouble began with his teachers. One of them must have been rather dull-witted, for Carlyle tells us he could never distinguish between him and another Carlyle youth, who had "red, carrotty hair, a scorched complexion, wild buck teeth, and was the worst Latin scholar in school." This may be taken as a caricature of Carlyle himself at fifteen or so; for unless the instructor was purblind there must have been some closer resemblance between the boys than their family name; yet within this rugged and uncomely exterior was a soul so fearless, puissant, aspiring, and so tender and devoted, that for two hundred years the like had hardly been known in Britain. These and fine perceptions are indeed the qualities of which genius is compounded. They begin to work at an early age, developing an internal something, like the pearl in the oyster, which only after long years becomes externally apparent.

For Carlyle was distinctively a man of genius. There are writers whom we admire and who fill a position in the literature of their country, and yet of whom we certainly cannot say this. Macaulay had a rare faculty of statement, and Addison was an elegant essayist, yet we hesitate to call them geniuses. In the London National Gallery there are two paintings of the same subject, one by Guido, and one by Caracci. They hang side by side, and we perceive at once that Guido's is a work of genius, but in regard to Caracci we do not feel sure. In Carlyle's case we feel as certain of it as that the sun will rise to-morrow. His work was *sui generis*, and in his peculiar line he is without a rival.

Peculiar is the word for it. He was a sublime kind of man, but peculiar also. What a strange sort of genius he had! Taine, who more than half appreciated him, was not far wrong in comparing Carlyle to a mastodon. He was truly a huge creature, and walked the earth with an elephantine tread; yet he walked quietly and harmlessly among his fellow-men,—looked at on all sides with astonishment and with not a little fear. He was sagacious also; minding his own affairs, and would cross no shaky bridges, preferring to flounder through the river beneath. He scorned the highways and beaten paths of mankind; but crossing the fields instead, and breaking his way through the woods,— occasionally uprooting a tree in his progress, and leaving a broad track behind him. A rather dangerous animal to irritate also, for he sometimes avenged himself quite out of proportion to the offence.

He had a mastodon-like way of devouring knowledge, literature, science,—anything that was intellectual. He read books by the hundred in five or six different languages, and always systematically. Gibbon's *Decline and Fall*, which it requires nearly a year for an ordinary man to assimilate, he mastered in twelve days, and never needed apparently to look at it again. It is doubtful if he bored people with his conversation—it was much too interesting for that,—but his friends often felt as fatigued after leaving his house as if they had accomplished a long journey.

While Carlyle was at work on the *French Revolution*, the poet Longfellow went to London with his family, and called on him. The mastodon did not happen to be at home; but almost as soon as Longfellow had returned to his hotel Carlyle appeared there also, and half an hour later, when a lady of Longfellow's party entered the parlor, she saw there (as she described it twenty years later) this strange man talking continuously about the French Revolution, while every eye in the room, young and old, was riveted on him with rapt attention. He excused himself for this finally, by saying that those pictures hovered before him day and night, and that he could not divert his mind from them.

How early he became conscious of his own superiority, Carlyle does not inform us. At about the age of twenty-two he wrote to his brother John, who afterwards made the finest translation of Dante's *Inferno*, " Two boys from Annandale will show the world what stuff there is in the Carlyles "; but it is likely that the truth came to him slowly and through many fears and misgivings.

A young lady whom Carlyle met while on a travelling circuit with Edward Irving was the first to announce to him his future good fortune, the highest perhaps attainable by man,—unless we except the hero's blood-stained laurel. Was it from looking into her pure, sympathetic eyes that Carlyle was stimulated on this occasion to exceptional elo-- quence ? It is love always that applies the torch to genius; and what a summer afternoon that must have been to her in the gray Scotch fells,—a day remembered so long as she lived, and growing continually brighter as the fame of Carlyle increased until it filled all Britain. Let us hope that she lived to read his own account of it, and knew that in his old age he still remembered her. How much wiser was this girl than Carlyle's pedagogues,—perhaps than his most intimate friends. She proved a true prophetess, and her portrait ought to have been painted by Michel Angelo. There are no pictures like those from real life if we have eyes to see them.

Broad natures make broad plans instinctively; as

the beaver builds his dam high enough to flood a sufficient area. Whether Carlyle foresaw his destiny or not, he prepared himself for it by a foundation of thoroughness and impartiality. He learned accuracy from mathematics, and a mental flexibility in the study of foreign languages. During the first half of the present century there was a feeling of profound contempt in Great Britain for everything that was not British. An hereditary respect was still paid to the ancient Greeks and Romans, but other modern nations were of no account at all.

Nothing is more repugnant to a high-minded soul than provincial intolerance; and when young Carlyle heard his instructors condemn a writer or a book, he felt the more inclined to make an examination for himself and learn whether or not the disparagement was just. In this way he was led to examine Voltaire and the French *philosophes* of the eighteenth century, which in course of time induced him to discern the causes underlying the revolution of 1789. In Germany he discovered a mine of literature, which not only gave the tone to his own writing, but served him as a strategic base from which to carry on his conflict with the traditionalism of his time.

If you will look in the *New British Cyclopedia* for the article on Goethe you will find the word printed between the columns in such large capitals as are used for the names of continents and nations. What a change is this since the erudite Mr. Dunlop designated the *Oberon* of Wieland as the finest poem in the German language. Byron, it is true, had offered a premium for a translation of *Faust,* but he did not know German enough to read Goethe himself, and the slight sensation caused by this had subsided again. Carlyle in his bold investigation of foreign writers read *Wilhelm Meister*, and recognized the true value of this author. He thus became the herald of a new intellectual era to the Anglo-Saxon race.

He wrote essays on Goethe, Lessing, Jean Paul, Voltaire, Diderot; translated *Wilhelm Meister*, and wrote a life of Schiller (which he afterwards criticised as " rose-water nonsense "). He had a monopoly of German literature in England, and no writer before had dealt with French literature from so thorough an understanding of the language. Such vigorous, earnest prose, so modest, and at the same time so keenly appreciative, had not been seen since John Milton's time. The clear, good sense which formed the tissue of his writing was enlivened by flights of imagination, and occasional snatches of humor, of a quality little inferior to the wit of Cervantes. These essays served as an entering wedge for his cause in the good opinions of the English public. Thirty years before Matthew Arnold set forth his dictum, that the true office of the critic was to celebrate the best that is thought and known in the world, Carlyle made a practical application of it.

The *Life of Schiller* was good material from the same mould. It was a youthful work but suitable to the subject; and three-fourths of mankind are more likely to sympathize with an ardent, impetuous hero, who sacrifices himself to achieve a great and glorious triumph, than the more calculating sort, who accomplish their ends with less friction to themselves and others. The hardship of Schiller's life was not owing to a lack of appreciation, but to an almost Quixotic idea of independence; and Carlyle could appreciate this feeling, although he could not sympathize with it; believing that the relation between man and man is best cemented by mutual obligations, and that it is as much our duty to accept benefits as to confer them. He might have laid more stress on this point if he had written the biography later in life, but his estimate of Schiller's genius and the value of his writings is just and delicately appreciative. He perceived that Byron and even Burns were in natural talent richer than their German contemporary, but that Schiller, led by a more elevated conception of life, had made a better use of his gifts and achieved results on a higher plane. Like Byron he was not only the popular poet of his own time, but has since continued to be so; yet there can be do doubt that the influence of Schiller is the deeper and more enduring of the two. It is Schiller's pathos, his sympathy with sorrow and suffering, which makes him dear to the heart of the German people; and in this respect he is at least superior to the best French dramatists. Carlyle's biography of him received the exceptional compliment of a German translation, and attracted the attention of Goethe, who quickly perceived the advantage of so able an ally.

It has been said that Carlyle's English was never so pure as when he translated *Wilhelm Meister;* and we may suspect the cause of this in the purity of the original. Carlyle did not develop the peculiar style by which he is proverbially known until some time afterwards, but he already had a style of his own, though not a very decided one. It was always different from the calm, self-possessed poise of Goethe, who in mastery of form has no modern rival excepting Voltaire. What is it that constitutes style except the individual taste of an author in his selection of words, and these, if properly translated into a language of similar construction, as from French or German to English, must produce nearly the same effect. The egotism of the translator, however, too often interferes with this, and the self-devotion of Carlyle to his work appears in total absence of his own personality in his rendering of the text. Dr. Hedge discovered a few slight mistakes in it, but that is of small account compared with the general character of the whole. It might be accepted as a standard of genuine, living English. There is no book which people stand so much in awe of it, though there are comparatively few who read it.

Carlyle's essays are the best account of eighteenth-century French and German literature that we have; and I suppose it may be added that Carlyle is the finest English critic either of our own or previous times. Wasson perhaps could have equalled him in a different way, but Wasson's work was of a more philosophical character. Dr. Johnson or Matthew Arnold cannot be compared to him. Lowell might be admitted to the second place, and his essays on the standard English poets may be credited as an authority; but Lowell's prose writing, though brilliant, is too labored and self-conscious to be altogether inspiring. His lectures on literature at Harvard University never created the enthusiasm among the students, for himself or his subject, which might have been expected. A large share of the satisfaction in reading Carlyle's essays comes from their freshness and spontaneity. He is too much interested in the subject to think of himself, and too much in earnest to think of his readers. He scorns all tricks of rhetoric, or attempts to make an impression on his audience. Truth is to him the finest of all rhetoric, and human sympathy the most persuasive eloquence.

I have often wondered how so rugged a nature could be united to such delicate perceptions. There is a *chiaroscuro* in his writing almost like that of Rembrandt. He goes straight to the character of his author, then estimates his talent, and observes how the two are woven together in the tissue of his writing. He seizes always on the salient point, stripping off what is either accidental or common, as a mathematician eliminates numbers that are common to his equation. Yet he would sometimes devote half a page to the elaboration of a single point if he thought it of sufficient importance; and then sum up the man in a sentence,—always holding fast to the spiritual side of things, which is his point of view,—whence the light comes for his picture. " Only the visible has value," he said, " when it is based on the invisible."

Although prone to scepticism in his youth, he penetrated the incredulous French philosophy—which it is not difficult to do—and accepted it for its true value, as a disintegrating element, instead of repudiating it as false doctrine.   It was at least more intellectually quickening than the dogmatic Scotch-English philosophy.   He had no anti-Gallic prejudice; saw Voltaire, Rousseau, Mirabeau, and the encyclopedists very clearly as they were.   " Voltaire was not the wisest of men, but the most adroit." Again Carlyle writes of him : " Given a subject, and he plunges boldly into it, to quickly reappear again perfectly satisfied that he has touched bottom, which is from three to ten miles lower down."   Nothing could describe better than this Voltaire's literary method.   Likewise, Mirabeau, who was in his way the Hampden of France, Carlyle accepted for such a torch-light hero as he was, burning himself out, when the revolution came, in smoke and glare, like a tar-barrel.   They were not an attractive set of men, half-demoralized themselves,—except Voltaire, who belonged to an earlier and stricter period.   Only their humanity and their patriotism have preserved them from oblivion.   Even Rousseau, the most disinterested of them, was by no means a sound kind of man, and yet his influence on the world has been enormous.

In Germany at the same time a group of men sprang up who were an historical contrast to the French; men of true constructive quality, with whom Carlyle could feel a much closer sympathy. The age of Louis XIV. resembled a great Strasburg clock, in which even poets and field-marshals played their parts as puppets and cog-wheels. This created great astonishment among mankind and was very effective in its way, but after a while the machinery became disordered, and the world heartily sick of it. The French naturalistic, or realistic, reaction took place, which was represented in America by the politics of Jefferson, and in a measure by the philosophy of Emerson.

In Germany, Winckelmann and Lessing laid the foundation of art and literary criticism, by recognizing the twofold principle of the natural as distinguished from the artificial, and the artistic as distinguished from the natural. Because art and nature are united in man, we should be the more careful not to confound them. " Art is called art," said Goethe, " to distinguish it from nature "; and yet no poetry is more true to nature than Goethe's. As prudent lawyers go back for precedents to cases under the best jurisdiction, so Lessing and Winckelmann returned to the great masters of antiquity, and from the principles thus evolved, laid the foundations for Goethe and Schiller to build upon. Carlyle, who never adopted Emerson's naturalistic views, recognized the validity of this method.

In personal character they pleased him better than the French, and were more in harmony with his Scotch notions of propriety. They respected morality for its own sake; and though they disagreed somewhat with the conventional religion of their time, they held in reverence the religious spirit of all times, as did Carlyle himself. Even Goethe, who, in assimilating French elegance, also adopted something from the French domestic idea, was altogether more of a Stoic than a voluptuary, and never lived, like Voltaire, in open intimacy with another man's wife. Schiller, Lessing, and Jean Paul are supposed to have been models of social uprightness. Heine, who formed himself wholly on French models, Carlyle did not like so well.

He also wrote essays on Burns, Walter Scott, Dr. Johnson: each the best of its kind, so far as I know, though the statement of Dr. Johnson might be improved on. Goethe was particularly pleased with his account of Burns, a poet whose pure, spontaneous melody was most like Goethe's own, and he made the following extract from it for his introduction to the German translation of Carlyle's *Schiller*, as a testimonial of the genius of this young Scotchman, and of the value of Scotch literature in general:

" Burns was born in an age the most prosaic Britain has yet seen, and in a condition the most disadvantageous, where his mind, if it accomplished aught, must accomplish it under the pressure of continual bodily toil, nay of penury and desponding apprehension of the worst evils, and with no furtherance but such knowledge as dwells in a poor man's hut, and the rhymes of Ferguson or Ramsay for his standard of beauty, he sinks not under all these impediments : through the fogs and darkness of that obscure region, his lynx eye discerns the true relations of the world and human life ; he grows into intellectual strength, and trains himself into intellectual expertness. Impelled by the expansive movement of his own irrepressible soul, he struggles forward into the general view ; and with haughty modesty lays down before us, as the fruit of his labor, a gift, which Time has now pronounced imperishable.

"A true Poet, a man in whose heart resides some effluence of Wisdom, some tone of the ' Eternal Melodies,' is the most precious gift that can be bestowed on a generation : we see in him a freer, purer development of whatever is noblest in ourselves—his life is a rich lesson to us ; and we mourn his death as that of a benefactor who loved and taught us."

This has a tone of youthful ardor and fresh enthusiasm, which after all is quite as valuable as the sagacious gravity of age. No wonder that Goethe admired it, for it bears close relationship to the handiwork of his own early days. Carlyle always insisted that Goethe saved his life, and when we consider the difficulties and embarrassment which surrounded him at this time, like a thorny hedge, we can readily believe it. What an encouragement it must have been to him,—like a message from the Delphic oracle predicting a glorious future.

Goethe concludes one of his last letters to Carlyle with the words, " So then—onward."

As a standard of the most pertinent criticism of his later years, we may consider this casual opinion of Gibbon, expressed in his *Reminiscences*:

" Gibbon's *Decline and Fall* was perhaps of all the books the most impressive on me in my then stage of investigation, and state of mind. I by no means completely admired Gibbon, perhaps not more than I now do ; but his winged sarcasms, so quiet and yet so conclusively transpiercing and killing dead, were often admirable, potent, and illuminative to me. Nor did I fail to recognize his great power of investigating, ascertaining, grouping, and narrating; though the latter had always, then as now, something of a Drury Lane character, the colors strong but coarse, and set off by lights from the side scenes."

This is all there is of Gibbon, all the mental faculty that he brought to his work. Though it is not to be despised, it was not fine enough or complete enough for the universal subject which he undertook to deal with. England, especially in his time, was a fraction, say one-fourth, of modern civilization,—a large one it is true,—but the Roman Empire was the summing up of ancient times.

Carlyle's struggles, doubts, despair, and final spiritual victory are related in a peculiar dramatic allegory, full of pathos and enlivened by penetrating jets of wit. How many have been through this experience, and yet only Carlyle, even in such an odd manner, has been able to describe it in perfect fulness. It is a dangerous state to fall into: it is not every one who comes out of it victorious, and there are those who have been killed by it; but it is necessary to the full mental development of the man. Some it touches lightly, so lightly that they hardly realize the fact; but deep, heart-throbbing natures, especially if their surroundings are unfavorable, it will often seize on like a violent fever. The simple faith we are taught in childhood will not serve us when we have become men and women. We are told that if we are diligent and virtuous success will be easy, but we find that kisses go by favor, and the world is not what we expected it. The indigent scholar, who has studied and toiled with his life in his hands, finds at last that all he has learned will not avail to keep him from starving. The maiden of cloudless skies suddenly discovers that the father whom she has loved and trusted is the enemy of her lover and her happiness. Neither do people who are more fortunate escape this mental-moral disorder, which has become well known as the Wertherian condition. Even the doctors are beginning to recognize it, and find that a simple change of air is not sufficient to cure it.

The *Sorrows of Werther* represents the same subject treated in a poetical and sensuous manner; whereas *Sartor Resartus* is internal and ethical. Goethe was rather too close to his own experience to do abstract justice to it, and afterwards rather disapproved of his own work, though it was the most universally popular romance that has ever been published. As an explanation of the matter, Carlyle's statement is the more valuable of the two; the more serious and of wider application. The book made a profound impression when it was published, for the world was ripe for it. A beautiful lady almost on her death-bed wrote, " I have no patience with some of Carlyle's writings, but *Sartor Resartus* is the beloved of my heart."

It is not written in so natural a style as many of his essays, more involved and tortuous in expression, —it would seem unnecessarily so; but the thought is fresh and genuine, and goes to the heart. We recognize in *Sartor Resartus* a human soul pleading its own cause before a jury of immortals. Three chapters contain the substance of it, and they are powerfully written: the everlasting NO, the centre of indifference, and the everlasting AVE. These names afford their own explanation. Fortunate is he who remains loyal to the truth and says with grim determination, " No, I cannot believe this, even if it lead him into the abyss of despair ": still more fortunate if he can say afterward, " There is somewhat I *can* believe," and then make this the corner-stone of his life edifice. The longer the night and deeper the gloom, the brighter will be that day to him, illumined by a sun that will warm his heart forever.

Such a man was Thomas Carlyle. He who would command others must first learn self-control; and he who is destined to reconstruct a race of men is first obliged to reconstruct himself;—for what is he with all his habits and traditions, and accomplishments, and second nature, but a sum of the world as it is. It is a most painful process, like the tearing out of the inside of a house in which even the laths and plaster have a sensation of their own; nor is the re-building accomplished without strenuous labor and sleepless nights, the spiritual occupant meanwhile being very uncomfortably situated. Carlyle expresses it thus:

" Some comfort it would have been, could I, like Faust, have fancied myself tempted by the Devil ; for a

Hell, as I imagine, without Life, though only diabolic Life, were more frightful : but in our age of Downpulling and Disbelief, the very Devil has been pulled down ; you cannot so much as believe in a Devil."

The most gloomy prophecy of our own time is that our educated young men use chloroform or laughing gas, of the moral sort, to go through this operation; and then, having suffered little pain, are content to believe for the future in nothing at all,— except such things as are plainly apparent to the senses; and thus go through life heartlessly conforming for the sake of appearances, and the mighty dollar. How different from the time when Carlyle's name was a spell to conjure with, even in the streets of New York! Now the Sunday newspaper takes its place.

Beneath the obelisk in front of St. Peter's Church at Rome, there is an inscription which says, " Christ preserves his people from abomination." We could wish that the Sunday newspaper were included.

The " Everlasting Aye " was a glorious assertion of the spiritual nature of man; an eloquent outburst of belief such as not even Jeremy Taylor could equal. That matter is nothing and spirit is everything, was the keynote of Carlyle's teaching, as it was of Emerson's ; only Emerson uttered it like a penetrating tenor recitative, while Carlyle gave it forth like a grand Messianic chorus. In *Sartor Resartus*, as in the Vedic hymns, poetry, philosophy, and religion are one.

Sir William Hamilton, and other high-church

metaphysicians of Carlyle's time, considered an elevated happiness the true end and object of human existence. Carlyle rises above that. He scorns happiness, as a serious man well may. Life means to him the service of truth and celestial obligation. He says :

" There is in man a HIGHER than Love of Happiness : he can do without Happiness, and instead thereof find Blessedness ! Was it not to preach forth this same HIGHER that sages and martyrs, the Poet and the Priest, in all times, have spoken and suffered ; bearing testimony, through life and through death, of the Godlike that is in Man, and how in the Godlike only has he Strength and Freedom ? "

Did Leonidas think of happiness at Thermopylæ; or Dante, in composing the *Inferno;* or Duperron, in his heroic quest for the *Zend Avesta;* or Washington, at Valley Forge ? These men were impelled by a wholly different impulse than that which carries people to the theatre. It seemed to them that they could not do otherwise, and it was in this obedience to a divine necessity that they became heroic. Much happiness no doubt they had—moments of supreme joy and satisfaction, but much more care, weariness, and pain. In healthy, active natures, happiness and discontent succeed one another as regularly as day and night. *The true end of life is rational development, in the individual and in the race.* Happiness is incidental, and an uncertain possession.

The French Revolution.

A broad, capacious mind requires great opportunities, and Carlyle was never altogether himself until he began to work on this subject. Then indeed he astonished the literary public only as *Childe Harold* had astonished it before him. The wonder is that such a strangely original work, strange in form and so difficult of apprehension, should have found a publisher. Here John Stuart Mill was Carlyle's good genius. His interest in Carlyle's work, and brotherly solicitude for Carlyle himself, is the best part of Mill's philosophy. They were both champions of liberalism, but Carlyle's deeper nature saw that liberalism was only a temporary phase of world history, whereas Mill conceived it as a permanent condition. It was Mill who first interested him in Mirabeau, and this led the way to the *French Revolution.* He was so actively interested in the subject, that he borrowed the first volume in manuscript of Carlyle, and it was burned up by some stupidity or other. The conflagration cost Mill a thousand dollars (for he assessed the damages on himself), and was something of an injury to that portion of the book.

Carlyle describes the re-writing of it as like walking on very thin ice. It is difficult enough to re-write a single page of manuscript that has dropped out and disappeared mysteriously; but to re-write a volume, what task were equal to it? We find accordingly an undercurrent of weariness and something like mannerism in the first few chapters, as of a man whose vitality has been exhausted; and it is not until Louis XIV. is fairly dead and buried that the spirits of the writer revive again.

Not a few of the finest passages are in the last portion of the first volume.

There is something magnificent in Carlyle's contempt for his audience.   He writes to tell you what he thinks and knows, and if you do not understand him that is no concern of his.   How different from Macaulay's advice to historians, that they should not take too much pains to be accurate for fear of losing popularity.   Carlyle's scorn is like nature itself; or like a monarch of the old style who refuses to make explanations.   For my part I find the effect of this healthy and invigorating.

Stuart Mill prided himself justly enough in having anticipated the critics of Carlyle's *French Revolution,* and prepared the public mind for it before print and paper were yet dry.   We doubt, however, if Mill or any other man has ever understood the whole of it, even with a biographical dictionary on his table. How, for instance, will the average Latin scholar know what is meant by "*Astræa Redux,*" unless he discovered the phrase in some author unknown to the schools.   There ought to be a glossary appended to the book, such as there is to the Waverley novels.

While the work was in progress, Carlyle wrote to Emerson: " I believe the true poetry is to be found in history," and this gives us the key to the standpoint from which he considered it.   Long before this was known, Carlyle's admirers had denominated it as the prose epic of modern times.   It is indeed an epic which describes not the wrath of Achilles but that of God Almighty and Divine Justice poured forth like hot lava upon political malefactors and other assassins of society. No other writer of the century could have done this with equal eloquence or power. A nature of sterling veracity finds itself brought in contact from its earliest years with imposture and small knavery, which it hates continually more and more until a reserve fund of indignation is accumulated; and only waits a fitting opportunity to break forth in words or action. Perhaps the French Revolution served Carlyle as a substitute for subjects nearer home, and afforded him that relief which every warm-hearted man requires at times for his righteous indignation. There is a certain satisfaction in seeing long-standing iniquity brought to its last account. Even merciful Shakespeare says: "The judgment of the gods which makes us tremble, touches us not with pity."

Such burning words had not been uttered since Dante composed the *Inferno* in his graceful Tuscan melody. Was it not a genuine Inferno, or hell on earth, which Carlyle set himself to describe. He was not a singer like Dante; but there is a rough sort of cadence in his sentences, not unlike the roll of the hexameter,—with an occasional crash in it too like a collision of the forces of nature, or like the waves of *time* breaking upon the rocks of *fate*. Otherwise its style is not unlike Browning's poetry, so that these two writers sometimes approach each other closely. It is a dramatic, pictorial style, well suited to the various phases and Tartarean horrors

6

of the Revolution, which have no apparent logical sequence, but appear successively like the shifting scenes of a stereopticon. That there was a logical connection between them cannot be doubted, but he will be a wonderful analyst who shall discover it. No other book has been written in such a style, and it would be a dangerous attempt to imitate it.

When Titian had nearly finished a picture, it was his custom to turn it to the wall and leave it so for months, until he had forgotten how it looked; then he would turn it round and scrutinize it in a searching manner to discover by what changes it might be benefited. This is the cause perhaps why, of all the great painters, Titian's work is of the most uniform, unvarying excellence; and it is this keenly observing expression which he has perpetuated in his own portrait.

It were well if Carlyle could have adopted such a practice as this. It were well if he could have spent ten years on his *History of the French Revolution;* and could have in the course of time detected the arid, uninspired passages in it, and brought them all to an equal standard with the rest. Then he might have produced an imperishable work, an *Iliad* in prose; but there was no possibility of this. Homer could live like the birds in that bountiful climate, which gave the tone to his poetry, but Carlyle required coal for his winter fire, and dresses for his wife to entertain distinguished visitors in,—the one experience which Emerson thought never lost its charm. Pegasus was harnessed to a horse-car and obliged to go forward at an even pace. However, we need not find fault if the whole of it does not rise to the level of Carlyle's description of the flight of Louis XVI. and his Queen from Paris; for he nowhere falls below excellence, and is at the worst superior to mediocrity. A cotemporary critic called it " History revealed in flashes of lightning."

The sole cause of the French Revolution of 1789 was misgovernment ; so Macaulay says. True enough, and let our legislators at Washington remember the fact; but was there something behind this ? What was the cause of the misgovernment ? It was not the abuse of a single reign, nor of a series of ministers; for it had been going on for nearly a century. In Martin's *History of France* (which is very good, as national histories go), the origin of the revolution is traced back deep into the reign of Louis XIV., at the very time that France seemed to culminate intellectually and materially. If a decline was necessary after this, why was it so rapid ? The misgovernment was realized and appreciated, and various attempts at reform were made before the final crash came, but they proved as futile a barrier as a board fence might against a tornado. Carlyle gives a more profound explanation.

"Faith is gone out; Scepticism is come in. Evil abounds and accumulates ; no man has Faith to withstand it, to amend it, to begin by amending himself ; it must ever go on accumulating. While hollow languor and vacuity is the lot of the Upper, and want and stagnation of the Lower, and universal misery is very certain, what other thing is certain ?   That a Lie cannot be believed !   Philosophism knows only this : her other belief is mainly, that in spiritual supersensual matters no Belief is possible.   Unhappy !   Nay, as yet the Contradiction of a Lie is some kind of a belief ; but the Lie with its Contradiction once swept away, what will remain ?   The five unsatiated Senses will remain, the sixth insatiable Sense (of vanity) ; the whole *dæmoniac* nature of man will remain,—hurled forth to rage blindly without rule or rein ; savage itself, yet with all the tools and weapons of civilization : a spectacle new in History."

The compact between church and state during the Middle Ages was highly favorable for maintaining our public order.   The influence of the priests over the laboring classes was the greater in proportion to the ignorance of the latter; and the doctrine that they inculcated, that every man should be contented with his position in life, and that it was wrong to envy those who were more fortunate, had great effect in supporting the strict subordination of classes.   So long as the different classes realize that they are essential to one another and act on this principle, the nation as a whole may be considered in a healthy condition; but as soon as the different orders of society become antagonistic, demoralization sets in.

The absolute contempt of the French nobility for man, as a human being, would seem to surpass anything recorded in history,—certainly among Christian nations.   To a French nobleman, a man was not a man but a dog; and to his wife, a still more degraded object.

This contempt for human nature, as such, had penetrated all classes of society more or less, and carried with it inevitably a disrespect for religion; for if you divest man of his spirituality he becomes simply an animal, and society reduced to such a level is, as Carlyle says, nearly cannibal. Voltaire's saying that the church is the beggar's opera, struck the keynote of French philosophy. French positivism, with its ally of literary realism, was performing the same work of disintegration. Whatever the priests might say, the mass of the French people recognized the fact that the human race existed only for the benefit of the few, and the more obstinately this was denied, the less respect was felt for the sacerdotal orders.

On the other hand, genuine constructive intelligence was absolutely wanting. If there was such discernible anywhere, it was to be found among a few isolated individuals, of whom Mirabeau was the chief. Constructive intellect (or we may call it common sense if we like) was replaced by a wild visionary sentiment; of which we know a little also on this side of the ocean. Wars were to cease forever; felons to be moulded into saints; capital punishment to be abolished; and a higher civilization to be produced like magic out of this rapidly decomposing chaos. An era of universal peace and goodwill to men, with money enough for his majesty's humblest subjects, was to be brought about as if by enchantment. Meanwhile Napoleon was reading Plutarch's *Lives* and studying military tactics.

It was significant of the times that, among numberless works on government and political economy published during the reign of Louis XVI., the one which received public approval and has continued to be of historical importance was not written by a Necker or a Turgot, men trained and experienced in the affairs of state, but by the morbid, enthusiastic novelist-critic, Jean Jacques Rousseau. Carlyle refers to it repeatedly as the " gospel according to Jean Jacques." It certainly was a political evangel to the Frenchmen of that day; one that when the time came to put it to the test proved a fallacious and misleading guide.

Rousseau's *Social Compact*, assimilated by Jefferson, formed the basis of what was called the glorious revolution of 1800, which finally resulted in state rights, nullification, and the glorious secession of the Southern slave-holding states. Perhaps no other small book has ever accomplished an equal sum of mischief. The very first sentence of it is a *non-sequitur*. Yet the fundamental truth that there is an unwritten contract between the governing and governed, like the unwritten code of personal honor, is eloquently expounded in it.

The chapter that Carlyle devotes to *The Social Compact* is rather a brilliant one, and he makes a strong point of the fact that in the popular romance of *Paul and Virginia*, it is for the sake of *etiquette* that the catastrophe takes place; but I believe there is not one word in it concerning Rousseau's book. This brings to our notice an idiosyncrasy of the man. We have observed before that Carlyle had the mind of an artist. He looked at life pictorially, and at history as a subject for his art. This did not prevent him from sympathizing profoundly with the sufferings and aspirations of mankind; but nothing could be more wearisome to him than to attempt to trace out a train of logical sequences. " Poor John Mill," he said, " is writing away in the *Fortnightly Review* on what he calls the philosophy of history. As if any man knew what road he was going to take with such a horse as that ! " Political science as well as practical politics were positively hateful to him.

It is not likely that he read ten pages of *The Social Compact*. His only idea of government seems to have been absolute monarchy; not so much an hereditary monarchy as the natural imperialism of Cromwell and Napoleon. It seems strange that he should not have perceived that, even if a succession of such men could be obtained, their form of administration would seriously interfere with the changing needs and habits of mankind. So far as Great Britain is concerned at the present time, however, he may not have been far wrong. What is evidently needed there now is a Cromwell, or a Von Stein, who will remove the time-honored excrescences, and do for England, and more particularly for Ireland, what the Revolution did for France, and Von Stein accomplished in a fair measure for Prussia.

Robespierre was an autocrat of a remarkable type,—an Utopian Cromwell. In his youth he refused to condemn a prisoner to the gallows; did not believe in capital punishment; was a reformer by profession; a theorizer on social science and model government, not unlike the abolitionists of 1832,—a class of men whom Carlyle always disliked. Hegel, who better understood the logic of the Revolution, asserts that Robespierre wished to establish a republic of *virtue*, and exerted himself to that end with unselfish devotion; and it is true that the younger Robespierre, who was at least the better man of the two, exclaimed when he was indicted by the Assembly, " I have tried to emulate my brother's virtues, and now I wish to share his fate." This is strong evidence.   Unfortunately, in the heat of partisan politics virtue soon becomes a matter of opinion.   The good were those who agreed with Robespierre, and the bad were those who disagreed with him.   There is no blood-poison like a political or philanthropic theory, when it has once obtained complete possession of a man.   He was the incorruptible Robespierre, but his eye was cold and stony.

After all, Mirabeau, Robespierre, and Napoleon were the three great figures of the Revolution, and Carlyle paints their portraits with a bold, vigorous handling.   The first represented resistance to oppression; the second, chaos; and the third, a return to common sense.   Only Mirabeau's death saved him from the guillotine; but he died because he also had drunk too deeply in the immorality of his time. Carlyle only gives Napoleon a few touches (" his bronze lips," " the whiff of grape shot "), but there is more about him in *Heroes and Hero-Worship*, a volume in which Carlyle's peculiar style becomes positive mannerism; nor has it much except a few brilliant passages to recommend it. All long-protracted and bloody revolutions have been followed by imperialism, and Napoleon happened to be the right man. He disciplined the French, and brought them to their senses.

Oliver Cromwell.

History takes its course from social and political movements, which either succeed or fail according to the momentum which they acquire and the skill with which the force thus developed is directed. The success of the Revolution of '89 was a foregone conclusion. It did not even require a Mirabeau to guide it; but to reap and secure the fruits of that Revolution required the most remarkable executive ability ever born in modern times.

Carlyle appreciated this, as one of the few Englishmen of his time, but he did not perceive it clearly enough to describe it, and it would hardly have been patriotic for him to have done so; for that, apparently, would have placed his own country in a false position with regard to history,—only apparently, however; for is not the spark that is struck from flint by steel a symbol of all light and enlightment, by which all mankind improves and progresses ? So by the same instinct which instructs the birds to fly southward in cold weather, he returned to a situation in English history closely allied to the position of France in 1795.

Mommsen compares Cæsar with Henry IV. and

William of Orange: truly a weak comparison. He had better have compared him with Cromwell and Napoleon, both of whom acquired the utmost power by mental force and strength of character, without the help of hereditary right. Cromwell, though he never wore a crown, was the greatest of English kings, and, like Frederick of Prussia, was equally admirable either as a statesman or a soldier. Marlborough and Wellington may have carried on war on a larger scale, but they were not more successful, nor did their victories produce such important results.

The *Life of Cromwell* is an invaluable book, and the student of history should by no means neglect it; but of Carlyle's more important works it is the least entertaining; the larger part of it being made up of Cromwell's letters and speeches which are practical, sensible, and often interesting, but unimaginative and full of religious repetition,* which has frequently been mistaken for cant; and it seems as if Cromwell might have spared us a portion of it. His letters are not as interesting as Napoleon's; whose grand ideas and comprehensive views, expressed so simply and forcibly, constitute a classic in French literature. Carlyle's interludes are often brilliant and witty.

Metternich, who was at the university when Louis XVI. was beheaded, never could see anything behind the French Revolution except a revolt of the lower classes against their more fortunate superiors;

---

* According to Cicero the word "religion" is derived from *relegere*—to repeat.

and there may be mossy old aristocrats in Europe now who view it in the same light. Their number, however, must be small. In dealing with that subject, Carlyle had public opinion wholly on his side, but in writing of Cromwell he was forced to contend against it. The Tories had always considered Cromwell the Satanic adventurer and arch-regicide, mitigated by his superior administrative abilities; while the Whigs regarded him as an ambitious usurper, and the Judas of his own party, Carlyle from his deep sense of brotherhood with all true greatness, recognized the man as he was. He combatted public opinion and won a signal victory. He is credited with having reversed the judgment of mankind in Cromwell's favor.

The chief critical interest of the book lies in Carlyle's explanations of Cromwell's assumption of autocratic power; and in this we find the same indifference to political science heretofore recorded. He says:

"Great lakes of watery *Correspondence* relating to the History of this Period, as we intimate, survive in print; and fresh deluges are occasionally issued upon mankind: but the essence of them has never yet in the smallest been elaborated by any man; will require a succession of assiduous series of many men to elaborate it. To pluck-up the great History of Oliver from it, like drowned Honor by the locks; and to show it to much-wondering and, in the end, right-thankful England! The richest and noblest thing England hitherto has."

"And now, if we practically ask ourselves, What is to

become of this small junto of men, somewhat above a Hundred in all, hardly above Half-a-hundred the active part of them, who now sit in the chair of authority? the shaping-out of any answer will give rise to considerations. These men have been carried thither by miraculous interpositions of Providence; they may be said to sit there only by a continuance of the like. They cannot sit there forever. They are not Kings by birth, these men; nor in any of them have I discovered qualities as of a very indisputable King by attainments."

He concludes briefly that a body of men so constituted was not capable of governing the country, whereas Cromwell was so. Might became right, and the weaker party was obliged to retire from the field.

This is good and true enough, but there is more to this subject. Neither the Parliament nor Cromwell were legally constituted authorities. As early as April, 1649, Lord Fairfax had requested Parliament to fix a day for its dissolution and arrange for a fresh election according to law. Parliament had appointed a day for adjournment, but when the time came declined to adjourn, and two years later the same Parliament was still sitting. There were only something more than half the original number represented in it. It exercised its authority as Cromwell did his, by the right of revolution. Charles Stuart, the only lawful authority for the kingdom by whom the summons for a new Parliament could be issued, was in exile. Yet there *was* a government in England; and the question arises, Was the real governing power vested in Parliament, or in the army of which Cromwell was the head ?

Carlyle might have hit closer to the truth by calling the Parliament a set of popes, rather than a set of kings. In addition to the fact that its members were more given to religion than to statecraft, parliamentary government as we now understand it had not yet been invented. The honest gentry and yeomanry of England would have been greatly puzzled at the notion of being governed by a party leader in the House of Commons. The office would have possessed small dignity in their estimation. The situation was analogous to that of France when Napoleon was chosen consul for life. The civil war was ended, it is true, but insurrection was liable to break out at any time. Prince Rupert was in command of a squadron of war-ships, and the young princes had established a permanent basis for future operations at the court of Louis XIV. Meanwhile the Dutch were taking advantage of the national evils to secure for themselves the foreign trade of Europe. There was peril without, and poverty within the realm. To attempt the formation of a republic would have been a tentative experiment, fraught with danger, as all political experiments are.

The popular impression has been that the Parliament was in favor of a republic, and that the army supported Cromwell in aspiring to the sovereignty. It is true that the army supported Cromwell first, last, and always; but the officers of the army, according to Bulstrand, favored a republic; while the members of Parliament favored a return to monarchy. The conversation reported by Bulstrand at Cromwell's *levée*, after the battle of Worcester, is intensely interesting. All the speakers but one favored a mixture of republic and monarchy, and Cromwell himself thought that " a republic, with something of a monarchy in it, would be more effectual."

It was Colonel Desborow who inquired why England could not, like other nations (that is, Holland), be governed in the way of a republic; and Whitlocke replied to him, that the laws of England were so interwoven with the power and practice of monarchy, that to arrange a government without something of a monarchy in it, would cause too great an alteration in the legal proceedings of the realm. Cromwell introduced the discussion with a request that those present should consult for the interest of the nation, so as to form a government that would preserve the civil and religious liberty which had been won by the sword.

There were not a few speakers on this occasion who favored the recall of the Stuarts, although having just defeated them on the field of battle;— enough to startle Cromwell into a knowledge of what dangerous stuff human nature may be, especially in the hour of triumph. He must have clearly foreseen, then and there, that the recall of the Stuarts would eventually be death to the regicides; and so it proved to be after the Restoration. He knew also that if they returned through the support of the French king, they would bring with them the despotic politics of the French court. The revolution would have to be fought over again. Shall we blame Cromwell because, with such a prospect before him, he concluded that the only person in England to be altogether trusted was *himself*, and that he must keep the reins of the government in his own hands? It was the most patriotic course that he could have adopted.

" In a multitude of counsellors there is safety." There was never such another solecism. In the multitude of counsellors there is confusion, indecision, vacillation, and compromise. A captain when he is guiding a ship in a storm does not want to be troubled with the advice of a select board of passengers. The question between Cromwell and the Parliament was one of life or death. The ease with which the Parliament was dispersed, and the strong support which public opinion gave Cromwell from that time forward, justify the measure, though an arbitrary and dangerous one. His army was the same irresistible army after his death that it was before; but it lacked a head, was irresolute and powerless.

Carlyle's formula, that *might* makes *right*, would seem to have been an awkward argument for the justification of arbitrary acts by Cromwell, Frederick, and others; and his constant repetition of it became a standing grievance with friends, like Emerson and John Sterling, who never could understand his meaning. The exercise of arbitrary power is not to be justified in that manner. The original object of government and of the development of law was to prevent *might* from becoming *right:* and so it always will be.   Much better is Macchiavelli's statement that a necessary war is always a just one. The true justification of Cromwell is found in what Secretary Seward called the " higher law," and Webster the " right of revolution."   When, as in England during the reign of Charles I., or in the United States under President Buchanan, law and government are turned into an engine of oppression, and there is no near expectation of a remedy,—then revolution is in order, and men like Cromwell and John Brown come to the front.   The grand convocation of pedantic stick-in-the-muds may carp at this till doomsday, and cry out in perpetual chorus that the trouble would have cured itself in due time; but good historians, and intrinsically great lawyers, have always recognized this principle.

I cannot refrain from introducing here Emerson's lines on Cromwell, supposed to have been inspired by reading Carlyle's history.   It is a shame that so few readers are acquainted with them.

> " Unknown to Cromwell as to me
>   Was Cromwell's measure and degree :
>   Unknown to him as to his horse,
>   Whether he or the groom are better or worse.
>   He works, plots, fights 'mid rude affairs,
>   With squires, knights, kings his craft compares,
>   Till late he learned through doubt and fear
>   Broad England harbored not his peer ;
>   Unwilling still the last to own
>   The genius on his cloudy throne."

Frederick the Great.

How grandly did Carlyle map out the work of his life,—if it were not after all the measure of his own mental depths. The three great events in history since the Reformation (of which Cromwell was the last champion) have the been the rise of Prussia, the French Revolution, and the growth of the United States of America. Two of these Carlyle has chronicled in such a manner that it will be long before any one will attempt to do his work over again.

Carlyle does not paint Frederick as a rose-colored ideal. In the very beginning he says:

" Friedrich is by no means one of the perfect demigods, and there are various things to be said against him with good ground. To the last a questionable hero, with much in him which one could have wished not there, and much wanting which one could have wished. But there is one feature which strikes you at an early period of the inquiry, That in his way he is a Reality ; that he always means what he speaks ; grounds his actions, too, on what he recognizes for the truth ; and, in short, has nothing whatever for the Hypocrite or Phantasm—which some readers will admit to be an extremely rare phenomenon."

This is what the stockbrokers call a conservative statement. Elsewhere he says, " Friedrich was not a great luminous intelligence," seeing deeply into the mystery of life and human affairs, " but rather a steel-bright soul," reflecting the best intelligence of his time with a basis of strength and tenacity to

resist the shocks and endure the conflicts of nations.
This was what was wanted for a man in his position;
especially for such times as Frederick lived in.   A
Dante or a Goethe, vibrating to the *cordex* with
tender sensibilities, could not have commanded an
army or even supported the daily strain of government business.

There is a prejudice against success as well as for
it.   Gustavus Adolphus loses his life by rashness on
the field of Lützen, and is canonized as the ideal
hero; Frederick, who was not more daring than
prudent, pulls safely through seven terrible years of
warfare, enlarges his dominions, and is looked upon
as an ambitious potentate greedy for conquest.
Charles Sumner made use of Frederick as an example of the menace which arises to the peace of
nations from the maintenance of standing armies.

After all, did not Frederick accomplish the
toughest piece of work which it was ever given to
mortal man to succeed in.   The whole continent of
Europe, except Spain and Holland, was leagued
against him; he had only three millions of people,
and a country as large as New England, to draw his
resources from; and yet his enemies could not crush
him.   At Rossbach, with an army of twenty-six
thousand, he utterly routed a French force of
seventy-five thousand.   At Leuthen he so dispersed
an Austrian army of eighty thousand men that they
never came together again until within sight of
Vienna.   Only Napoleon, in his Italian campaign,
has ever achieved such successes.   Certainly this is
one kind of heroism, and if not of the highest order

it was a kind exceedingly useful to Prussia, and to all Protestant Germany. Gustavus also might have wished for territory, and the Swedes certainly claimed it when the Thirty Years' War was ended.

Frederick did not go to war because he had a well-disciplined army. A standing army may supply the means of warfare more readily, but it is also the most effective means of preserving peace. If the United States government had possessed a regular army of sixty thousand in 1861, we should not have had four years of fratricidal strife in this country. By the treaty of Westphalia nearly one half of Silesia had been conceded to Prussia, but after the Swedes had evacuated Germany the Austrian government refused to surrender it. Such a claim could not be outlawed in less than a hundred years, and Frederick finding himself in a strong position demanded his rights, and marched his army in to take possession,—to the great rejoicing of the inhabitants. The act, however, had an effect on the course of Prussian history which Frederick could not have foreseen.

In the perpetual wars which occurred between France and Austria from that time until 1859, Prussia had been obliged to act an apparently dubious part. To permit France to obtain a sufficient advantage to seize on German territory would not have been patriotic, and Prussian statesmen, with the exception of Haugwiz, have always recognized this as an absolute principle of their policy. At the same time it was important that Austria should not become powerful enough to deal at pleasure with the other German states. This gave a superficial appearance of fickleness to Frederick's policy, which the facts did not justify. He was not the ally of France in the first Silesian war, and had a perfect right to make peace without consulting the French government. Afterwards, when the French were overmatched, and Frederick saw there was danger that the victorious Austrian army would be turned against him, he attacked the Austrians again.

So, in 1858, when Napoleon III. had defeated the Austrians in two engagements, the king of Prussia placed his army on the Rhine, and both sides hastened to make peace; Napoleon, for fear of losing what he had gained, and Franz Josef, because he did not like to be under obligations to Prussia for assistance. You will often hear of the unprincipled policy of Prussia, and this is the explanation of it. The present reorganization of Germany has brought it to an end.

There seem to have been various underlying causes for the Seven Years' War. It was an alliance of all the Catholic powers of Europe against the Protestant powers. This fact has attracted much attention of late among German writers; and Carlyle also notices that France, Spain, Austria, and Russia were governed by women, or their parasites, at that time, and Prussia and Great Britain by men. Both Carlyle and Macaulay exonerate Frederick from the responsibility of the war, and it is amazing that Sumner or anyone else should have held him responsible for it.

Looked at broadly, it was a war of sham against

reality, of pretension against plain dealing, of super-stition against intelligence, of stagnation against progress, of mis-government against good govern-ment, and of injustice against justice. Frederick did not pretend to be a high-minded man. He was more like Augustus than Aurelius; but he knew how to govern, and succeeded better in the reforms he undertook than Joseph II., who was the nobler nature of the two. It may be said to the everlast-ing glory of Frederick, that he was the first to estab-lish popular education on a broad foundation; which, if looked upon as a human invention, may be com-pared to the motive power of steam, or to the uses of electricity. He not only provided the essential means of it, but had the law enforced, so that it was impossible for a boy to grow up ignorant in Prussia, as it is still in France and Italy. He reformed the Prussian law, which was more involved than those of most other countries, fifty years before Na-poleon's code; abolishing the profession of attor-ney altogether, and compelling all suits before the courts to be finished within one year,—two highly important reforms.

Prussia thus became the first nation in the world's history founded on universal intelligence; and when we consider that fact we need not be surprised at any events which have since taken place there. There is a remarkable prediction in the preface to Carlyle's *Life of Frederick*, which I believe was written about 1855; a prediction fulfilled in the Franco-German war, and the hegemony of Bismarck. Met-ternich was filled with jealous admiration for the progress of Prussia in his own time, and attributed it to the energy, and administrative faculty of the early Prussian kings.   An English writer on tactics considers the Prussian staff the most formidable military organization since the time of the Romans.

Frederick could not have accomplished what he did without the earnest support of all Protestant Germany.   A strong military power was necessary as the basis for that grand epoch of German literature and scholarship which has since astonished the world.   Nations instinctively feel their destiny, and Frederick was as much the product of German consciousness, as Goethe and Beethoven.   Goethe's father was an ardent partisan of Frederick, although he dwelt far from the Prussian boundary; and thousands of recruits were gathered to Frederick's standard from Swabia and the Rhineland, just as the young men of Maryland went over to Lee's army, and the mountaineers of Tennessee enlisted with General Thomas.   Rossbach was to Goethe what the battle of Marathon was to Sophocles.

Such was Carlyle's work : to describe this man who was the most important person living in that time; and he has done it without palliation for his faults, or exaggeration for his virtues ;—the most veritable presentment of a great administrator known to literature.   Emerson wrote to Carlyle after reading the book, " It is easily the greatest of histories," and that is what I said myself half a dozen times while perusing it.   Whether I should say so now I do not feel sure.   They told me in Berlin that it was one of the best biographies of Frederick; but what German literary genius has been born in this century equal to Carlyle. There may be German historians who represent the logic of events better than he, but it is doubtful if any have given such a grand pictorial account of the Seven Years' War. The sketch of German history also which fills his first volume, and through which he traces the rising fortunes of the Hohenzollern family, is most interesting reading,—animated and full of wit. Nothing entertains like imagination.

The severity of Lowell's critique on Carlyle,* and deliberate depreciation of the *Life of Frederick*, is measurably excused by its being written during the war for the Union, when Carlyle's lukewarm sympathy with the slaveholders' revolution was only too notorious. Had the essay been written ten years earlier, or ten years later, it must have expressed a different and a better feeling. Cynicism has often been charged against Carlyle, but I think it must have arisen from a misunderstanding of the difference between satire and cynicism. Of deeply enjoyable, heart-warming humor he has always enough, and also some pretty keen satire; but I do not remember any cynicism. A cynical writer is my abhorrence. It is the language of Mephistopheles. It is one with snobbishness; and who would suspect Carlyle of that ?

Satire often seems rather sharp when it is used as an argument against us. Carlyle said during the civil war to some New Englander, " Why don't you

* See Appendix A.

let those bad people in the South go to the devil if they will, and then you good people in the North get to heaven *if you can."*   This is very witty, and seems sensible enough from an outside point of view; but here political science steps in to tell us that a government will never permit its authority to be disputed so long as it can prevent it.   The sense of national unity lies at the base of patriotism, and when a people once become divided they cease to have much historical value.   In his old age Carlyle read the Harvard Memorial biographies, and said in a contemplative manner, " I doot I have been wrang."

His support of negro slavery was a strange thing. How could the man who sympathizes so closely with the sufferings of the French peasantry under the old *régime,* who in *Sartor Resartus* venerates the hand hardened by manual labor, and who could speak of the humble toil of the Silesian farmers as something beautiful to him,—how could he refuse an equal sympathy to other suffering millions merely because they were black ?   His friends argued this question with him all through life, but without ever persuading him to change his position. He thought slavery was the best thing for "Sambo." Elizur Wright, a tough Ohio utilitarian radical, once shook him a little in argument by asserting that slavery was worse for the white owner than it was for the negro chattel.

Despite the peculiarities of Carlyle's style, which became a kind of mannerism as he advanced in life, the *History of Frederick* is written in a plainer and less poetic language than the *French Revolution;* and though it contains more than three thousand pages, the last chapter is as instinct with vitality as the first. There may be dead sentences in it, but no dead paragraphs. No other work of equal length is so well sustained, and so free from monotone. Lowell did not find the subject an interesting one, but I think we may conclude this to have been his own fault. It is impossible for an unprejudiced reader not to sympathize with Frederick in his barbarous treatment by an eccentric father (instigated by the Austrian court in one of the vilest intrigues in history), with his love for his noble-hearted sister, with his respect for learning and literature, and finally with the almost superhuman struggle of the Seven Years' War. Frederick's friends were mostly a disappointment to him, and this may have been largely his own fault; but it is a rare chance when a man elevated by both rank and genius above his cotemporaries can make intimate friends for himself. He was beloved by his own people, and I have been enough with the common people of Prussia to know that they regard his memory much as we do the name of Washington. He was not so virtuous as Washington, but he was one of the bravest, wisest, and most skilful of men.

Memoirs and Correspondence:

When Carlyle's friends desired him to write an autobiography, he replied that he did not consider that his biography was worth writing. Fortunately he reconsidered the matter and wrote his *Reminiscences;* divided into sections, and inscribed respectively to his father, to Edward Irving, to his wife, and to Lord Jeffreys. It is the most modest account that any celebrated man has given of himself, and an equally graceful tribute to his relatives and friends. His pictures of Scottish country life, of his schoolmates and his school-teachers, of the struggles of his youth and the distinguished acquaintances of his later years, are drawn with the quiet, simple fidelity of Albert Dürer's woodcuts. How vivid is his description of Wordsworth, quietly eating his dates behind a green shade, amid the glare and clatter of a London dinner-party. How clearly that incident stands forth to the mind's eye. How amusing his account of the Scotch merchant who informed Carlyle that '' Poetry was the proodooction of a rude aage,'' which his auditor listened to without remonstrance.

Matthew Arnold estimated the Carlyle and Emerson correspondence so highly that he ventured to predict that the two authors would survive in it rather than in their deliberate publications. Without believing this too readily, we can recognize it as the capstone of a literary and artistic edifice, such as there are few enough examples of. Whether the future generations will find the same interest in it that we do, who have felt the personality of these two mighty men, is somewhat uncertain. Meanwhile let those read it who wish to know what Emerson and Carlyle really were at heart; remembering always that what was written therein was never intended for the public eye. Emerson especially it places before the world in so favorable a light that none can refuse to recognize. The strong, sensible kindliness and friendliness of these letters is their chief attraction, but they are also full of delicious humor. Carlyle thought that Emerson was the whitest soul on the planet; but he should have known Rev. Samuel Johnson of Salem.

Carlyle's correspondence with Goethe is more formal and less sympathetic. Goethe was over eighty at the time, and some of his letters are a trifle drowsy; but there are passages also full of intellectual fire which proclaim the superiority of the great master. It is, if anything, the more valuable book of the two.

Froude's Biography.

Carlyle's *Reminiscences* left small need of a biography; and the story which Froude has told in three bulky volumes is not so well expressed there as in the two smaller ones. Froude deserves credit for his sincerity, especially as he was the most trusted of Carlyle's friends; but it is still an open question how far the biographer has a right to reveal the secrets of domestic life to the public eye. There certainly must be a limit, and if we ask where the line is to be drawn the answer must be, " Only good judgment can decide." A finer sense of delicacy than Mr. Froude's would have refrained from lifting the curtain from over the Carlyle household in the way he has done. His determination to tell the truth has resulted in producing an erroneous impression.

Carlyle never talked against his wife, and his tribute to her in his *Reminiscences* is most tender and appreciative. It is enough to say of it that there are no finer passages in modern prose.

Jane Carlyle was not only devoted to her husband's well-being, but she could give him full sympathy in his intellectual strivings ; and this rarely happens to a man of genius.

Carlyle's life, however, was one of unremitting toil. His writings brought him little money, so that it was not often that he could look forward with certainty to the means of subsistence. His nerves were as sensitive as Bismarck's, without Bismarck's excellent digestion. Such dyspepsia as he suffered from has led weaker men to suicide. No wonder if his writing assumes a gloomy tinge in places, and that he was troubled with unhappy forebodings. He must have possessed an heroic constitution to have lived through it all; for it is said that the German who translated *Frederick* into his own language was killed by the exertion. It was Jane Carlyle's fate also to fall by the way, in this life-long campaign of forced marches.

There is even more to be said on the other side. Mrs. Ireland's admirable biography of Jane Carlyle has certainly succeeded in vindicating Carlyle himself from ill-treatment or neglect of his wife. You may read the book through, and then ask yourself what cause for complaint Mrs. Carlyle might have had. She was jealous of Lady Ashburton, at whose house Carlyle received the only social recognition of his life; and she was even jealous of Emerson, whom Carlyle never met but three times, at long intervals apart. In such cases the irritating cause is something that never appears on the surface. Mrs. Ireland, with exceptional frankness, gives even stronger testimony.

" She, as well as Carlyle, had a strong disposition and fiery temper. When provoked she showed a thoroughly unamiable side of her nature—inflexible she was—and her words cut like knives. Another element of her blood, pointed out by Dr. Japp, does much, in his idea (and I agree with him), to account for many traits in her character. It has been somewhat overlooked, though told with some pride by Mrs. Carlyle in speaking of her own ancestry, that she had a decided strain of gipsy blood. That famous gipsy chieftain, Matthew Baillie, who could steal a horse from under the owner, if he liked, was yet said to be a thorough gentleman in his way."

Only the Reign of Terror could equal such a piece of human mechanism: a woman attractive as a siren, a true heroine withal; yet with the reckless idiosyncrasy of a gipsy, and a tongue in her like a whip-lash. Truly a man who has endured such an infliction on earth might require small punishment hereafter. Is there need of further explanation on this subject? If Carlyle sometimes became enraged with her, it is no more than other men would have done. Honors were even. They both struggled faithfully, if not always successfully, and we cor-

dially respect them in spite of their inherited weaknesses.

What I feel especially in regard to Carlyle is that
he was a man with a Heart in him.   He meant what
he said and felt what he wrote, more than Emerson
or Byron or Thackeray or Tennyson.   He has often
been called a pessimist, but the question is whether
the effect of his words is cheering or discouraging.
In this world of perversion and misrepresentation
such a truth-teller shines like a light-house to the uncertain and dubious mariner, giving assurance that
civilization lies not far beyond.

Carlyle sometimes sacrificed truth to his love of
humor.   What he wrote Emerson about Sterling's
Secret of Hegel was exceedingly witty, but although
it might apply to Hegel's own writings, it was not
appropriate for Sterling's book at all.   He was also
fond of practical jokes.   About six years before his
death an adventurous young lady from Boston requested the permission of an interview with him.
This having been granted, after a long conversation
she produced an album, at which he laughed and
volunteered to write in it of his own accord.   " I
will give you," he said, " an old Scotch proverb,
which contains the wisdom of the world in four
lines "; and then wrote the following:

> " Jamie Geddes had a coo :
>   He lost his coo, and nowhere could he find her.
>   When he had done a' mon could do,
>   The coo came home, and brought her tail behind her."

FROUDE

WHENCE do we obtain our historical opinions? Are they not mostly instilled in us in our homes in early years, or at the first schools which we attend, before we are able to reason with regard to them? The impressions of our childhood are the most lasting, and if erroneous the most difficult to eradicate. What we learn at home becomes a matter of feeling with us, stimulates patriotism, and assists in the formation of a national character. This is very valuable; but what we learn at school from immature and abbreviated text-books often warps the mind and stultifies the judgment. Books that are written in order to make history entertaining and popular to young people, also frequently do a deal of mischief.

Dickens's *Child's History of England* belongs to the latter class. At the time it was published, forty years ago, Dickens was the most popular writer on either side of the Atlantic, and the book was everywhere given to children as a highly moral and amusing work. It was bright, witty, sentimental, and the young people liked it. Their parents also read it, as they afterwards read Miss Alcott's *Little*

Women. I think the popular opinion of English history in this country, until within the last ten years, was derived from Dickens rather than any other source. I feel as if I had scarcely yet recovered from the impression his book made on me; though it was no more deserving of respect than the tales of an uneducated nursery woman. The manner in which he speaks of the Anglo-Saxon chronicle, for one item, shows conclusively that he was writing at hazard and cared little for the truth.

On one occasion, after the reading of Shakespeare's *King John*, a lady present quoted Dickens's opinion of John's brother Richard to this effect: '' He was a king who seemed to have but one idea in his head, and that, the rather uncomfortable idea of breaking the heads of other people. He is said to have had the heart of a lion, but I think it would have been much better if he had had the heart of a man.'' This sounded well, and was applauded by the company; but nothing could have been more unjust or mean-spirited,—for Richard the First, though he was fond of fighting, always fought in a good cause, and it should never be forgotten that he forgave and liberated the man who caused his death. What other king, potentate, or soldier has done the like ?

Dickens regarded history as a humanitarian, and as material for his pen; but Froude, like Macaulay before him, from the standpoint of a statesman. When his *History of England* was published and reasons were discovered in it for supposing that Henry VIII. was not so bad a man as had been believed, a storm of indignation arose which raged

along the whole Atlantic coast. Fair-minded persons, who liked to hear both sides of the controversy, and have the case thoroughly sifted, were
unable to speak in Mr. Froude's defence. In public and private alike their mouths were stopped by
an universal clamor. Even at his own hearthstone
a man's wife would say to him: " Don't talk to me
of a king who had six wives, and put two of them to
death: the thing speaks for itself." It would seem
as if public opinion was afraid of being cheated of
its prey; and this would have been reasonable
enough, if anything had been known of Henry
VIII. except the external facts; and the external
facts of history are like pictures in an old illustrated
paper or magazine, which we have to be informed
about before we can understand them.

James Anthony Froude was an English gentleman
of fairly independent fortune, born at Dartington in
the county of Devon on April 3, 1818,—the anniver-
sary of Shakespeare's birth, as has been supposed.
He studied at Oriel College, Oxford, and there came
under the influence of Francis Newman, whose exalted spirituality collected about him the most high-
minded young men of that day. It was evidently
from Francis Newman that Froude derived the
liberal theology which marked his earlier publications, and which may be perceived as an undercurrent
in his later and more mature writing. He cannot
be considered liberal so far as Catholicism is concerned; but as between Puritanism and the Established Church of England, it would not be easy to
find a fairer or more discriminating judge; though

he considered Puritanism the sheet-anchor of the Protestant cause, without which it would have been lost forever.

The apostasy of John H. Newman and his imposing train of followers (chiefly persons of rank and fashion), between 1850 and 1870, may have led Froude to investigate the period of the Reformation in England, and to give the result of his researches an historical form. Froude considered if he reminded his countrymen of the high price their ancestors had paid for their religious faith, with its established church and thirty-nine articles, that they would value it better; and his expectation was not disappointed. Napoleon said at St. Helena that, as a rule, it was best for men to continue in the religion in which they were brought up. How sensible and far-sighted this is. All forms of religion have their value, and are suited to different races and nationalities; the Catholicism of to-day is not the Catholicism of Leo and Clement; but that an educated Protestant should return to the Catholic faith would seem to show a lamentable weakness. Human souls falling down an abyss of time are ready to clutch at anything that will give them a temporary support.

Froude's father was an archdeacon, and he contemplated taking orders himself, but he found after graduating at Oxford that he could not do this with a clear conscience. He foresaw that he would be obliged to preach what he did not believe, as so many of the clergy are doing at the present time. In this emergency Carlyle appeared to him as the type of an independent life, of all others most worthy of imitation. He therefore resolved to follow Carlyle's example, and fought his way boldly and bravely.

The London *Times* published rather a mean obituary of Froude, but it confessed that after all " he was to be classed among the ' immortals.' " If his *History of England* was not received by English critics with unanimous approval, yet a substantial majority gave it a hearty commendation; and it may now be looked on as a standard work. The Catholic party naturally attacked it in a vehement manner.*

Froude's style as a writer is much in his favor. It is not so impressive as Carlyle's, nor so pleasant-flavored as Thackeray's; neither does it have the splendor of Burke and Bacon; but for clear crystalline English there is hardly its superior in the present century. Froude is sometimes slightly melodramatic in feeling, but the purity of his language is beyond dispute. It would seem as if he wished to place his case before the world in the plainest possible manner, considering good sense the finest ornament of speech. His writing can be read with great rapidity and yet be perfectly intelligible.

If we are to suppose that the faults in Macaulay's style result from peculiarities in his character, we are justified in believing that Froude's English is representative of the man himself. This corresponds with what we know of his character. I met him in

---

* The daughter of Byron's old friend Trelawney wrote to a friend in 1872: " Of course I pin my faith on Froude. I think his style is perfect,"—which I give as an example of English opinion. The Trelawneys were liberals.

Boston in the winter of 1873; the lean, angular type of Saxon, reminding one slightly of Emerson in the cast of his features and in the cheerful serenity of his expression: a fine example of a modest, self-possessed gentleman, who preferred the quiet pleasure of his work, and the society of his friends, to public performances and fashionable entertainments. Especially was the sincerity of the man apparent in everything he said and did.

At a banquet given in his honor in the city of New York, Emerson said, " Mr. Froude surprises us by the novelty of his conclusions, but we cannot help respecting the earnestness and sincerity of his argument."

There is no shadow of ostentation in his writing, nor any sophistical attempt to force an unfair conclusion on the reader; and yet it is not without a slight peculiarity. If the tendency of Macaulay was to turn history into an oration, and Carlyle to make poetry out of it, Froude's danger is continually to give it the form and character of a novel. This is not apparent in his first two volumes, and may have resulted from the enjoyment of his work, and the overflow of genius, which led him to a fancied perception of the thoughts and motives of his actors beyond what a prudent judgment should permit. The dramatic poet can take historical characters and mould them at his will. He can expose their most secret thoughts, and the desires which lie closest to their hearts; for they are after all men and women of his own creation. The historian must also do something like this, but he should beware of carrying analysis too far. We are too often mistaken in regard to the motives of those with whom we live, to judge with certainty of persons whom we have never seen. Two notable instances of this kind are, Froude's account of the regent Murray of Scotland and his diagnosis of Cicero. The historian has a right to his opinions, and may bring forward arguments in support of them, but he should be cautious of too didactic an assertion.

If, however, Froude sometimes idealizes his characters, he never romances in regard to his facts. Perfect accuracy would seem to be a human impossibility where the ground to be covered is so extensive and the information has to be obtained from documents in three or four different languages, but Froude has at least not fallen short in this respect of what might be expected of him. Macaulay is continually being cross-examined by critics of the present day, and Carlyle also made some mistakes, which he was ever ready to acknowledge. The numerous foot-notes in Froude's history referring to a variety of writers, state papers, and other material, such as no historian had ever collected before, bear strong testimony in favor of his truthfulness. When in 1873 an American priest, assisted by Wendell Phillips, attacked his veracity, Froude came forward with an offer to any person who might consider himself an impartial judge, to examine any hundred pages of his history in all the languages from which his information was derived, for which he (Froude) would pay the whole expense, including a suitable compensation, on condition that the investigator would make a public statement of the result of his inquiry. No one accepted the challenge, but it produced an excellent impression; for people realized better how difficult it is to ascertain the truth in regard to past events.

Son of man has rarely set for himself a more difficult task than this of analyzing the course of the religious reformation. The chief distinction between the English and Germans lies in this, that the English care more for the form than the spirit, and the Germans more for the spirit than the form. In Germany, owing to the clear popular perception of right and wrong, and with the help of some enlightened princes, the revolution was quickly accomplished and without much confusion or loss of life. For this same reason the German Protestants were less prepared for the counter revolution a hundred years later.

In England events took a wholly different course. The English respect for custom and tradition is the true safeguard of English political freedom, but it makes them as a people slow to accept innovations and even salutary improvements. Horse-cars, which are a decided advantage to the weaker sex, were readily adopted in Paris, and christened with international courtesy, " *chemin de fer Américaine,*" but they did not succeed in London. The useless and troublesome distinction in England between " barrister " and " attorney " was abolished in Prussia by Frederick a hundred and twenty years ago. The English people in the sixteenth century were as much alive as the Germans to the corrupt administration of the Catholic Church. They recognized the inconsistency between the sensual lives of the priests and nuns, and the doctrine they professed; they suspected, justly enough, that the money expended in building magnificent Roman palaces had been filched from the superstition of the poor; and they cordially supported their king in his effort to cleanse this Augean stable. They wished, however, to preserve their allegiance to the pope, to rehabilitate the old structure, to purify the Catholic Church within itself; and when this was found impossible they tried to establish an English Catholic Church, in which their king should be the highest spiritual, as well as temporal authority. At one time they approximated to German Lutheranism, and again recoiled violently from it. It was not until the reign of Elizabeth, and after Mary had attempted to reestablish the old creed with all its enormities, that English Protestantism adopted a form like that by which we now know it.

Religious toleration was a thing unknown, and men were more likely to become intolerant while stimulated by party passion. Heresy, even in regard to a single article of faith, was a higher crime than high treason. Fire was the only punishment it was supposed that would eradicate it. Thus those high-minded, patriotic souls who foresaw the ultimate result, and had labored to bring it to pass, were the ones most in danger. The confusion that each successive change produced in the community may be imagined. The king himself was not safe unless he could steer his course so as to always secure the support of a majority of his nobles.   The man who only cared for his own life could not tell what to believe or say; and he who was at the top of affairs to-day might be decapitated to-morrow.   '' The idea of a people changing their religion,'' says Macchiavelli, '' is enough to strike terror into the stoutest heart.''

The picture reminds us of France in 1793, but with this difference: what was condensed in the French Revolution within a space of two years, was spread out in the English Reformation like a long panorama, and all the more trying and difficult on that acount.

It was a transition period, and such are of all periods of history the most troublesome to deal with. What was the dark ages but a transition period ? A hundred years afterward both Catholics and Protestants looked back on the English Reformation with intense disgust; for, superficially considered, neither party could take much credit for it.   Both sides agreed, however, in heaping obloquy on Henry VIII.; for he had persecuted both Catholics and Protestants.   Of course there was a reason for this, as there is for all things; but the reason lay concealed.   All the engines of party virulence were therefore set to work to blacken his memory.   To clear away this historical rubbish, and discover the true lineaments of the man, was a task of the first magnitude.

It were well if we could congratulate James Anthony Froude on his success in dealing with this fourfold problem, but a thorough-going justification of Henry's career is more than we can readily accept;

yet it is a natural error for a writer to fall into when he is obliged to contend against preconceived prejudices. It is certainly better than a thorough-going condemnation, for there is much that can be said in Henry's favor, from whatever point of view we choose to look at him. Dr. Frederick H. Hedge, who was one of the most learned of American scholars in the literature of the Reformation, has given Henry the chief credit of establishing the Protestant faith in the British Islands.

We should distinguish somewhat between his character as an individual and the peculiar traits of his family. The Tudors were different from the Plantagenets, who were a warlike, adventurous, free-hearted, and almost reckless race of monarchs. Henry VII., Henry VIII., Mary, and Elizabeth form a series in which the first and the last are the most alike, and decidedly the best of the four. They were all peaceable, and preferred cultivating their own territory to interfering with that of their neighbors. They encouraged improvements in manufactures and the arts, and, with the exception of Mary, proved good shepherds of the people. During the hundred years and more of their administrations, England made rapid progress in civilization; else we should never have had Shakespeare and Bacon and Johnson. They were, however, reserved, suspicious, and extremely self-willed, as well as the most unmerciful race of sovereigns that Europe had seen since the dark ages. Their victims were put to death according to form of law, whether justly or not it is now impossible to tell;

but even Elizabeth rarely made use of the pardoning power ; Mary and Henry VIII., perhaps never. They were perhaps the first, and certainly the last, rulers in England who sent women to the scaffold for political reasons; that is, for sympathy with the treason of their relatives. The conjugal infidelity of a queen is high treason and punishable by death ; but other sovereigns have commuted it to banishment to some remote castle, where the offender might wear out the rest of her life in small conversation with her retinue of servants. On this point, also, the Tudors were inexorable.

Giustiniani, a Venetian envoy at the English court, has left an invaluable description of Henry VIII., written in 1519, seven years before his divorce from Catherine was first mooted. It is in a report addressed to the Venetian Senate that he says:

" And first of all, his Majesty is twenty-nine years old, and extremely handsome ; nature could not have done more for him ; he is much handsomer than any other sovereign in Christendom, a great deal handsomer than the King of France ; very fair, and his whole frame is admirably proportioned. On hearing that Francis I. wore a beard, he allowed his own to grow, and as it is reddish, he has now got a beard which looks like gold. He is very accomplished ; a good musician ; composes well ; is a capital horseman ; a fine jouster ; speaks good French, Latin, and Spanish ; is very religious ; hears three masses daily when he hunts, and sometimes five on other days : he hears the *office* every day in the Queen's chamber, that is to say, vespers and complins. He is very fond indeed of hunting, and never takes this diversion without tiring eight or ten horses, which he causes to be stationed beforehand along the line of country he expects to take, and when one is tired he mounts another, and before he gets home they are all exhausted. He is extremely fond of tennis; at which game it is the prettiest thing in the world to see him play, his fair skin glowing through a shirt of finest texture.

"He is affable, gracious; harms no one; does not covet his neighbor's goods, and is satisfied with his own dominions, having often said to the ambassador: 'Domine Orator, we want all potentates to content themselves with their own territories; we are satisfied with this island of ours.'"

This is a brilliant Venetian picture, and gives one rather a pleasant impression of this young monarch with the golden beard: a strongly objective nature, serious and yet fond of pleasure, one who enjoys life and wishes others to enjoy it. If he was handsomer than Francis I. he must have been a remarkably fine-looking person at this time; for Titian's portrait of the French king is one of the most attractive in the Louvre. How differently does Henry appear in Holbein's portrait painted fifteen or twenty years later: a blear-eyed, truculent, beefy-looking man, yet not without a certain stamp of sincerity to his face. Great changes must have taken place within him during that time.

His interest in religion is remarkable and rather surprising. His controversy with Luther is a still further evidence in this direction. It was evidently a serious matter to him, and no little to his credit to condescend to such an effort with a German monk.

It is easy to say that his bishops may have supplied the arguments. We may suppose that they assisted him, but why should he claim the work if it was not his own ? We do not hear that Henry was vain, and he certainly was not ambitious. Luther's forci‑ ble logic may have made an impression on him. It was the beginning of the change in his belief. A king, born to rule by natural right, he certainly was not. At twenty-nine we still find him leaving the affairs of state chiefly to his ministers, and so he con‑ tinued until after he was forty; he was not like Louis XIV., Frederick II., or the present Emperor of Germany. Of all forms of activity, statecraft is the most interesting and absorbing, and no one who has the capacity for it will ever willingly relinquish it. Neither was Henry a soldier by temperament. We do not hear that he was lacking in physical courage. He was in fact the average Englishman of his time : frank, fearless, good-humored, and unimaginative ; living in his nervous and muscular system rather than his intellect.

This appears to me the true explanation of Henry VIII. He was a strong-willed and determined man, but lacked the foresight and sound judgment which are required for a statesman. Such a man necessa‑ rily was obliged to depend on others, and where he placed his confidence he placed it for the time being absolutely. Wolsey, Anne Boleyn, Cromwell, and Catherine Parr all had the same experience with him. He trusted them implicitly, indulged them, encouraged them to become autocratic, and as soon as they overstepped the limits of their proper position he turned on them and destroyed them. Shake-speare recognized this peculiar method in him, and has so represented him in the noted scene between Henry and Wolsey, " By your leave, Lord Cardinal, we 'll have but one king here."

There are few people living who heard one of Daniel Webster's speeches, but Webster's manner was so impressive that an imitation even at second hand may still give us a fairly good conception of his style. *Henry the Eighth* is the most highly individualized of Shakespeare's plays, and by following such traditions no doubt he has made the man so life-like that we may almost hear the tones of his voice. As Shakespeare has delineated him, and so far as he has done so, we may trust he actually was.

Neither has Shakespeare been unjust to Cardinal Wolsey. Here also the Venetian ambassador comes to the support of the dramatist with a telling piece of evidence.

" This Cardinal is the person who rules both the King and the entire Kingdom. On the ambassador's first arrival in England he used to say to him,—' *His Majesty will do so and so* '; subsequently, by degrees, he began to forget himself, and commenced saying, ' *We shall do so and so* '; at this present he has reached such a pitch that he says, ' *I shall do so and so.* ' "

Froude gives Wolsey credit for great designs; for planning an alliance with the king of France to release the pope from the power of the emperor, and protect Christians in the East from the increasing tide of Turkish conquest. This may have been the reason for his accumulating such an amount of property, though the plan of course included his own elevation to the papacy if possible. Froude does not seem to have noticed Giustiniani's statement, which is in the appendix to his *Letters from England.*

Wolsey was a man " learned, eloquent, indefatigable, and of vast ability." We may presume that he governed England as well as it ever has been governed; but for all that the king could not permit the royal authority to be overshadowed by him. He presumed too much on Henry's favor and was instantly hurled down.

There has been little difference of opinion in regard to Wolsey's fate; but the divorce from Queen Catherine is a more delicate and difficult question. The common opinion, that Henry was infatuated with Anne Boleyn, and therefore wished to separate from his wife, is a woman's reason. No man who is possessed of large properties would entertain it for a moment. An English nobleman would remind you of the reply of George II. to his dying wife when she advised him to marry again. " *Non, j'aurai maîtresses.*" The family of Anne Boleyn might have felt proud of such a relationship.

A lawyer who wished to ascertain Henry's motives would look for parallel instances. Now, divorces among royal families are rare, for they are sure to occasion political complications, even at the present day; and in the sixteenth century, when kingdoms lost their independence through the hereditary principle, they were simply a thing unknown. Charlemagne, however, divorced two wives, and Napoleon one, and both for political reasons. Napoleon's avowed object was to obtain an heir to the throne, and so was Henry's. If such an act can be justified, this is the only true justification; and he would be a narrow moralist who did not hesitate before such a problem.

Napoleon's divorce has been generally condemned in America, because we feel there was no need of his founding a dynasty, if for no other reason; but Henry had firmer ground to stand on. He had been married, while still a minor, to his brother's widow, and this was contrary to English law. It is a sufficiently absurd law,* quite contrary to common sense, but the English people clung to it, and still cling to it with the same tenacity that they do to their barristers and omnibuses.

Pope Julius II. had granted the young pair a dispensation from the law; but there were many in England who doubted if he had the right to do this, and the fact that all their children excepting "Bloody Mary" (who was frail and delicate enough) died in early youth, gave strength to the

---

* Sumner Maine says of inheritance under the Salic law : " When it was transplanted to England, the English judges, who had no clue to its principle, interpreted it as a general prohibition against the succession of the half-blood, and extended it to *consanguineous* brothers ; that is to sons of the same father by different wives. In all the literature which enshrines the pretended philosophy of law, there is nothing more curious than the pages of elaborate sophistry in which Blackstone attempts to explain and justify the exclusion of the half-blood." The law against marrying a brother's widow may have originated in the same manner.

idea, in those superstitious times, that it was the judgment of Heaven on an iniquitous marriage. Whether Henry shared in this belief is uncertain; but a man who wishes to obtain release from an unfavorable contract would be likely to catch at all such spiritual straws.

Henry appealed to Pope Clement VII. to sanction his divorce by granting him a dispensation from his previous marriage, and Clement might have done this willingly enough; but unfortunately he was wholly in the power of Charles V., who was Catherine's brother. The Pope therefore could not and would not give a definite answer. Years were wasted in fruitless negotiations: Clement had a genius for equivocation, and the hope that the emperor's power might in some way be diminished proved a fallacious dream. The universities of Europe were appealed to, to attest the validity of Henry's claim, but there the agents of Charles again met and defeated him; shameless bribery having been resorted to on both sides. Clement died and Paul III. became pope without the question coming nearer to a settlement. Then Henry called together his parliament; and the representatives of the English people solemnly decreed the well-known Act of Supremacy, which placed their king at the head of the Anglican Church, and separated themselves forever from the Roman See. The divorce followed as a matter of course.

Froude perhaps goes too far in supposing that Henry acted in this matter from a sense of the justice of his cause. His motives, if they could be known, would probably be found a good deal mixed,

—as the motives of most men are. He appears to me to have acted rather from a feeling of necessity, than of justice. His anxiety to place himself before the world in a favorable light is significant, and shows that he must have had a conscience, and that his conscience troubled him.

If Henry waited six years to make Anne Boleyn his wife, we can at least admire his constancy, such as it was; for a middle-aged man is not likely to retain an attachment for a woman longer than a year or eighteen months, unless it be consummated by marriage or otherwise. He knows the nature of women better than a younger man and does not enjoy the same hopes or the same illusions. The act was justified in an historical sense ; for the result of his second marriage was Queen Elizabeth, who inherited the best qualities of both her parents, and to whom the Anglo-Saxon race is as much indebted as the Germans are to that electoral prince of Saxony who protected Luther.

Now if Henry VIII. had only lived happily with Queen Anne until the close of his life, posterity might have condoned his divorce. Unfortunately this was not to be. Who was rightly to blame, it is no longer possible to tell. Superficial opinion says, as before, he became tired of her and wished to marry Jane Seymour,—not noticing the inconsistency of a man's becoming tired in one year of a woman whose society he had been accustomed to for eight or ten years. Although in fact he did marry Jane Seymour after Anne Boleyn, the disappearance of the Spanish nun was not a stranger mystery than the tragic fate of this unfortunate woman. That she should have been guilty of the terrible crimes imputed to her seems as incredible as that, in honest and manly England, she could have been unjustly convicted before the highest tribunal of the realm.

The fatal mistake in dealing with the history of this period arises from the supposition that Henry was an absolute despot; like a Roman emperor, who could send people to the Tower and the scaffold at his will. He was a constitutional sovereign, and, what was most remarkable for those revolutionary times, he never attempted to infringe upon the constitution, but in the most desperate passes of his life always acted according to the form of law. He had no standing army, and his household troops were hardly a more effective force than the present London police. His nobles were not more afraid of him than he was of them.

It should be borne in mind that, of the Plantagenet kings from Richard I. to Richard III., all who proved themselves culpably weak or vicious were either deposed or subjugated by their nobles. There had never been a time when English manliness and sense of honor had not risen to the public need. The national loyalty was fully equalled by the national love of justice. Wrong-doers might be able to sustain themselves for a time; but it rarely happened that they escaped punishment in the long run. The number of executions ordered by Henry VIII. greatly surpassed those of Richard III.; and yet during his long reign there was never a serious rebellion against him, nor popular discontent.

I was once acquainted with a worthy merchant who purchased a handsome edition of Froude's *History of England*, and read it until he came to the statement of Anne Boleyn's trial. There he closed the book, and would never open it again.

This is an illustration of the way in which we may be dominated by preconceived opinions; for nowhere has Froude made a clearer or more impartial statement than in regard to this sad affair. He evidently believes that Anne was guilty; but he never relinquishes the possibility that she may have been innocent, and the whole business a terrible mistake. It is true he prepares the mind of the reader by some unfavorable statements concerning Anne Boleyn's early life, but he purposely nullifies this again by saying, " We are unable to form any trustworthy judgment of Anne Boleyn before her marriage." He describes her conduct when taken to the Tower with tender and pathetic delicacy. It is like a scene from one of the plays of Sophocles; but he justly adds, " While she wins our sympathy, there is nothing in it which helps us to decide whether she was innocent or guilty."

This is true enough. Not many years ago a New England woman was brought to trial for the murder of her nearest relatives. It seemed impossible that she should not have committed the deed; the evidence was strongly against her; and yet she was acquitted on her trial on account of her beautiful behavior in the court-room. If Anne Boleyn had been tried before a jury of Massachusetts mechanics and shopkeepers, she would probably have been acquitted likewise. But she appeared before a sterner tribunal. The jury that indicted her was composed of the highest nobles of the kingdom, and the most trusted servants of the state. Her own uncle, the Duke of Norfolk, the conqueror of Flodden, was president of the investigation, and foremost in catechising his niece. Francis Bacon at a later time was obliged to appear against his former patron in order to avoid the suspicion of being implicated in his foolish insurrection against Elizabeth. This was a sorrowful thing to do, but there was no reason why he should throw away his life for the sake of an unworthy friend. But there does not seem to have been any occasion for such humiliation at the trial of Anne Boleyn. The Duke of Norfolk held the highest reputation of any man among the English people, and if any man could afford to decline serving on this jury, he was the one to do it.

The court was composed of a mixed commission of nobles and gentlemen commoners. It could not be compared with the courts held by the infamous Jeffreys in the reign of James II.; nor is there any reason to suppose that Anne was refused a fair trial. The testimony of witnesses, which would now be more interesting than any other portion of the proceedings, has not been preserved ; but the queen was convicted on every indictment.

If the gentlemen on this tribunal stultified and incriminated themselves by assisting Henry VIII. to judicially murder his wife, the case is not only exceptional in England, but the pontifical tribunal which condemned Beatrice Cenci is the only one with which it can be compared. I cannot believe there has ever been a time since Richard I. when such a deed could be perpetrated in England; when, from among twelve respectable men selected in this manner, half of them would not prefer to be themselves put to death rather than commit such an enormity. The probability would seem to indicate wrong on both sides. Either the king was unfaithful to Anne Boleyn, or gave her reason to believe so by his conduct towards other ladies; and she either retaliated by making reprisals or incurred grave suspicion of doing so. We have learned from a notorious scandal in the present century, how impossible it is sometimes to eliminate the truth in such matters. The jury disagreed, but the opinion of the legal fraternity was against the defendant. The letters said to have been written by Anne to the king, while she was confined in the Tower, are either forgeries or support the view we have just now advanced. They are not such letters as Desdemona or Hermione would have written to a jealous and merciless husband; yet Anne Boleyn may have been the victim of an unjust suspicion as well as Henry Ward Beecher.

In the midst of these horrid details there are passages in Froude's history which give us the pleasant sensation of green, sequestered valleys among barren and horrific mountains. One such is his account of the early life of Bishop Latimer, and another his sympathetic narrative of the martyrdom of the monks of Charter House. The two taken together are convincing proof how Froude *could* be just and fair to both sides of the same question. In delicacy of feeling and simple earnestness of statement his language reminds me of no one so much as President Lincoln, whose Gettysburg address has become as famous as the Declaration of Independence.

Latimer was the noblest man of his time; of finer mental quality, and infinitely more useful than Sir Thomas More. His charming humility was only equalled by his fearlessness in the service of truth. His independent speech attracted the attention of the old devouring bishops, who persecuted him with academic intolerance, and would have destroyed him like tigers in the arena of the Coliseum, but for the interposition, first of Wolsey, and afterwards of the king himself. There is no other proof so convincing of Henry's veracity of character than his protection and support of Latimer from first to last.

Of that self-education, which, in forming a man of true intellectual power, is more important than any university training, Froude says: " Like the physician, to whom a year of practical experience in a hospital teaches more than a life of closet study, Latimer learnt the mental disorders of his age in the age itself; and the secret of that art no other man, however good, however wise, could have taught him."

It is only by taking a share in the practical activity of mankind that the scholar can escape from the benumbing influence of continuous study. Otherwise he stagnates, and his learning becomes like a lump of lead.

The Act of Supremacy, passed by Parliament in

1534, served as a temporary expedient, like Sumner's civil-service bill, to give the Anglican Church a substitute for papal authority during its first years of separation from the Roman pontiff. That Henry VIII. could no more mould Parliament to his will than Charles I. was able to, appears from the stout resistance which Thomas Cromwell gave to a bill of impeachment against Wolsey which had already passed the House of Lords; and it was not long after that when Cromwell was chosen Lord Keeper in Wolsey's place.

All other religious fraternities bent before the storm, but the Charter House monks of London alone preserved their allegiance to the pope. They were an isolated community of the sixth century cast down into the sixteenth, the living embodiment of that heroic self-sacrifice which converted the semi-barbarous hoards that overran and destroyed Roman civilization. Inclosed by the walls of their monastery, what did they know of the progress of events? Their world was stationary, and they supposed the church of Borgia and Clement was filled with the same holy spirit as that of Augustine and Gregory. Neither threats nor entreaties could induce them to subscribe to the Act, and they were broken into fragments: as the Southern army was in defence of Richmond, fighting gloriously for the preservation of African slavery. It would seem as if such heroic devotion to a petrified idea was only a waste of noble material, but Froude perceived in it a higher significance. He says: " They fell gloriously and not unprofitably. They were not allowed to stay the course of the Reformation; but their sufferings, nobly borne, sufficed to recover the sympathy of after-ages for the faith which they professed. Ten righteous men were found in the midst of the corruption to purchase for Romanism a few more centuries of tolerated endurance.''

These ten were executed for treasonable opposition to the government, according to the barbarous method of the age, and the rest were distributed among different monasteries.

Still more worthily does he speak of the unfortunate Anabaptists, who were sacrificed for differences of faith which would even now excite horror in the minds of strictly devotional persons; though one of them, namely that children born of infidels may be capable of salvation, shows a spirit of enlightenment beyond that of Luther and Melanchthon. On the other hand their doctrine of irredeemable sin after baptism would be subversive of all morality.

" For them no Europe was agitated, no courts were ordered into mourning, no papal hearts trembled with indignation. At their deaths the world looked on complacent, indifferent, or exulting. Yet here, too, out of twenty-five common men and women were found fourteen who, by no terror of stake or torture, could be tempted to say that they believed what they did not believe. History for them had no praise; yet they too were not giving their blood in vain. Their lives might have been as useless as the lives of most of us. In their deaths they assisted to pay the purchase-money for England's freedom,"

This is one of Froude's finer passages which are like music in the ear.

He is perhaps too zealous in his praise of Sir Thomas More and Bishop Fischer. They were men of pure minds and uprightness of character, but they had not the same excuse as the Charter House monks, that they were ignorant of the world and the great changes that were taking place in it. It is a sin of itself, to be internally blind, when we have not only eyes to see with, but an intellect to reflect on the objects of our vision. A German writer, Professor Lötze, thinks that tragedy does a finer kind of justice than historians, by condemning those who set themselves against the general order of things. Thus Egmont, More, and Anne Boleyn were naturally tragic characters. More and Fischer were permitted comfortable imprisonment so long as they would remain quiet; but they continued to write and agitate, and so the axe was sharpened for them. More's virtues were of the domestic order, and in that light he appears to great advantage. For Froude to call More the most illustrious man of his time is rather a rash statement while Luther and Michel Angelo were still living. It is the Latimers and Cromwells and Sewards, who help civilization forward; the Mores and Metternichs and Everetts, who retard it. Even Henry VIII. was a more useful personage.

Henry's marriages certainly are a bog for any historian to navigate, and the general public is not to be blamed for holding an evil opinion of him for them. However, if we accept the sincerity of his explanation for the first divorce, all succeeding cases can be explained in a similar manner. His wedding with Jane Seymour, so soon after the execution of Anne, is suspicious enough; but the fact that Jane Seymour was willing to marry him is also suspicious. No one could have known his true character better than she did. Parliament passed a resolution at once requesting the king to marry again for the sake of an heir to the throne; and there is no reason to doubt the sincerity of this. For England to have been left without a king in those days would have been as great a calamity as for the United States of America to have one now. The people could not imagine any other form of government.

Anne of Cleves was another bad blunder. The king declared that he could not live with her, and thought Cromwell had deceived him by a flattering portrait. No one has ever doubted Catherine Parr's guilt, and that completes the sorrowful list. The court of Henry VIII. must have been a fearful place; but not worse, perhaps, than some private habitations in our own time.

The fall of Cromwell has been considered the most enigmatic of all the terrible incidents in Henry's reign; but I think we may find in it the true solution of other enigmatic cases. Froude stated it just as it appears to have happened, and his only commentary is that Cromwell, like Wolsey before him, had presumed on the king's favor, and that he made free use of the public funds. His foisting Anne of Cleves on Henry with the help of a flattering portrait, for the sake of a shallow German alliance, was the blunder which precipitated his fall; but more serious causes lay in the background.

Cromwell had risen from being a poor adventurer to be Earl of Essex; and the hereditary nobility were not only jealous of him for this, but they were terribly afraid of him. He had destroyed the Earl of Exeter and most of his family. Where would the next blow fall ? He was trusted implicitly by the king, for it was one of Henry's peculiarities that where he placed his confidence he placed it wholly. Cromwell's enemies only waited for an opportunity, and the king's disaffection for Anne of Cleves exactly suited their purpose. The man who came forward in this emergency was the Duke of Norfolk.

Shakespeare represents the Dukes of Norfolk and Suffolk as conspiring against Wolsey. It was the Duke of Norfolk who presided at the trial of Anne Boleyn. He was considered the best soldier in England, and appears to have possessed the entire confidence of the English nation. He may have been the power behind the throne. He was always a member of the king's council, and remained in favor to the last. He arraigned Cromwell at a meeting of the council.

Thomas Cromwell possessed some noble qualities, and his actions may have been prompted by motives of public expediency. The fact remains, however, that most of the so-called atrocities in the reign of Henry VIII.—and the execution of the Countess of Salisbury certainly was such—were perpetrated during Cromwell's administration, and after his death they came pretty much to an end. His fate resembles that of Robespierre, and would have been called in the East a revolution in the palace,

The practice of decapitating an outgoing chancellor during the Middle Ages was not peculiar to England; though there was much less of it in France, and in Germany the numerous princes, landgraves, and grand dukes lived with their subjects in an amiable, patriarchal manner, like the Hebrew kings of old. The banishment of Dante is an example of the treatment that defeated candidates received in the Italian cities,—Venice always excepted.

It is equally a mistake to consider princes as exceptional persons, and to judge of their actions as if they were ordinary men. They are mentally and physically like other men, but their lives are very different. Henry VIII. might have been president of the Metropolitan Bank without ever attracting attention except for his fine physique and proud bearing. Judged by the standard of his time, he does not appear to have been a very bad, or a particularly good man. He was not a great statesman, but a more fortunate king for England than Edward IV., Charles I., or George III. would have been in his time. That a man is known by the company he keeps, is an adage which throws light on many a political problem, and Henry's association with Wolsey, Cranmer, Latimer, and Hertford should always be remembered to his credit.

There is rather too much of Froude's history, as there is of Macaulay's. It might have been condensed into ten volumes, if not into eight. We feel this especially in his account of the brief reign of Edward VI. and in the intermittent chapters on Irish affairs. It is all interesting, however, and much of it highly entertaining. Froude is not a humorist himself, but he appreciates humorous situations. One of the best of these is his description of an Irish woman, a female corsair, called Grannie O'Neal, six feet in height, who sailed about the coast with a cutlass strapped to her waist, and who gave the English authorities more trouble than any man in the country. Neither can we avoid a smile, in spite of the awful gravity of the occasion, at the Spanish merchant in Antwerp who offered to assassinate the Prince of Orange for eighteen thousand dollars, and who sold out the business for three thousand to his " undersized, paltry-looking clerk," who thought he could become invisible because the priest had stuffed a dried toad in his pocket.

People who read for entertainment always have plenty of time, but those who are in quest of knowledge find life short enough.

The most brilliant and also most interesting portion of Froude's history is his last five volumes on the reign of Elizabeth. He may be said here to have cultivated virgin soil; for a comparison with Hume, Smollett, and others shows almost at a glance how little has previously been known of this period. The material which he collected for this portion of his work will be the wonder of investigators for centuries to come. Not only has he resurrected Elizabeth herself, with her two great coadjutors, Burleigh and

Walsingham; but he has obtained the reports of the Spanish ambassador, together with cipher dispatches in the archives of Madrid, the secret diplomacy of France and Scotland, letters from William of Orange, all sifted and distributed in their proper places; so that we seem to stand in England in the sixteenth century, and receive telegraphic dispatches from all parts of the world,—not bare external facts, but messages laden with significance. As a literary feat this formerly seemed so incredible, that even such a scholar as George S. Hillard doubted its possibility; but after he became acquainted with Froude himself, he changed his opinion. These volumes contain, besides, the best account of Mary Queen of Scots, as she is poetically called; and if it is not altogether sympathetic, it is nevertheless so clear and complete as to enable us to form a just opinion of her. The history closes with a description of the Spanish *armada*, whose destruction represented the final triumph of Protestantism in Great Britain and the Netherlands.

Froude did not understand women much better than Henry VIII. himself. He criticises Elizabeth exactly as if she were a man, and though his portrait of her is lifelike and real, we feel on that account that he has barely done her justice. A good deal has been said about the sphere of woman, and there is some truth in it. Her proper sphere is domestic and social life; and that is certainly enough. It is the best part of life. A banker said to me: " I leave the management of everything in my house to my wife. She sometimes consults me, but I rarely interfere with her. In that way, as soon as I leave my office I am free from care." Women can write poetry and novels, paint pictures, and do many other things that men can; they even make good doctors; but they cannot go to war, nor understand politics; and this is perhaps the reason why no woman has yet written a good history even as a text-book. If you meet with a woman who talks well on political subjects, you may be sure it is the echo of some talented man of her acquaintance.

When women interest themselves in politics it is as often for evil as good. In the arts of persuasion and dissimulation they are more skilful than men; for they are obliged to be so. Persuasion and dissimulation are necessary in politics because unreasonable men have to be won over and bad men have to be deceived; but they make only a small part of the true statesman, and are more likely to be associated with a political charlatan. They are the devil's machinery, though sometimes used for good purposes.

When, however, a woman is obliged to fill the position of a man, and does it to the best of her ability and with good intent, the admiration she wins for her partial success is enhanced by our sympathy for her disadvantages. It is thus that Elizabeth of England and Maria Theresa of Austria have obtained places in history beside the most renowned.

Elizabeth was not without serious faults. She was as obstinate and implacable as her father. Her parsimony was such as to be almost ruinous to the civil service; and while she enriched worthless favorites like the Earl of Leicester, she permitted Walsingham to impoverish his estates, and die without reward for his splendid public services. She gave stingy and ineffective succor to the Netherlands in their mortal struggle with Spain, though everyone but herself could foresee that the conquest of Holland would be followed by a three-cornered attack on England by the Spanish, Irish, and Catholic Scotch, for the purpose of deposing Elizabeth, and making Mary Stuart queen of a Catholic Britain.

Elizabeth's whole diplomacy (on which she greatly prided herself) consisted of continued procrastination, and such small intrigues as jealous women practise in the social warfare of a provincial city. Froude says:

" Elizabeth saw no reason to risk her throne for a cause for which at best she had but a cold concern. She preferred to lie and twist, and perjure herself, and betray her friends, with a purpose at the bottom moderately upright; and nature in fitting her for her work had left her without that nice sense of honor which would have made her part too difficult."

This seems like rather harsh language. It is true that she worried her ministers almost to insanity, by interfering with their well arranged plans at the last moment, and upsetting their work like a house of cards. But these are mainly feminine traits, suited to domestic life, but exaggerated to ugliness upon a throne. Froude does not fail to point out that but for her constancy to Burleigh and Walsingham they would not have been able to accomplish what they finally did.   This too was a feminine trait, for it is in the nature of a true woman always to maintain her confidence where she has once placed it.   It is the true glory of Elizabeth, and of Maria Theresa as well, that they accepted the wisest men of their times as counsellors, and held fast to them through all changes of fortune and public opinion.   This is the reason why Elizabeth's reign is more illustrious than that of any English kings excepting Henry II., Edward III., and Cromwell.   So far as she herself interfered in public affairs it was only to create mischief.   Froude has made this somewhat too painfully evident.

The honor of guiding the ship of state through those dangerous seas belongs to Burleigh before all others.   Macaulay speaks of him carelessly, as belonging to the adroit class of politicians who knew how to adapt themselves to the humors of their sovereigns, and therefore remain in power when better men would be displaced.   Burleigh possessed this faculty, but also all other faculties pertaining to the thorough statesman.   Froude has separated his line of personal activity from the general medley of English affairs, as an anatomist dissects a nerve or an artery; and as he has presented him, Burleigh appears before us one of the grandest figures in English history.   It was a terrible element he had to deal with,—the order of the Jesuits poisoning mind and body, conjuring up superstition as an engine of destruction, worse than dynamite.   The noblest men of that period fell by the hand of the assassin, and Elizabeth's life was only saved by Burleigh's incessant watchfulness. Open war would have been a relief to him; but he was obliged to fight an invisible enemy, countermining underground through quick-sands and fire-damp. We see the reflection of it in the portraits of him.

Elizabeth's true work, which Froude, absorbed in tracing the course of politics, allows her small credit for, was giving to English society a more ele-vated tone. Her court may not have been as ele-gant as that of Louis XIV., but it was more moral, learned, and intellectual. English manners had been at their best from Edward I. to Henry V. During the War of the Roses they had suffered a serious decline, which had only been partially arrested by the good example of Henry VII. In such mat-ters a queen is much more influential than a king, and the good effect of Elizabeth's discipline becomes apparent in the dignified language and fine courtesy of the characters in Shakespeare's plays,—which may have been partly due to Spanish influences. The manners of Hamlet, Othello, and Rosalind and Portia are not what we should call well bred, but more in the fashion of noble manners. It was only this social background of magnificent men and wo-men that could give Shakespeare the material for his dramatic work. It was then also that the Eng-lish language is supposed to have been at its best.

It is a poetic picture that we have of Mary Stuart, the beautiful girl scarce twenty-one, sailing across from France to Scotland to take possession of her royal inheritance. She was a courageous young woman and charming to everyone, but her life was being involved in a contradiction which could only lead to one misfortune after another. How could she, a Catholic and so inexperienced, succeed in ruling the sternest of all Protestant communities? If she had possessed Elizabeth's intellectual fibre, and been prudent enough to surround herself with wise counsellors, she might have prospered for a term of years; but she was injudicious from the first. Her choice of Darnley was an unlimited blunder. Carlyle thought that she preferred him on account of his handsome legs. That she was in love with him is not likely; and we must contrast this with the veracity of Elizabeth, who often tried to make a match for herself, but never could find a man whom she liked sufficiently. Mary's familiarity with Rizzio, innocent and harmless as we suppose it, was certainly imprudent. A young wife who causes her husband to be jealous lacks both judgment and consideration. The murder of Rizzio was fearfully atoned for by the homicide of her husband,—whether justly or not it is impossible to decide. Of course she could not live with Darnly after the death of her favorite, nor could she separate from him after the manner of private persons. Her second marriage with the Earl of Bothwell was equally injudicious, and in its manner discreditable.

It is easy for a beautiful young woman to be pleasant and amiable while those about her are paying her incessant homage. In such cases her amiability is nothing more than an external reflection. Both men and women often possess a charming manner, which makes them popular, and yet is all the capital they have. Mary Queen of Scots appears much like George Eliot's character of Gwendolen, a woman of fine physique, good spirits, and not without a share of intelligence, but indifferent to everything outside the small circle of her own affairs.

We would not say that the sympathy that has been excited by her misfortunes has been wasted, but it might have been better expended on her uncle the Earl of Murray. It is the privilege of historians to disinter illustrious characters who have been buried under the *débris* of time, and set them forth again in the clear light of day. Such a hero is the Earl of Murray, who was regent of Scotland after the flight of Mary into England. When Froude becomes melodramatic, we know that his cup of admiration is full to overflowing, and we even like him better for this weakness. He has not represented Murray, however, as a general type of hero, but so highly individualized that we readily place confidence in the portrait he has painted for us. Murray was one of those men that come so rarely to the head of affairs, who are determined to have right and justice done, even if the skies should fall,—which they did before very long in the form of an assassin's bullet. He shared the fate of William of Orange and Henry of Navarre.

Froude's veracity has been persistently called in question in regard to the execution of Mary of Scotland, whom he holds to have been justly condemned for high treason. The prevailing opinion has been that she was judicially murdered in order to protect

Elizabeth from assassination; the vulgar notion, that Elizabeth put her to death from motives of jealousy. As the evidence on which Froude mainly relies is taken from the dispatches of the Spanish ambassador, which it would require a journey to Madrid to examine, the question is likely to remain open in this country a long time. The testimony of Throgmorton, which implicated her, was obtained through the use of torture, and such testimony is not wholly reliable; for even a brave man will finally be driven by suffering to say almost anything that will end the pain. Froude affirms, however, that Throgmorton's disclosures were substantiated by the reports of Mendoza, and there is no reason why we should not believe him. At the last he is unnecessarily severe with poor Mary, and his account of the death scene seems pitiless.

From Mary's standpoint, the conspiracy was not a crime but an attempt at revolution; and she was led into it by her friends.

Froude says that when Throgmorton had finished his confession he drew himself up on his seat and sobbed in misery: " Now I have disclosed the secrets of her who was the dearest Queen to me in the world, whom I thought no torments could have forced me so much to have prejudiced. I have broken faith with her, and I care not if I were hanged." No tragedy could be more pathetic than this.

Queen Elizabeth went from a prison to a throne; Mary of Scotland, from a throne to a prison. Frederick and Napoleon also knew what imprisonment was like before they began to rule.

There are occasional sentences in Froude's history, so compressed with deep significance that they elevate him for the moment above all other historians of the century. One such is the following: " Innocent persons have suffered by millions in this world, but the community which permits the injustice to be perpetrated will afterwards be obliged to compensate for it, to the last drop of blood that has been shed." This reminds us of the course of the slavery question in America.

Julius Cæsar.

If you would distinguish good historical work from that which is not, compare Froude's *Life of Cæsar* with the one by Napoleon III. Napoleon's book is written in a fair literary style, and some chapters in it show decided ability,—it has a tribute to Cæsar's mother (which was probably intended for his own) which does him credit as a man of sensibility; but we cannot obtain from it either a clear conception of Cæsar, or of the times in which he lived. Louis Napoleon was not the astute gentleman whom a New York editor supposed in 1866 would make a dupe of Bismarck. He succeeded in the earlier part of his career by the good genius of Count Cavour; and it will be observed that after Cavour's death all his undertakings failed. He may have left the *Life of Cæsar* unfinished because he realized that, after all, he did not understand the subject. If Froude had been the controlling authority of France from 1850 to 1860, there would have been no Mexican expedition nor a Franco-Prussian war.

Froude's *Life of Cæsar* is the most brilliant of his works, and one of the most entertaining books in the English language. It is a book that everyone should read, for nowhere else is so much political wisdom presented in such an attractive form. His view of the subject is not a new one, being directly traceable to Mommsen, and before Mommsen to Hegel, who perceived in Cæsar not only the greatest soldier, but the greatest statesman of antiquity. Froude has however given it a finer and more complete development than any writer before him. He calls this biography a sketch, but he could not have made a more full use of his material unless he had included two or three of Cicero's orations. The ancients had a happy faculty of concentration which characterizes everything pertaining to them.

Rome itself was a political concentration, such as the world has not seen since, except during that short period when Napoleon was master of the continent of Europe. It is that which makes their great men stand out before us in such prominent relief. From the destruction of Carthage in the second century before Christ, to the defeat of Maxentius by Constantine in the fourth century after Christ, the fortunes of civilization were dependent on the fate of a single city; and men were produced there to correspond with the vast political forces which were brought into play. In the sequence of events thus effected, there came a time where the further progress of affairs depended on the exertion of a single individual, and this person was Julius Cæsar. He would seem to have been ordained by divine providence for the purpose.

Froude was not an imperialist, like Carlyle; and it is a fatal mistake to suppose this. Like nineteen Englishmen out of twenty, he believed constitutional monarchy to be the best form of government, though the Austrian or Italian governments would probably be nearer to his pattern than the English. Above all things, however, he believed that a government should be justly administered; and if justice could not be obtained in one form, the time for revolution was at hand. This is the cardinal principle in his biography of Cæsar, as it was of Cæsar himself. The government of Rome during the third century B.C. was the best that had been devised in ancient times, but it had become like a ship whose timber had been honeycombed by borers. Governments, like men, have their periods of youth, maturity, and decrepitude ; and change is the universal law of creation. Cæsar perceived that the rotten old structure could not last much longer, and he recognized, like Bismarck, that the only remedy was blood and iron. Cicero perceived it, but lacked courage to deal with the situation. Cato, who was an earlier Sir Thomas More, shut his eyes obstinately and went over the cataract.

Napoleon III. should be credited with one very wise statement. He condemns the destruction of Carthage by Rome (which was indeed a political crime only avenged at last by Genseric and his Vandals), and alleges as the reason for it that nations lose their mental balance like individuals. It was caused by the jealousy of the Roman mercantile interest. The Roman Senate, which, in the time of Pyrrhus, had been an assemblage of kings, an hundred years later had changed into a combination of greedy capitalists who cared little for the honor or welfare of the state, and were altogether absorbed in the accumulation of wealth. By the introduction of slave labor they ruined the small free-hold farmers, who were the backbone of the Roman army, and drove them to the cities, where they were obliged to live largely by crime and vice. At the same time, these lords of creation demoralized the community in another way, by the introduction of Asiatic luxury and extravagance. They corrupted the public elections by every use to which money can be applied, and gained an illegal possession of the public lands. It was as impossible for a plebeian to obtain justice against a patrician as if he had been a negro slave.

Froude is, as usual, clear, logical, and penetrating. He detects the gradual growth of the monarchy out of the republic, and makes this so plain that only a strongly prejudiced person can fail to perceive the fact. It began ninety years before the battle of Philippi, with the proposal of Tiberius Gracchus compelling the patricians to restore the public lands which they had illegally occupied. He carried his point for the time being, but as consul his power was limited to a single year, while the senators held their office for life. He foresaw that his work would be overturned as soon as his successor was elected, and to prevent this he illegally stood for the consulship a second year. The patricians consequently declared him an enemy to the state, and he was killed like a dog. Ten years later his brother Gaius came forward with equal heroism in support of the same cause, and obtained a longer period of success; but was finally disposed of in the same manner. In both instances the offence which the brothers were charged with, was the crime of seeking arbitrary power.

First of the Romans, Gaius Gracchus obtained the passage of a law that no citizen should be put to death without a public trial. In this connection it is noteworthy that the rights of man as an individual were first established and carried to perfection under the Roman empire; inconsistent as this seems with the proceedings of the bad emperors.*

The invasion of the Germanic hordes brought a cessation of hostilities between the two classes, but as soon as the danger was over, civil dissension broke forth again with fresh fury. The plebeians had saved Italy from the greatest danger that ever threatened civilization. They were united and confident and soon had everything their own way. If the patricians however had proved themselves unfit to govern, the plebeians in their popular assembly were still more so. As in all such cases, they immediately became the prey of demagogues—proceeded to violent and short-sighted measures, which brought about the aristocratic reaction under Sulla.

History in its more perfect development is governed by the same principles as a work of art; and

* My authority for this statement is Professor Burgess of Columbia College.

from the time of Cæsar's birth until his death was revenged by Anthony and Augustus, the Roman republic was in a state of intermittent revolution. First came the discord just referred to; then the war broke out between the Roman state and its allies in southern Italy; next came the civil war between Sulla and Cinna, and their respective dictatorships— a reign of terror over Italy like that of France in 1793; then came the servile insurrection, and afterwards an insurrection of the debtor class against their exorbitant creditors, the rate of interest being one per cent. a month. The compact between Cæsar and Pompey restored order for a time; but as soon as Cæsar had taken his departure for Gaul the popular outbreaks in Rome were renewed, and chaos reigned supreme, until at last the war between Cæsar and the Senate put an end to it by the establishment of a military despotism,—just as Napoleon gave a quietus to the disorders of France.

Now are there any so blind that they cannot read this handwriting on the wall,—a government convulsed and writhing in the agony of death? Yet educated men have written histories without number, and treated this subject as if all the trouble had been caused by the rivalry of Sulla and Marius, and the ambition between Pompey and Cæsar. That there were enormous political forces behind these men, driving them onward with an irresistible pressure, was not dreamed of even by Shakespeare, who looked at the matter as a dramatist, and not as a statesman.

Though there were many opportunities during the

following century to restore the republic, no attempt was made to do so, even by men who died under the tyranny of Nero and Caligula with heroic fortitude; and Galba, in his speech on the adoption of Piso, is represented by Tacitus as saying that he would gladly restore the republic if he thought the Roman empire could be possibly governed in that manner.*

The first two pages of the *Annals* of Tacitus are the best justification of Cæsar's policy; for he says that Augustus demanded the tribunitial authority for the protection of the plebeians, and this testimony is the more valuable since Tacitus himself belonged to the senatorial party. It was not Cæsar's purpose to establish a military despotism, and it was in trying to avoid this that he lost his life. The military despotism began in the reign of Tiberius.

For the last twenty years in America, writers have been busy trying to prove that our civil war was an unnecessary extravagance, and that a little diplomacy and a few more concessions to the Southern slaveholders might have prevented it; that the invasion of Virginia by John Brown and the election of Lincoln were the sole causes of a conflict which cost five hundred thousand lives and seven thousand million dollars.

Nothing can be more frivolous than such calculations. If a five-story house is about to fall, as happened not long since in New York City, can a man prop it up with a pole? If an elephant dies, can we

* "If the mighty fabric of this empire could subsist and balance itself without a ruler, the glory of restoring the old republic should be mine."—Tacitus, *Historia*, 116.

prevent his body from decomposing ? A book has lately been published applying the same principle to the French Revolution, which the author supposes resulted chiefly from the weakness and indecision of Louis XVI. Such considerations are puerile. The true historian does not ask himself what might have happened, but *how* did it happen; and he usually finds this a problem sufficient to tax his whole strength.

Louis XVI. represented the time in which he lived. It was a period of weakness and vacillation. So Webster and Clay were compromisers, because their political education belonged to a period when compromise with slavery seemed possible. Success in politics is only practicable on a large scale for men who represent and sympathize with the spirit of the age; and a king feels this on his throne as much as a senator in Congress. " The world," Froude says, " is not ruled by intrigue and diplomacy, but by right and justice." There is at least a constant tendency to right and justice in progressive races, which continually interferes with the schemes of politicians.

Mommsen compares the Roman patricians to the slave-holding oligarchy of America, which fortunately is now extinct. There is still a class of persons, however, in this country, who resemble the great land-owners of Italy, and it is remarkable how close a sympathy exists between the Roman aristocrat of two thousand years ago and this native aristocrat of the present time. One of the latter, who was formerly a professor in Harvard University, informed his class every year that " Mr. Mommsen never lost an opportunity of kneeling down to lick Julius Cæsar's boots."

The best results in ancient Greece were obtained after the change of monarchy to democracy; and the best results in Rome after the change from a republic to an empire. In both instances some credit should be allowed to the preceding period; " for," as Thucydides observes, " the influence of new laws and political methods does not take effect until some years after they have been in operation."

We should not fail to remember that the republic only existed for Rome itself, and the territory about it. The government of Italy, and of the provinces, was as autocratic in the days of the Gracchi as in the time of Domitian; and even more so, though the names " justice " and " virtue " may have been hateful to such a man, for it was not for the emperor's interest to permit his subordinates to enrich themselves in the way the senators had formerly done. It was under the empire that the development of the Roman law took place which must have been the greatest possible blessing to the Mediterranean world. Nevertheless, after this was accomplished, civilization steadily declined.

Mommsen estimates Cæsar as a statesman; but Froude also as a man. We may not go so far in our admiration of him as this author does; but there can be no doubt that he was one of the best-hearted men that ever lived. His unfailing kindness and fidelity to his friends is a less signal proof of this than his merciful disposition toward his enemies. There was no one in antiquity comparable to him for magnanimity of this kind, and even the best Greek and Roman writers could not understand it. He anticipated the spirit of Christianity fifty years before the birth of Christ. Froude's comparison of Cæsar with the Messiah is rather startling. One hardly feels that he was a philanthropist; but the fact that he virtually gave his life for the benefit of the poor and oppressed cannot be gainsaid. The common people of Italy still reverence his memory as a helper of mankind. Strangely enough Dante tacitly made the same comparison as Froude, associating in the last canto of the *Inferno* Judas Iscariot with Brutus and Cassius; but this shows plainly how Cæsar was considered in Dante's time.* His bequest of seventy-five drachmæ to every citizen of Rome, friends and enemies alike, is an affecting testimony to his patriotic good-will.

Froude makes rather too much of an effort in attempting to defend Cæsar from the small accusations and calumnies of his time. They seem dreadful enough to an Anglo-Saxon; but they were nothing to a Roman, or even to a modern Italian. Suetonius retails similar scandals of Augustus, Titus, and Nerva, who were all the best men of their time. Cæsar seems to have been like Napoleon, a man naturally gentle and amiable. He was a greater historian than either Froude or Macaulay, and he was even a better writer. The account of the conquest of Gaul is rather dry but nevertheless invalu-

---

* Satan is represented in Dante's *Inferno* with three mouths; in one of which he is chewing Judas, and in the others Brutus and Cassius.

able, and his history of the civil war is intensely interesting.   His sentences sometimes remind me of Wordsworth.

Froude has improved on Mommsen's judgment with respect to Marius and Cicero.   In spite of Mommsen's breadth of view he is a good deal of a pedant.   Like most German professors of his time, he knew little of practical politics,—no more perhaps than Marius himself, who spent his whole life in war and should not properly be called to account for the extravagancies of his party after the defeat of the Cimbri.   Froude recognizes this fact, and also the advantage it was to Cæsar that he should have been a politician before he became a general.   Cicero was a rare man.   Mommsen condemns him as an equally empty and voluminous writer; but Matthew Arnold, whose opinion is certainly of equal weight, considered him a very valuable author, and Froude admits that we are chiefly indebted to Cicero for our information of this remarkable period.   Such a writer can not properly be called empty; in fact, his orations light up the era in which he lived, so that no other portion of Roman history is so plainly visible to us. Froude makes use of him too much as a contrast and a foil to Cæsar; dilates too much on his vacillation, his indecisiveness, his vanity: but the conditions in which Cicero found himself were not such as are favorable to a man of letters.   They required a man of the sword.   For some mysterious reason, great orators seem to be always the precursors of political catastrophes; and the game they play is a losing one.   Cicero's death was heroic even for a

Roman; and one of the noblest pieces of antique sculpture is a bas-relief of Cicero holding the hand of his daughter.

Ireland.

Froude came to America to lecture on Irish history at an unfavorable time—while the memory of English assistance to the Southern Confederacy was still active in the public mind,—and the newspapers condemned his argument even before he had begun to deliver it. Many went to hear him from curiosity, and a few also to hear both sides of the question; and they found him a lecturer in manner not unlike Emerson and quite as vigorous in his language. He was calm, dispassionate, earnest, and, as well as one could judge, fair and unprejudiced in his statements. His lectures were a brilliant success.[1]

He showed that the English occupation of Ireland was both an historical and a military necessity; but he did not deny that English statesmen had made grave mistakes in legislating for the Irish people. Especially the English Bishops had caused serious mischief in their zeal for propagandism; and rapacious acts of Parliament had been passed intended for the advantage of English commerce at the expense of Irish trade. He credited the Irish people with many virtues,—the men are brave and generous, the women faithful and kind; but they are even more inflammable than the French, and lack the self-control which is requisite for popular government. The difficulties in dealing with the Irish question

[1] See note B in Appendix.

11

were three: their religion, their temperament, and the constitution of Parliament, which was so distracted by political parties as to prevent any continuous and systematic treatment of the case. Mr. Froude's audiences were satisfied that he had the sense of the matter; as the course of events has subsequently proved.

These lectures were afterwards elaborated into a work of four volumes, which is of equal value and interest as Froude's English history. The London *Daily News* did not consider that Froude was altogether just and fair to the Irish character; and in a certain sense this is true, because he looked at it from a political point of view. Froude was a Stoic and a severe moralist, and he did not seem to understand that it is possible to err by being too frugal as well as too luxurious.

In 1880 he addressed a letter to the English public in which he said: "If the Irish are a reproach and a byword here, and in America and Australia, *it is we who have made them so*, and the reproach is our reproach. If we cannot take the responsibility we had better let it go altogether." He concluded, however, that the net result of leaving Ireland to the Irish would be a civil war; the English government would have to interfere to preserve order; and the previous condition of affairs would commence again.

Froude's grammar is not always accurate. He writes " eldest " where it should be " elder," and " each other " where he should say " one another," and such occasional lapses,—which are rather a comfort to the rest of us; but his English, as a rule, is purer than that of more fastidious writers; for language, like water, requires (mental) activity to prevent it from stagnating and becoming insipid.

WALTER SCOTT

A MAN'S activity in the world might be represented by an irregular figure, in which the length corresponds to the extent of his work, the breadth to the ground which it covered at any particular time, and the height, or depth, to its superiority or weight. The extent of his work may be measured in years of public service, either in some political capacity, or what is quite as important as a director in banks, railroads, or insurance companies; or it may be counted by the number of books he has written, the pictures or other works of art he has produced; or by his usefulness in a private capacity as a faithful husband, a wise father, and a patriotic citizen. In like manner may the sphere of his activity be limited to a farm, or to a small neighborhood; or it may extend over a large district, or even over a continent. Likewise his occupation may be so humble as not to attract passing attention, or it may be so exalted as to serve for a beacon-light in his own time, and become a monument to after ages; it may be so trifling as not to make the weight of a feather in the balance of human economy, or it may have such a weighty character that it determines the destiny of millions.

All bodies, however, are distinguished by quality as well as quantity, and it is quality which gives them a permanent value. The Tartar king who re-conquered the empire of Alexandria had as ephem-eral an existence as the day-laborer or the news reporter; while the words of Ruth to Naomi are as enduring as precious stones, and as beautiful to-day as a fresh-blown rose. It is the unlimited combina-tion of these different conditions which causes the infinite variety we observe in human life.

It is a temptation to apply this form of measure-ment to Walter Scott, for few other writers could so well illustrate the value of it. Homer, Dante, and Shakespeare seem almost immeasurable. They are not everything certainly; but in that which they are, they seem almost beyond human reach, and even in Browning we meet with qualities which border on the infinite; but it is not the same with Scott. Although he lived in an age the most re-dundant of great men since the Reformation, and was more widely known as a genius than any others, except Goethe and Byron, he never aroused enthu-siasm, nor is he spoken of in that undertone of affec-tion used by admirers of Wordsworth and Schiller. Although a cordial and warm-hearted man, univer-sally liked by those about him, he never sympathized deeply with his fellow-men, nor does he appear to have taken more than a passing interest in those humanitarian movements which distinguished the close of the eighteenth century. He accepted the world as he found it, with perfect confidence that everything would go on as it had done formerly, and that the future would provide for itself without any particular effort on his part. He was conservative in politics and religion; but he also accepted liberalism, not with any high-toned impartiality, but simply as an inevitable opposition. He was a poet without being impassioned, a thinker without being profound, and a patriot without being ardent. Although he belongs to the nineteenth century and is quite modern both in style and material, he lived actually in the past, and was more interested in a mediæval castle, than in the strategy of Napoleon.

Scott was in fact the type of a popular writer; and as a writer so he was a man,—sensible, good-humored, with a fund of cheerfulneess in him, and not likely to say anything that would puzzle his hearers, or go over their heads. He had a natural inclination for the bright side of life, and avoided the dark and gloomy side, except so far as it was necessary for his own moral well-being, and to give a kind of relief to the figures that he drew. Such a person can have no divine message for mankind; but what he could do Scott accomplished to perfection, to provide his countrymen with pleasant, wholesome entertainment. Carlyle considers the best quality in Scott's writing to be its *healthfulness*, and this goes to the root of the question. Compared with Scott, Hawthorne, Dante, and sometimes even Goethe, are morbid writers. No man ever preserved a more perfect mental balance,—until near the close of his life. The basis of this is his unfailing good judgment, which carries him through the artistic difficulties of his work in an easy and graceful manner. I have heard his novels recommended as a cure for insomnia, and I should think this quite possible; for his writing is like a stimulant and a sedative combined, which produces a healthful tone, by energizing the mental faculties, while avoiding all superfluous excitement,—a favorable mental condition for a good sleep, as it is for noonday work. A monstrous, morbid production, like Victor Hugo's *Hans of Iceland*, would keep the reader awake more than half the night. Scott was also the first to introduce that refinement and chastity in the writing of fiction which has so greatly enlarged as well as improved its influence. Young ladies now go to the theatre instead of to a convent, and perhaps it is better for us all that we are obliged to respect them.

So much for the quality of Scott's prose, which has given it a permanent value; and though in our own time he is not so much admired as formerly, this is true also of Milton himself, and there can be no doubt that public taste will come around to him again in due course. With respect to the extent of his work, he is even more remarkable, for few have ever exceeded him in the amount performed, and as few may be said to have equalled it. Quantity also has its value, and as one swallow does not make a summer, so neither will a single volume constitute authorship.

There is not much variety in the character of his work, whether prose or verse, and *Waverley*, *Ivanhoe*, and the *Heart of Midlothian* may be taken as types of all his novels; but the quantity is undeniable,

Yet it is in breadth that Scott makes evident the true greatness of his mind. If he does not show much variety in plan, the variety in detail is inexhaustible. It would seem as if few men were so free from personal ambition; for he did not begin to publish as a poet until nearly thirty, and was close to the half-way house of life when he wrote his first novel. Meanwhile he was laying up a wonderful store of material from which he drew afterwards for twenty years before the supply became exhausted. He was a prodigious student, an insatiable reader, and his historical or antiquarian researches were like those of Gibbon or Hallam. His wanderings, too, about Scotland supplied him with an extensive topographical knowledge; and his love of nature, which gave him an interest in everything living and beautiful, added to this an extensive local information. At the same time, he studied human nature in all its different phases; and if not so profoundly as some, yet in their variety and wide range the sum total of his characters exceeds that of any other novelist. If they are not delineated with the skill of a Titian; if they are somewhat shadowy, and unfinished in details yet they have the rare merit of existing altogether separately and distinct from their author, and for the most part so individualized that they would seem to have been portraits from life, and to have lived at the time in which he represents them. They have, as we say in painting, a very good *chiaroscuro.* Walter Scott was a genius of the continental order.

There are four great English novelists and only

four—Fielding, Scott, Thackeray, and George Eliot or Miss Evans. Dickens came close to making the fifth, but he missed it from an insufficient love of truth. Better judges than the present writer have considered Fielding as the greatest of them all. As an English humorist he has either the first or the second place, and it matters little which; his characters are depicted with the solidity of a Van Dyck; and the essays which are interspersed in his novels would alone give him high literary rank. To delineate a pure-minded young woman, so that we may even perceive the beating of her pulse and the blue veins of her wrist, there is nobody like him; but Fielding lived in an immoral age which was steadily gravitating toward the " general overturn " of society, and his work partakes of the strangely contrasted good and evil of his time. A portion of his material is so low and coarse as to be positively offensive, and his volumes have been relegated to the highest shelves, where they will attract the least attention. The gap between Fielding and Scott is a wide one, and is filled in by as great an intellectual revolution as that of '93. Goethe was of course the leading spirit in this, and it is noteworthy that one of Scott's earliest publications was a translation of Goethe's earliest play. He had, however, neither the courage nor the inclination to follow the skyward track of Goethe's chariot, but relapsed rather into the amiable conservatism of Chateaubriand. But the Revolution had its effect on him, and though he did not learn from it what Carlyle and Wordsworth learned, that is, ideality of *thought*, he did learn ideality of *form*.   He acquired that dignified, self-respectful style which distinguishes him both from French and English fiction of the eighteenth century.   Scott was a gentleman of the old school of punctilious manners; and yet, intellectually, he belongs to the new epoch.   He was to Great Britain almost exactly what Chateaubriand was to France.   Scott, Byron, and Wordsworth formed a period of their own, and differ essentially from the writers we have hitherto been considering. Coleridge and Charles Lamb may perhaps be placed with them.

Before we consider Scott as a novelist we should first understand him as a poet, for it was in poetry that he made a beginning in literature.   Burns and Scott are the two most distinguished names in the literature of their country, but they are different from one another as poets well could be.   It might almost be said that since the *Iliad* there has been no such natural, genuine poetry as that of Robert Burns.   This was partly owing to his lack of education, which saved him from any preconceived notions of poetic composition.   His verses are like roses that have grown up among weeds and stones by the wayside.   Scott's poetry, on the contrary, is, I believe, wholly imitative; a scholarly imitation of mediæval lays and ballads.   It may pass for very fine poetry, but it is to the original what moonlight is to the light of day.   It possesses a romantic charm, but is not warming or fructifying. Compare the opening of Scott's ballad called *Lochinvar ;*

> " O young Lochinvar is come out of the West ;
> Through all the wide Border his steed was the best ;
> And save his good broadsword, he weapon had none ;
> He rode all unarmed, and he rode all alone "—

with the first verse of the *Childe of Elle*, a poem of those rude ages which we are taught to look back on with self-complacent horror:

> " The Childe of Elle to his garden went
> And stood by his garden pale,
> When he was aware of a little foot-page
> Come tripping down the dale."

The former is a spirited description, but also slightly rhetorical. How much more simple and sympathetic and humanly tender is the description by this unknown minstrel. His unconsciousness is delightful. One of the finest passages in Scott's idyls is the hunting scene in the *Lady of the Lake*.

> " The stag at eve had drunk his fill
> Where sleeps the moon on Monan's rill,
> And deep his midnight lair had made
> In lone Glenartney's hazel shade."

And though it seems as if this description of a deer hunt could not be excelled, when we recollect Mendelssohn's hunting song we recognize a similarity between the two, and that Scott, though spirited and musical like Mendelssohn, has not much strength. The octosyllabic couplet, which he uses, is in itself a limitation. It is an excellent metre for concentrated poets like Pope and Emerson, but Scott is not concentrated,—rather the reverse. It is much to his credit that he could use this sing-song verse, and produce so spirited and even dignified effect. In strong dramatic contrast, however, the old English ballad singers have the advantage. If you want the life of the Middle Ages, you must go to them or to the German *Niebelungen*, rather than to Scott's *Marmion* and *Rokeby*. The old ballads have not Scott's nicety of diction or form, but they have much more powerful light and shade; they are more circumstantial, and hold a deeper pathos.

Such by a natural transition from poetry to prose was the foundation of the romantic novel; which differs from the mediæval romance in always keeping within the bounds of probability, and from the modern or classic romance in its fulness and variety of incident. It is in fact a compromise, or perhaps rather a combination, between the novel of Fielding and the romance of Goldsmith. Bulwer, Dickens, Charlotte Bronté, Disraeli, Miss Sheppard, and to a certain extent also George Eliot, as well as many lesser lights of fiction, all belong to this class. The romantic novel has run through a career of nearly eighty years, but latterly it has fallen into the hands, almost entirely of the more gentle sex, and now seems to be dying out. It has had its imitators also in France and Germany, but not of much celebrity. Victor Hugo was largely influenced by it; though in his case, as also in Dickens's, it was combined with the philanthropic element.

Although Scott's poetry is imitative it is still sufficiently original to pass for genuine verse; but it was in novel-writing that his spirit first found freedom and the largeness of his nature a sufficient field for its growth and development. I am aware that his prefaces are of extraordinary length,—as the sailors say, long as a bowline,—and that there are descriptive passages here and there which may be compared to them; but it is all good, and the freshness and vigor of his mind make even common situations interesting. What Scott tells us in his plain straightforward manner, without any ornament or more than an occasional touch of rhetoric, is frequently more surprising than the most skilfully devised plots of French novelists.

This is particularly noticeable in *Waverley*. With female novelists it often happens that their first work of fiction is their best; and the reason is that there has been a long accumulation of pictorial ideas and fancies before the first concentration takes place, and afterwards they have no such large store to draw from. Charlotte Bronté, Miss Sheppard, Miss Mulock, and Mrs. Stowe are examples of this. *Waverley* is not the best of Scott's novels, but it contains almost a superabundance of intellectual material, which the writer has not yet quite learned how to dispose of. The first half of the book may be considered experimental: the writer is endeavoring to find his way into his work, and to learn the secrets of his art at the same time that he applies them. It was the same with Raphael's dramatic picture of the *Entombment*. While Scott's account of the old manor house of Bradwardine, and its occupants, is exceedingly picturesque, we notice that Waverley's first two days there occupies nearly fifty pages, and meanwhile small progress has been made in the movement of the plot, or in the exposition of Waverley's character. The repeated expression of " our hero," for Waverley, is ingenuous and faulty, but it does not occur elsewhere to the same extent, and it would be quite unfair to judge of Scott's literary method by this portion of his work.

Waverley, Ivanhoe, Henry Smith, Osbaldistone, the Knight of the Leopard, and perhaps others in Scott's novels, are substantially the same person. It is an ideal type of youthful excellence, a comparatively faultless young man around whom all the other characters in the story, with their various peculiarities, are grouped. There are such personages in real life, though they are not common, and do not usually make the ablest and most serviceable men. It is the type of Christian manhood which belongs to romantic art; an ideal which may be said to have been grandfather to the modern gentleman.

Shakespeare introduces such characters sometimes,—as Orlando in *As You Like It*, as Ferdinand, in *The Tempest*, and as secondary characters in other plays. Generally, however, they do not serve the purpose of dramatic poetry. In the novel we follow them, stand by their side, and view the other *dramatis personæ* from their perspective. We become attached to them from the closeness of their relation to us, but for that very reason we do not perceive them so distinctly as the others.

Such is the peculiarity of the romantic novel; and its writer as well as its reader acquires a partisan feeling for the so-called hero which prevents him from doing full justice to human nature. It is well enough to introduce perfect characters into fiction, but to call them heroes, and refer to them as heroes, is a mistake. Anything which tends to dispel the illusion produced by a work of art is an injury to it; though I am aware that in making this rule I am placing myself in opposition to some of the highest judges. It should be left to the reader to decide whether the leading character in a novel, or play, deserves to be called a hero or not. The word itself should always be respected.

Neither can I agree with those who consider Sir Walter the true standard of a Scotchman. He seems to me much more English than Scotch; and this is an advantage to him in rendering an account of his countrymen. He looks at them from an outside standpoint. The *bona fide* Scotchman, if he has intellect, is either a philosopher or a humorist. Carlyle was both, and Scott was neither. He was, however, enough of a Scotchman to sketch humorous situations, though we cannot be confident that he was always aware of this.

One such is the arrival of young Waverley at Bradwardine Manor. With the feeling of uncertainty which a young man has on strange grounds, he approaches the massive knocker on the hall-door, uses it more and more vigorously but with no response. Then he finds his way around the corner of the house into a court where two young women are washing clothes with their feet; and these dart away at the first sight, leaving Waverley in possession of the wash-tubs. Feeling now somewhat embarrassed, he proceeds farther, and meets with a half-witted fellow dancing and singing, who detains and hampers him after the manner of such characters; and at length, when he is quite in despair, conducts him to the butler, who gives an intelligent answer to his inquiries. The baron himself is of course the last person that he meets with. The twofold significance, also, of the motto on the baron's ancestral drinking cup, " Beware the Bar," is a second case in point. There is a genial, hospitable tone running through Scott's writing which is a fair substitute for humor. He is never severe or satirical, but endures the follies and trespasses of mankind with the patience of an ox at the plough.

Old Bradwardine reminds us of Fielding's *Colonel Bath* in his sincerity, stilted manners, and bellicose spirit; but he is amplified and elevated. Only Scott, perhaps, could have handled such a character. A letter of introduction carried by an eligible young gentleman to an old family friend, living with an only daughter, is rather suspicious of the way in which the story may end; and we begin to wonder how the author will obviate such a transparent opening; when Waverley is suddenly spirited away by Scott to a castle in the Highlands, where he encounters another young woman of stronger will, and more magnetic, than Rose Bradwardine. After a series of lifelike and quite probable adventures, fate leads him back to his first acquaintance, who has all the while been secretly in love with him.

Though the plot is a simple one, its development is, or was at that time, quite original. The tender, easily blushing Rose is finally contrasted with the spirited and brilliant Flora Mac-Ivor, a character almost worthy of a place among Shakespeare's heroines. Both are intellectual and high-minded, and yet the distinction between them is strongly marked. Fergus MacIvor is also a grand character; and if Scott's description of the Highlanders is somewhat idealized, it is much more credible, as well as creditable, than Macaulay's.

Such is *Waverley* in general terms; and of similar quality are the majority of Scott's novels. *Guy Mannering*, the *Heart of Midlothian*, the *Bride of Lammermoor*, and perhaps *Rob Roy*, rise above it; the *Antiquary* and some others fall below it.

The picturesque variety of English, and especially Scotch life, in the eighteenth century is what gives Scott the advantage over either French or American novelists of the nineteenth century. Especially at the present time people are (as it were) so nearly run in a mould, like leaden figures,—social regulations are so exacting, that both eccentricity and its corresponding virtue, originality, are nipped in the bud while men and women are almost too young to be aware of the fact. Independence of character thus becomes an obstacle to advancement in life. A young man who is obliged to make his own way in the world soon finds, if he has opinions of his own, that he had better keep them to himself.

A former editor of the Springfield *Republican* was accustomed to say to his assistants: " I shall not tell you how you are to write this, but if you do it otherwise than as I like, I shall complain." This

12

of course made them servile imitators of his mental methods. A younger partner in a banking-house wished to subscribe to a testimonial to Walt Whitman the poet, but he was advised against doing so by the chief magnate of the firm as it might slightly discredit the character of their house. Edwin Booth the actor was fond of dressing in a crimson vest, but it made so much comment and unfavorable criticism that he was obliged to relinquish it. The railroad carries the formulated life of the city into the country: the servant girl imitates the dress of her mistress; and one has to go among wood-choppers or plantation negroes for a picturesque subject either in poetry or painting. The time is approaching when it will be difficult to distinguish a yachtsman from the skipper of a Cape Ann schooner.

This similarity of different people and different classes makes it difficult to give the characters in a novel such a description as may serve for artistic contrasts. Walter Scott met with no trouble of that kind. The *dramatis personæ* of *Guy Mannering* are even more firmly drawn and strongly marked than those in *Waverley*. In what other novel are such dramatic characters as Meg Merrilees, Dominie Sampson, Dandy Dinmont, and Mrs. McCandlish grouped together. Meg Merrilees alone would suffice to give energy to the plot, and will long be associated with one of the noblest of American women, who made a sanctuary of the greenroom, and almost converted the theatre into a temple of the virtues. When a distinguished actor was regretting that there were no ladies on the stage, he added, " I must of course except Miss Charlotte Cushman." Scott himself might have felt a full measure of gratitude for her impersonation of Meg Merrilees.

Perhaps the opening of *Guy Mannering* was intentionally a contrast to the long introductory description in *Waverley*. The story certainly begins in a bold manner, and the reader finds himself involved in the fortunes of the Bertram family before he has time to consider whether he likes them or not. In both instances, however, the leading character, or nominal hero, is a young Englishman who is wandering in Scotland for amusement or adventure; but the appearance of Meg in the second chapter shows the forethought of genius and sounds the key note of the book.

I am not aware of any realism which equals for imaginative reality the scene between Meg Merrilees and Dominie Sampson in the hut; in which she first throttles him,—in order to make a reasonable man of him,—and afterwards makes him comfortable and happy over a good supper. A still more remarkable passage is that in which young Bertram suddenly appears before Guy Mannering,—who supposes him to have been killed in a duel,—his own sister, who does not recognize him and takes him for an assassin,—and Miss Mannering, who is in love with him, and afraid of divulging it to her father. The varied emotions and ideas which his presence inspires, are so vividly depicted that not even a greater genius than Scott could have added anything to the scene. As an example of the perfect disinterestedness with which Scott could place himself in the position of another person, take the speech of Dirk Hatterick, when the villain Glossin inquires of him if the lost heir of Ellengowan is not in India: " In India,—a thousand deyvils, no: here on this dirty coast of yours."

Now the coast of Scotland nearly resembles the eastern coast of Maine, and a cultivated Scotchman is naturally proud of its picturesque scenery. Not a few sea captains may also be found who can appreciate this. A landsman certainly would never think of it as a dirty coast; but a smuggler would only have in mind its heavy tides, dangerous promontories, and the difficulty of landing on it.

The story would be more according to probability if young Bertram had also been killed at the close of it; for in real life tragedies are much more common than melodramas; but this would have been too great a tax on the sympathies of the reader, who also has to be considered. The course of a novel is too long drawn out for it to end unfavorably. Tragedy should be swift, and hasten by rapid strides to its completion.

If Scott has anywhere risen to a higher plane than *Guy Mannering*, it is in the *Heart of Midlothian*, for there he has delved more deeply into human miseries and sorrows than anywhere else. The principle of *Guy Mannering* might be called virtue blindfolded, and wrestling with open-eyed avarice; but in the *Heart of Midlothian* there may be noticed two distinct principles from which the story is evolved. One is the same that Miss Evans has treated so powerfully in *Adam Bede,*—the danger to which young women of the lower classes are exposed from the ignorance of their parents and the superior fascination of more cultivated young men; and the other is the same on which the tragedy of *King Lear* is founded,—the pride of innocence which makes self-defence hateful to it. He has mapped out these two lines of fate in all their intricate windings, so that they may be legible till the day of judgment. It is sometimes to the advantage of the novelist that he can comment on his own dialogue, and give explanations such as the dramatic poet is unable to do.

As the plot reminds us of Miss Evans, so Dickens is foreshadowed in much of the detail. Many writers since Aristophanes have questioned satirically the wisdom in certain cases of legal procedure, but neither Fielding nor Dickens has exposed the uncertainty or abuse of a legal tribunal in so clear and comprehensive a manner as Scott has done, in the examination of Rev. Mr. Butler before the Edinburgh magistrate. It was only necessary for this purpose to give a quite credible account of the course pursued in taking the clergyman's testimony, and the conclusion arrived at by his examiners; which the reader involuntarily compares with the true facts of the case as narrated in the previous chapter. Legal pedantry is one of the sorest evils of society, and never has it been penetrated by keener sarcasm than in this instance.

In spite of Scott's conservatism, he was too much of a poet, and lived too close to nature, not to have a very friendly feeling for those rugged, earnest characters who oppose conventional right and take the law into their own hands, for the benefit of mankind. A chord of this sort vibrates throughout his literary work. He carries it perhaps too far in the *Pirate*, but it is the mainspring of *Rob Roy*, and both Meg Merrilies and Robin Hood belong to that resolute class. Probably the most eloquent passage in the length and breadth of Scott's prose is a speech of Rob Roy to Osbaldistone in which he defines his position with regard to civil authority: " They shall hear of my vengeance who refused to listen to the story of my wrongs." It begins vehemently, but ends sadly enough: it hurts him to think of his sons leading their father's life. Scott's sympathy with Rob Roy is complete, and he comprehends with broad vision the exceptional situation in which he was placed. It is this, quite as much as the novelty of his scenes, which makes the Waverley novels so refreshing. A narrow, pettifogging moralist is be-numbing to the intellect, and a weariness to the spirit. Such characters as Madge Wildfire and Davy Gellatley serve Scott the same purpose that the clown does in Shakespeare's plays.

There may be observed three distinct classes in the Waverley novels: the romantic novel, such as we have been considering; novels like Scott's poetry in imitation of mediæval romances, such as *Ivanhoe* and the *Tales of the Crusaders;* and true historical novels, which both in time and character are midway between the two others.

Ivanhoe is properly a book for boys; for only a youthful imagination is likely to indulge itself in the illusion that it creates. It is so much a romance as to border closely on fairyland. Yet it is full of such vivid scenery, and gorgeous descriptive pageantry, that even the most mature mind can hardly escape its influence. In no other novel are there such bold contrasts of character; and yet they are figures drawn in outline, which need to be filled up to give them solidity. Those portions of history which are sufficiently lighted up for us to see how men and women lived in them are few and far apart. Even the dark ages are not more obscure to us than that great integrating period of modern Europe, during which the cathedrals were built, constitutional government arose in England, and jurisprudence again became a science. We recognize from these monuments that it was one of the most vigorous ages since Rome was founded, but of the lives which men and women lived in that time we know very little.

The *Talisman* has something of the same splendor as *Ivanhoe*, but *Count Robert of Paris* and *Castle Dangerous* possess small value either as romance or history. The introduction of an ape for dramatic effect in the *Count of Paris* is sensational, and has been rightly characterized by Ruskin as an evidence of waning mental vigor.

Scott may not have been the first writer of historical novels, but he was the first to give that species of fiction a decided stamp. His followers and imitators in that line have been as numerous as the pinnacles on Milan Cathedral. None of his books have received less admiration, and with good reason. The mixture of great historical personages with what one may call every-day characters, as in *Kenilworth* or *Quentin Durward*, give a sense of disproportion such as we feel when we see a few grown persons dancing with a number of children. This is avoided in the *Talisman* and *Ivanhoe* by the antiquity of the subject. Is not the swineherd hero of Ulysses as precious and remarkable to us as an old Greek coin ? So Gurth and Wamba and Friar Tuck become only less illustrious than Richard Plantagenet.

Guizot complains that Scott has done injustice to the burgher class of the Middle Ages, in his description of a citizen of Ghent in *Quentin Durward ;* and this may be well-grounded, for Scott gave the landed gentry rather more respect than they perhaps deserved. His reverence for George IV. as hereditary monarch does not appear to have been mitigated by an appreciation of the weakness of that unworthy figure-head. A little of Byron's dash and independence would often be efficacious in Scott's prose and verse.

The poetical extracts with which he adorns the chapters of his novels have rather a stilted effect, and I think his readers usually pass them by without taking much notice of them. Miss Evans also adopted the custom in one or two of her novels, and in her case it must be considered a success. There is no reason why a poetical heading should not be given to a new chapter, if one that is particularly appropriate chances to enter the author's mind. At the same time this is not likely to occur on all occasions, and there is no need of going to market for such culled flowers of erudition. The original verses, which are interspersed through the Waverley novels, are an ornament, and an advantage, and may well be envied by such prose writers as do not possess the rhyming gift.

Scott's *Life of Napoleon*, though intentionally honest, was written under the influence of strong party prejudice, and may now be fairly called obsolete. Its sole value is the evidence it affords concerning the means employed by the British government to contend against their greatest enemy. That a cargo of assassins should have been landed on the coast of France by a British man-of-war is only rendered credible by Scott's repeating this statement without perceiving the enormity of the transaction. It is also true, however, that Charles James Fox wrote to Talleyrand to warn him that a conspiracy was on foot, and it was by this means, and by Napoleon's own sagacity, that the plot was frustrated. Fox thus absolved the British nation, and left the ignominy to Pitt.*

There are no better books to place before young people than the Waverley novels. We read them at sixteen for pleasure; at thirty for appreciation; and in our old age for comfort, and, as Pericles said, to chase away the sadness of life. Scott was a great artist,—much greater in prose than in verse. If he had no special mission to mankind, yet he was true to himself and true to his art; and much may be learned from him from this very fact. We may also learn this (which there is much need of at the present time), a respect for individuality as the basis of all sound character.

* For further information see John C. Ropes's *Napoleon.*

THACKERAY

THERE is a bust of Thackeray in Westminster Abbey, and it is the only one there, whose expression I recollect distinctly; chiefly from the lines about the mouth, which are similar to those of a doctor who is prepared to undertake a surgical operation. Otherwise the face is remarkable for its fulness and tenderness,—a thoroughly human face,—and the eyes have an expression of brooding observation. It is not a portrait of rare excellence, but so much can be distinguished from it.

Carlyle mentions him in a letter to Emerson as calling at Cheyne Row, but the only remark that he makes about Thackeray is that he was a very " hungry man," a man who is fond of a good dinner. How did it happen that Carlyle, who often took such pains to describe personages of whom we know nothing, should have missed the opportunity of revealing to us the character of such an interesting man.

Thackeray himself relates that in his childhood, while on the voyage from India to England, he disembarked at St. Helena and went with his preceptor to a place from which they could see Napoleon walking back and forth in an enclosed garden,—a sight never to be forgotten. Subsequent to his university life he went to Weimar, as the capstone of his education, and there saw and was introduced to Goethe in his old age. What a meeting was that! We might almost call it the setting sun looking to the rising moon. Only once in his whole life had Goethe clasped the hand of such a genius. It is not likely that either of them was aware of this. "His complexion," says Thackeray, "was still bright and fair; his eyes were remarkably large, dark and brilliant." He was too young at that time to make Goethe's acquaintance.

What influence these two spectacles may have had on Thackeray's future life, does not appear on the surface. He satirized the *Sorrows of Werther*, and spoke of *Wilhelm Meister* as an immoral book; though there are passages in his own writing which are quite as immoral,—if that be the proper word for it. Yet he is distinguished above all his contemporaries except Carlyle, for his breadth and catholicity of mind; and no other English writer has described a Frenchman with such a clear appreciation of the national character. He understood the strong points and the fine points of the French, as well as their weaker side.

Carlyle was right in calling Thackeray a " hungry man." He had a great physique, which, with his active temperament, required fuel to keep it going. In early life he wasted a small competency in convivial entertainments. He was fond of dinners, clubs, evening parties, and junketing. He was not only a " hungry man," but a very sociable one.

He not only liked fine conversation, but also the coarser kind, if it had a background of human nature behind it. However, this dissipation, as it seemed to his friends, proved in the end a paying investment; for it was thus that he obtained his peculiar insight into the character of men and women. Hawthorne learned the secrets of human nature by silent observation, but Thackeray drew people out of themselves by genial discourse, and tempted them to be confidential. Probably no one, except the greatest dramatists, has known human nature so well. He might even be called an every-day Shakespeare. In this respect Milton, Goldsmith, or Byron hold no comparison with him. The London society in which he was immersed is the richest soil for studying life to be found anywhere. His acquaintance was one of the largest in the city. He was a favorite with English noblemen, was acquainted with all the distinguished writers and artists, belonged to an exclusive circle in the upper middle class; and at the same time was on friendly terms with actors, news reporters, and all sorts of impecunious Bohemians. Yet he never laid aside his dignity: he was always the same Thackeray under all conditions, and could smile without condescension on an acquaintance of the wine cellar, if he were walking with an earl.

The gap between Scott and Thackeray is as wide as that between Fielding and Scott. In fact Thackeray abjured Scott and his methods altogether, and went back to Fielding for his models,—so far as he did not take them from actual life. Like Fielding, he was by nature an humorist; and humor is the natural enemy of romance, for as soon as we begin to laugh the fine illusion disappears. The humorous novel, therefore, is essentially realistic; but it is no hard, uncomfortable realism. We find relief from the actual in one of two ways; either by creating an ideal for ourselves, which we follow as a guide and strive to accomplish, or by comparing the present state of things with a possible ideal, thus taking revenge on its deformities. Shakespeare made use of both these methods, but I believe never at the same time. His comedies are never heroic, and the comic scenes in his tragedies are taken from the lowest life. A plain, prosaic realist like Tolstoi may interest and even instruct, but he can never quite satisfy us; for he cannot go beyond a certain point. A writer, to be really great, must possess ideality. Without that he is like a bird with clipped wings.

The line between romance and poetry is difficult to define, but it can be illustrated by the subject before us; though there is as much poetry in Thackeray, perhaps, as in Scott, the few poems which he published, albeit on ordinary subjects, are the more distinctly poetic on that account. On the other hand, Scott's poetry depends on romance for its consistency. Scott's humor, when he is humorous, is usually so introduced as to have the effect of very sharp irony. An instance of this in the *Heart of Midlothian* is Captain Knockdunder's asking Mr. Butler for his " pell ropes " with which to hang Jeannie Deans's nephew. Holbein's *Dance of Death* has nothing in it so trenchant as that. Where a situation is naturally comic, like young Lochinvar's carrying off another man's bride, right from the altar, Scott treats the subject in such a high-toned manner that the humorous side of it, though plainly seen, is kept in the background. Readers of Thackeray can well imagine how he would have described such an event; but he wrote in an age when such events were no longer possible.

The sudden meeting of an old acquaintance in altered conditions is a trying circumstance, and the discovery of Colonel Newcome by Pendennis as an indigent Brother of Greyfriars might be called a piece of high comedy, not unlike the return of Rip Van Winkle after his protracted sleep; but Thackeray draws forth from it the noblest poetry, and it is doubtful if Scott would have succeeded so well.

Thackeray proves his ideality in his humor, his style, and the quality of his thought. Like Albert Dürer, he drew his figures from real life, imitating every peculiarity, so as to make them the more individual; but as Dürer gave his faces an ideal expression, so Thackeray surrounded his characters with an atmosphere which emanated from himself. His style I conceive to be one of the finest in English literature: so simple, flexible, and expressive. His writing is as pleasant as a wood-fire, full of English warmth and cheerfulness. It has not the grave dignity of Hume, or the high-spirited tone of Froude, for these would have been unsuited to his subject. He wrote not of public life, but of social life, and his manner is conversational. It is a lively colloquial style, which carries the reader onward at a good pace.

The incidents of human life are of little consequence to him. He calls *Vanity Fair* a novel without a hero, and he might have said as truthfully, that it was a novel without a plot. His plots are of the simplest description; such experiences, for the most part, are familiar to all of us. George Sedley was killed in battle, but he might as well have been lost on a sea voyage,—a fatality which has happened to a number of my acquaintances. Neither are his characters more remarkable. There are worse women than Becky Sharpe and better men than Henry Esmond. They are not remarkable people, but such as one meets with every day. At the same time they are not commonplace, but usually interesting; and after we have followed the course of their lives, in one novel, we are pleased to meet with them again, incidentally, in another. They have their peculiarities, as we all have, but they are not ear-marked by any eccentricity. There are neither born fools nor lunatics among them. They are highly inividualized portraits, and so represented that we know them not by one characteristic but by many. They neither say nor do remarkable things, and yet their proceedings always have an interest for us. We live with them and see them in flesh and blood. It is their behavior toward one another which Thackeray records, and those mental conditions which influence their behavior. We perceive the whole machinery of their lives, as if their minds were transparent. It is only genius that could do this.

He was not only an humorist, but a satirist; and

this accounts, perhaps, for the expression of his mouth. Satire is a keen weapon, and a satirist is truly a spiritual surgeon, who operates on the tumors and diseased members of society. It was after the first hundred years of the Roman Empire that satire first made its appearance, and since then it has been customary to associate the prevalence of satire with national decline. This was certainly the case in France during the eighteenth century and perhaps also, in Spain during the seventeenth; whether the rule applies to England is doubtful. The position of India, the extension of British commerce, and the increase of manufacturing capacity by the use of steam power, caused a rapid accumulation of wealth in Great Britain, the larger portion of which fell into the hands of those who were ignorant of its uses. This produced, or inflicted, a congested condition of society, such as was sure to lead to great extravagance and folly; a condition of affairs not unlike that in Rome during the period when Juvenal and Persius flourished. The body-politic had become too full-blooded and required cupping. So Carlyle, Ruskin, Thackeray, and Matthew Arnold appeared, and were politely paid for their services.

People who are themselves fit subjects for satire, such as snobs, gourmands, and parasites, never like to read it, but there are many others who consider its employment uncharitable, unchristian, and ill-natured. Truly enough, it is so when misapplied; but when all kind and conciliatory methods have failed, what are we to do? A spoiled child of fashion, arrogant with prosperity, and infatuated with self-love, is hardly a subject for kindness. Conciliatory methods are wasted on him; he spurns interference no matter how well intended; and if he laughs contemptuously at our feeble efforts to reform him, it is after all no more than we deserve. He may puff tobacco smoke in our face, and scoff at the virtue of respectable women. How are we to protect ourselves from his contempt and insolence ? How shall we deal with the self-infatuated person who cannot be made to understand the simple reason of things, but continues to insist that black is white? Satire is the only refuge we have,—except profanity; and it is certainly better than that. '' Make way for me, sir '' said John Randolph to the impudent officer who blocked his way on the sidewalk. '' I never make way for an infernal rascal,'' was the reply. '' I always do, sir,'' said Randolph, bowing and passing to one side. This contains the whole question in a nutshell. We are not all as ready-witted as the satirical Virginian, but even the record in a book of such an adventure will do much good and finally reach the ears for which it was intended. The only vulnerable point in such people is their self-love.

An aristorcratic lady had a favorite pug that after a time became sickly and declined to eat. So she consulted a skilful doctor on the subject, who carried the dog to his own house for a fortnight; where, according to his statement afterward, he starved him and whipped him around a tree. He then returned the dog in a frisky and healthful condition. Human nature, also, sometimes requires treatment of this sort.

Although Thackeray did not spare the clergy when he met with an undeserving incumbent, and even if he did inquire of Prof. Ticknor, while in Boston, for an introduction to Theodore Parker, no one who has read the last five chapters of *The Newcomes* would suspect him of being irreligious. He was not the first to reprehend the practice of shoving younger sons of the gentry into the fold of the church, so that they might be provided for, irrespective of their fitness for the holy office. We recollect some fine lines of Milton, which come to this point also; and it has been said in America that not a few young men studied divinity, because they knew not what else they might do. In this way a kind of life-long pretence is created which often leads to pathetic, as well as to humorous situations. Clergymen are human beings, and if they cannot obtain honest work, or, as the saying is, are thrown out of line, they are obliged to live by begging, or stealing, or some other knavery. Rev. Mr. Honeyman places himself in the hands of a Jew, who organizes a congregation for him, and advises him to cough so that the ladies shall think he is consumptive and feel more sympathy for him. This is a terrible sarcasm, but we may trust Thackeray for its truthfulness, and in real life we could point to an instance quite as sacrilegious. Still more impressive is his description of the squalid Hunt, parasite, gambler, and prospective felon, dragged before a police court to pay the fine of a common drunkard.

Truly an awful warning this for youthful follies and levity. It may be regretted, perhaps, that Thackeray did not pay more consideration to the brighter side of clerical life, and give us examples worthy of imitation in that line.

He was no respecter of surplices nor of hidalgos. The proverbial cloak of respectability which covers so many sins, was a perpetual target for the shafts of his wit, and his keen arrows penetrated all pretences and protections, which were not of genuine metal. A favorite of George IV., noted for his vices and daring misdeeds, he has held up to the detestation of posterity, under the name of the Marquis of Steyne. Even royalty could not escape from him, and his criticism of George IV. was so severe, that many of his friends blamed him for it; on the ground that the office ought to be respected even if the incumbent proved unworthy, and the publication of his censures had all the effect of an argument for republicanism. A few of his titled acquaintances fell away from him, but this did not concern him much. He considered that his business was to tell the truth, and that his excoriation of George IV. might serve as a warning to Victoria's son.

Thackeray always felt a particular aversion to snobs, and no other writer has analyzed this species of civilized humanity so thoroughly. His treatise on this subject is one of the most amusing of his books, though he has perhaps given it more importance than it altogether deserves. A man whose social position is clearly defined, and whose mind is occupied with important affairs, does not trouble

himself much, whether casual acquaintances treat
him with the respect he deserves or not.   If they
are not polite to him, so much the worse for them,
Emerson would say.   Thackeray's social position,
however, was not fixed, but fluctuating.   His association with people of various classes, and different
professions, may have caused a feeling of uncertainty, in the minds of his friends' relatives, as to
how they ought to behave toward him.   Thackeray
was not only a writer, but an artist, in a literal sense,
and like all artists, as he says himself, sensitive, im-
pulsive, excitable.   The expression of his face gives
evidence of rare tenderness of feeling.   His sensibility may often have been wounded,—humiliated
he could not have been,—without his realizing the
cause of it; but he also must have suffered from a
great deal of impudence, bad manners, and the
patronizing airs of people who were actually his inferiors.   At the time of the exclusion of a Jewish
banker from a Saratoga hotel, a venerable Boston
lawyer said to me, " Purse-proud millionaires are
very disagreeable, whether they are Jews or not."
In all large cities there are self-important people,
male or female, who go about tramping on the toes
of others, with haughty indifference,—like the heavy
bodies whom Goethe describes in the *Walpurgis
Night* who wear out the sod on the Brocken.   No
person is to be blamed for taking an amiable and just
revenge on these folk, and no one could be better
qualified to do it than Thackeray.

In America we pretend not to recognize distinctions of classes, though such distinctions exist in all

communities, except the most barbarous, whether they are recognized or not. There are decided advantages in this unformulated condition of society, but it also increases the difficulty for modest men and women to maintain the position that belongs to them. This it is that gives an American gentleman the suspicious, unfriendly look with which he regards others. This is not so bad as formerly, but it cannot be wholly avoided in a community where no authority exists to decide on social rights and privileges. Distinguished people, very wealthy people, and men of political and mercantile importance are obliged to cultivate a fair amount of reserve in self-protection. The best people are accused of exclusiveness, because they are the ones whom everybody wants to know. The problem is largely a physical one: it is a question of time and strength; though some allowance must also be made for personal taste and inclination. So there is much complaint on this head which is quite unreasonable, and by persons who would be even more exclusive were they in the same position. Everybody knows the governor, but the governor cannot be expected to know everybody.

Yet there is much real snobbishness in America, ill-mannered and disgusting enough to every person of refined sensibility. I remember at the university, a young man from one of the oldest Boston families, otherwise a pleasant and sensible fellow, but who was in the habit of speaking of his suburban classmates as the " dirty little King," the " dirty little Thompson," etc. Still worse was the speech

of a literary man at a public dinner, given in honor
of a most democratic novelist, stigmatizing a portion
of his own city, which was inhabited by respectable
shopkeepers, as the '' abomination of desolation.''
Another instance might be taken from a lady at a
sea-shore hotel, who said, referring to a group of
ladies and gentlemen from central New York: '' They
seem to be enjoying themselves, and it is interesting
to meet with people so different from those we are
accustomed to, but of course we do not think of
speaking to them.''   There is the New York woman
who thought that no lady could be said to be dressed
unless she had on her diamonds; and the Philadel-
phian notion that, in order to be genteel, people must
live between Chestnut Street and Spruce Street, no
matter how inconvenient this may be, or how difficult to obtain a suitable residence.   Such cases
would be humorous, if they were not so lamentable.
Snobs are always the readiest victims of adventurers
and impostors; for, as they have no true criterion
of worth and culture, they are easily deceived by
external appearances.

.If, as stated by Thackeray, the word humbug was
derived from the city of Hamburg, it must have
been a malicious libel on the most honorable class
of merchants in Europe.   Both Hamburg and
Bremen, before their consolidation with Prussia,
were diminutive but model commonwealths ; as perhaps they are even now.   Absolute poverty was unknown in them ; crimes were of the rarest occurrence ;
and property holders were so honest that they were
permitted to assess their own taxes.   However that

may have been, the word came into use at the time when it was needed,—about one hundred and fifty years ago,—to express a new phase in the history of civilization.

After the accession of William of Orange, great improvement in legal administration took place in England, and this has continued ever since. The same thing happened in Prussia during the reign of Frederick, and somewhat later in other countries. Previous to that time nine points of the law, so far as practical application was concerned, might be summed up in the formula, might equals right. Acts of robbery and acts of violence were open and high-handed, but there does not appear to have been so much secret knavery: at least the work that was done in old times was remarkable for its honesty, and it is significant that Voltaire could have accumu-lated a fortune by such methods as are now too transparent to be imitated with success. Human nature, however, is extremely plastic. If repressed in one direction, it will always expand in another. So when open robbery could no longer prosper, all sorts of impostures were practised by which covet-ous persons could defraud others without coming within the danger of legal indictment. The form of imposition by which offices, preferment, and social advancement were gained, is called humbug; and this has increased to such a degree, that it is al-most impossible now for a young man to rise in life without the help of it. The excuse of Barnum, the showman, for his stuffed mermaids and other impostures, was that people like humbug, and if he did not provide it for them, others would do so and take his business away from him.

Thackeray was the first writer of English to realize the extent to which this evil had permeated society, and his attacks on it were vigorous and incessant. If he has not accomplished its reformation, it is not from lack of a thorough exposure. He has at least taught us better how to recognize it in all its various forms and protean disguises. A great deal of his finest humor is derived from this subject. In fact, some of his characters seem to be wholly made up of it, like Blanche Amory in *Pendennis*, of whom he says: " a sham enthusiasm which she had, a sham hatred, a sham love, a sham taste, a sham grief, each of which flared and shone very vehemently for an instant, but subsided and gave place to the next sham emotion." There are persons more or less like this, of various gradations, shading off to reality on one side of their character, and back again to pretension on the other.

It has been said to me, " I do not like Thackeray, because he makes everybody appear so mean and selfish, and if I read him I seem to see selfish motives in what everyone says and does." It is true that he helps us to see the selfish motives of action, but we should not see them if they did not exist. The man who knows human nature thoroughly, must realize how large a part self-interest plays in it; but he also knows that this is to a great extent justifiable. The question properly is not whether selfishness is right, but when it is right: time and circumstances making all the difference between vir-

tue and vice.   Thackeray was no conventional moralist, and his philosophy was rather Epicurean than
Stoical.   He composed a song which has for a refrain :

> " Then sing, as Dr. Luther sang :
> Who loves not women, wine, and song,
> He is a fool his whole life long."

As Martin Luther perceived that chastity did not
consist in celibacy, but rather in a virtuous married
life; so Thackeray knew that true virtue was not to
be found in conventional forms, but in the moment-
ary decision which precedes every important action.
He considered habitual self-denial as vicious as self-
indulgence; and to the young man who said he
never allowed himself to eat cake, he replied: " The
reason is, because you are a glutton."   The seven
cardinal virtues were reduced in his mind to one;
that of doing the right thing at the right moment.
If he was relentless in railing at the follies of
mankind, he delighted also in representing human
nature at its best, when the plot of 'his story made
this admissible.   He delineated virtue with so fine
a point, and shaded it so delicately, that many of
his readers pass it by without recognition.   The last
portion of *The Newcomes*, is all aglow with moral
enthusiasm; and I think there is no other writer
that discriminates more clearly between the genuine
article, and its contrary.

> " And marked so well the high behavior of man or maid
> That he from speech refrained, nobility more nobly to repay."

This quiet and elevating manner of representing virtue is nowhere more conspicuous than in *Pendennis*, which is much of an autobiography, though not to be trusted in regard to details. He published his subsequent novels under the name of Arthur Pendennis and was often called Pendennis familiarly by his friends. The prodigality of this young man,—Thackeray never calls him a hero,—his period of idleness after leaving college, and his readiness to fall in with his uncle's plans for a lucrative match are all set forth in bold relief; but we should also notice the handsome manner in which he retrieves his character and fortune, the sincerity of his nature, by which he escapes from the matrimonial snare, and the magnanimity he shows to his clannish townsman who had previously spread evil reports of him. Pendennis is not an ideal character, certainly, but if there are some better young men, there are many more who are worse. He is a more favorable subject for the central figure of a novel than his friend Warrington, who spoiled his own life from a sense of duty, would have been. Thackeray does not condone his own faults, and leaves us to discover his real merit.

The Fotheringay incident, with which the book opens, could not be exceelled. The ardent, imaginative schoolboy falls in love with a beautiful Irish actress, who cares nothing for him, but accepts him for the benefit of her family. She has neither head nor heart; her acting is mere machinery, and she only understands in a dim way the meaning of the part she plays. Then the circumspect manner in which the old major undertakes to extricate his nephew from the trap he has fallen into, which he finally succeeds in doing by an incident which no one could have foreseen,—the apparition of a lawyer who has a list of debts against the theatrical company.

Pendennis is not written in the best English, and there is a good deal of slang in it, a reflection of academic life; but it has a youthful freshness and buoyancy which we prize more highly the farther we advance in years. It is remarkable that Thackeray, who was so much given to clubs and male society, should have understood so well the nature of women. Laura, Blanche, Lady Rockminster, and Fanny are all sufficiently feminine, and yet very different from one another, without being in the least typical characters. Pendennis does not fall in love with Laura, simply because he has always lived in the house with her; but after he has been separated from her, and has had experience of the frailty of other women, he appreciates her superiority.

Vanity Fair is the most powerful of Thackeray's novels, if not the most powerful of all works of fiction; but it is also the most terrible. Taken by itself, it would seem to be too cynical a representation of society, but considered as a part or section of a whole series, we recognize that it has a right to existence. The Marquis of Steyne was taken from real life and is not overdrawn. In my youth there was such a man in Boston, who used his wealth for most shameful purposes, and that in an open and flagrant manner; and yet was able to maintain himself in society. Becky Sharpe, that is, " a sharp beak," is his proper feminine counterpart, and, as the personation of an adventuress, will no doubt last while the English language lives. Shakespeare delineated Iago and Shylock and Richard III., but he did not find occasion to picture such women as might correspond to them. Women exist, however, or have existed, quite as wicked as the worst male specimens, and it remained for Thackeray to represent these. His Campaigner in *The Newcomes* outshines or outblackens Becky Sharpe, and Beatrix Esmond is at least as heartless and unprincipled. The mischief that women do is more secret and easily concealed than the evil deeds of men, and, therefore, there is even more reason why it should be exposed. The talent that some women have for covering up their tracks surpasses that of the cuttle-fish.

The Newcomes is delightful. It is generally considered the best of Thackeray's novels, and it surely deserves that reputation. A mild radiance pervades it throughout; the intelligence of a warm-hearted, clear-sighted, sympathetic man who has attained the full fruition of his power,—who knows the world and knows himself. Its tone is as tranquillizing as some of Raphael's pictures: there are no void passages in it, and few inequalities. The book has a mellow tone, and the knowledge of human nature displayed in it is marvellous. Colonel Newcome would endure for ages as the standard of an English gentleman; and his mental limitations only serve to make this more conspicuous. I do not know how many American girls have been named for Ethel Newcome. She is a lily, growing among tares, a gazelle among jackals, and we watch the course of her fortune, her dangers and narrow escapes, with breathless interest. She is the queen of English fiction, unless we except Sophia Western, who is not nearly so well known. Ethel is a true heroine, but still a human being, and her pride prevents her from forming an alliance with her half-cousin Clive, at the moment when she might have done so. For this mistake she is obliged to suffer years of sorrow and loneliness, but finally triumphs by a grand stroke of magnanimity. The true character of the Campaigner is kept in reserve until near the close, when she springs into notice like a tigress from her den. This terrible woman caused the death of Colonel Newcome, her daughter, and daughter's child; and, but for the interference of Ethel, would evidently have destroyed Clive also. This is explained so clearly that we can see the mental and physical working of it, even to the last pulsation of the heart. The last scenes in *The Newcomes* might not unjustly be compared to the last scenes in *Faust*; and it should always be remembered that Hawthorne and all his family wept over this portion of the novel. The arrangement is rather too artistic to be wholly natural, and yet we could not wish it to be different from what it is.

The Adventures of Philip has its faults, but is smelted from the same ore as *The Newcomes*, and is even more remarkable, as a study of human nature.

Brandon, who is to fight a duel, on the following day, with the young painter Fitch, looks very pale at the evening entertainment, but as soon as he drinks a glass of punch his face turns very red. This is the way stimulants affect people while in a state of nervous agitation; but how did Thackeray know it, and how did he happen to think of it at the right moment ? He must have realized the scene pictorially as he wrote. When we read the chapter in which is described the family battle at the French boarding-house, and Colonel Bunch challenges General Baynes, " his face as red as a lobster, and eyes starting out of their sockets," we lay down the book and exclaim, How could he know so much. Read his description of wicked old Mrs. Baynes after the defeat of her mercenary scheme: her grim loveliness, her rebellious tears, and sullen grief at the obstinacy of her husband in not breaking his word to Philip Firmin and rendering his daughter miserable for life. Thackeray places himself so perfectly in her position, that he says finally, " I shall have to stop or I shall sympathize with her,"—and we feel so ourselves. " One, two, three rattling sonatas Minna and Brenda played "; how much more poor music there is in the world than good music, and how often does a pianoforte become an instrument of torture. There is more mannerism in *Philip* than in any of his novels except *The Virginians;* but the character of the Little Sister is unique, and stands by itself.

Lovell the Widower is a short story, but compact with humor. The prudent and enterprising young woman, who dances in the ballet to support her family, and afterwards becomes governess to Mr. Lovell, keeps three or four admirers on the very edge of acceptation until Lovell himself offers to marry her,—when she takes him in a twinkling, and leaves her former suitors to their various reflections. Here satire sits enthroned; and yet there is an undercurrent of pathos in the story which elevates and beautifies it.

Celebrity always has its effect on a man. If he does not become vain from it, he loses interest in his former pursuits, neglects his friends, or becomes more ambitious. Its effect on Thackeray evidently was to make him desire a place among classic authors. He had already obtained this distinction, but was not aware of it. For the attainment of his purpose he considered the classic style essential, and so he wrote *Henry Esmond*, a tale of the last century, in the manner of Scott and Fielding, or something between the two. Though in this way his writing acquired a more dignified style, in a certain sense it was a mistake; for he lost by it both humor and fluency. When a writer deserts his own manner for another, he loses power. Yet in its way, it is the most perfect of Thackeray's works, and its freedom from satire recommends it to a large class of readers; and those who cannot perceive the finer points in Thackeray, prefer it to *The Newcomes.* We do not, however, find the same comfort and refreshment in it. Esmond himself is an ideal character; a small, compact, handsome, and alert man, without a fault. Perhaps this is the reason why he does not engage our sympathy to the same extent as Clive Newcome and Philip Firmin. Beatrix Esmond, a portrait of great solidity, is as unprincipled as Becky Sharpe, but this want of principle is united with a feminine charm which Becky did not possess. The novel concludes in a manner as surprising as the events of real life.

There never was a sequel equal to its original, whether it be the second part of *Faust*, *Paradise Regained*, or Thackeray's *Virginians*. In the latter instance this may have been partly because the story was written for a New York magazine. In Virginia, Thackeray feels himself on foreign ground, and proceeds accordingly with slowness and caution; as soon as he succeeds in bringing over the two grandsons of Henry Esmond to England, the tale becomes more interesting. Beatrix appears in it again, to prove how even such a woman can be of use, though unrepentant; and the determined little American heiress who marries Lord Castlewood, and tyrannizes over his whole family, is admirable. Thackeray did not live very long after writing *The Virginians*, and there are places in it which indicate that he was losing interest in his work. The worst of his faults is always the confidential attitude which he sometimes assumes toward the reader.

M. Taine's account of Carlyle, Byron, and Tennyson, though inadequate, is interesting; but his criticism of Thackeray is no better than a rigmarole. It seems a shame to apply this word to the work of so amiable a writer, but there is no other that suits the case. He writes and writes continually, attempting to grasp his subject, but always without success. He quarters the ground like a hound, in search of a lost scent; but without coming to any conclusion of importance. He quotes long passages, comments on them, and just as we expect to learn something from him, he starts off in another direction. It is doubtful if any Frenchman could understand Thackeray to the same degree that he appreciated the French. Only the author of *Tristram Shandy* has done them equal justice.

I once said to a noted Berlin critic, " Thackeray is the most dramatic of our English novelists." " No," he replied, " he explains too much." This, however, is only true of the *form* of his statement, which is not dramatic in narrative. He is always sketching dramatic situations.

There was formerly a ship-owner in Boston, a grave, taciturn man of business, who never told his joys or his sorrows, but when he came home at night and took *The Newcomes* from his bookcase, his family knew that something, that day, had gone wrong with him. Is not this the best criticism we can make on Thackeray. Yet I think we can also add what Wasson says in his essay on *Wilhelm Meister*, that Thackeray opens the door into a hospital, and Goethe opens the door out of a hospital, into the fresh air and sunshine. There is this limitation to satire: it corrects, but it does not invigorate.

14

DICKENS

I HAVE heard a story, though it may be a myth, that at the time when *Dombey and Son* was being published in monthly instalments, while an English steamer was closely approaching the wharf at Jersey City, ·some person called out to those on board, "What is the news from Europe," and the reply came back, "Paul Dombey is dead." Whether true or not, the story serves to prove how widely extended was the interest in Dickens's novels forty years ago. The death of Paul Dombey was of international importance.

Dickens is the Macaulay of novelists; vigorous, careless, rhetorical, with a good deal of mannerism; but nevertheless valuable from real and intrinsic merit, which it would be useless to deny. His virtues outweigh his faults, and from the satisfaction which two generations of English readers in both hemispheres have derived from his novels it seems probable that Dickens will hereafter be counted among English classic writers, though hardly a classic himself.

There are said to be seventeen distinct classes in Russian society,—that is, those who are in it, and those who are not,—but in Christian countries the people may be divided into those who are very wealthy; and the upper-middle class, the lower-middle class, tradespeople, and peasants. Now Thackeray belonged to the upper-middle class, and Dickens very decidedly to the lower. He was not well educated, and if his mother was really the prototype of Mrs. Nickleby, she must have been a foolish and rather vulgar woman; or her son has done her great injustice. This is the more surprising as Dickens, speaking of the best of England's early kings, says that, like most great men, he had a good and intelligent mother. The influence of a wise mother on the moral development of her children cannot be overestimated; but there have been men who rose to greatness without this advantage, and Dickens would seem to be one of them. The vicissitudes of orphan boys and girls were a favorite theme with him; and though David Copperfield has a mother, she is a gentle, timid, and rather shadowy figure, quite unable to protect her son from the rude world in his tender years, or to provide against the dangers that threatened him. No one could sympathize with the sorrows and troubles of childhood better than Dickens, for he had known its neglect, its injustice, its unprotected weakness, and the lack of sympathy and consideration which properly belonged to it.

The lower-middle class, then, was the material from which Dickens elaborated his romantic tales, and, to judge correctly of his work, we must know something of that element ourselves; yet nothing is more difficult. If a cultivated man goes into one of our country towns, at a distance of fifty to one hundred miles from the Metropolis, and makes it his residence for a short time, he will find at first that the people whom he meets there seem to be under a kind of enchantment. Wherever he goes, silence precedes him. People are pleased to meet him and will talk with him, but not apparently of their own free will. If he enters the tavern of an evening, and finds six or eight men conversing together, they wind up their talk as soon as he appears and only recommence it in a languid manner, while two or three go into a corner of the room, and the circle soon breaks up. If he calls on their wives and daughters, he is received with much appearance of satisfaction, but presently there comes a chilling pause, and before long he becomes aware of the relief that will be felt after his departure. This class of people corresponds nearly to the army of shopkeepers and clerks in the large cities. Shopkeepers and clerks are continually dying off, from their unhealthy mode of life, and their ranks are recruited from the country.

If, however, he remains long enough with them to make them feel assured that he is a good-hearted man, who means well by them, and respects people for what they are worth, he will in course of time discover much that is interesting and admirable. He will encounter narrow prejudices in plenty; but he will meet with men and women of such solidity of character as he has rarely known before. He will discover families in which religious devotion is as sincere as among the early Christians; and where the economy is not more strict than the practice of virtue. He will find young men, perhaps studying for a profession, whose self-denial borders on heroism, and young women whose perfect modesty would shame many of his fashionable acquaintances. He will also encounter mixed characters enough, as well as rudeness, coarseness, and provincial bigotry. The one thing he is not likely to meet with, is a sense of beauty and elegance.

Isolated individuals of natural refinement and a keen sense of beauty may appear anywhere. Hawthorne came from the lower-middle class of New England, like a lily in a cornfield; Turner was born in the same class of Englishmen; Carlyle was the son of a stone-mason, and Burns of a peasant: but the rule is, that the sense of beauty and elegance comes either with domestic culture, or is an inherited tendency, or is developed by a liberal education. At the university a young man first learns to associate objects in harmonious groups; he perceives that the physical sciences are co-ordinated in a harmonious manner, and the abstract beauty of this appeals strongly to his sense of fitness and his idea of things as they should be. If he finds pleasure in writing letters to his friends or family, or has any other literary taste, the translation of Greek and Latin authors gives him a sense of style, and he discovers that a graceful method is both the easiest and most effective. Beauty, says one of my friends, is the line of the least resistance. It is only through a liberal education that a man first learns the value of knowledge for its own sake, independent of any use he may be able to make of it. Before that, everything has been to him a matter of utility; but it is only by rising above utility that we can appreciate the beautiful. Wealth is not essential to it, but a certain amount of leisure is essential. The Alcott family lived for many years in Concord, on an income like that of a ship-carpenter; but their house was not only beautiful internally but all its suroundings were so.

Dickens, therefore, could not have derived much sense of beauty and elegance from either of these sources. It was not a part of his birthright; nor could he obtain it from the home culture; nor from a higher education, except such as he might find for himself, on the way through life. Consequently his work was deficient in this respect. His style is heavy and lumbering,—somewhat like an old stage-coach on a bad road. His manner of reading narrative passages was similar to this, as some people may recollect; though in the dramatic portions he was in voice and expression equal to the best comic actors. His *Child's History of England* is more smoothly written than his novels, and I think this is to be accounted for by the necessity of condensation; whereas most of his writing if not diffuse, has at least a great deal of *language* in it. There is a sentence at the close of his first chapter in the *Child's History* which is quite exceptional of its kind. "On Salisbury Plain Stonehenge yet stands, a monument of the olden time, when the Roman name was unknown in Britain, and the Druids with their best magic wands could not have written it in the sands of the wild sea-shore." This is poetry, and it would only require a few changes to transform it into verse.

His Christmas stories, especially *Marley's Ghost*, and *The Haunted Man*, rank next to the *Child's History* in purity of style.

Neither could Dickens find much that was beautiful in his material. He did not, like Schiller, idealize the common people, but exaggerated rather than diminished their peculiarities. As a picture of English life he has even done them injustice; though as an accomplished American lady said on her first day at Liverpool and Chester, "You cannot caricature these people." Many of his characters are interesting, but few of them are attractive. Even David Copperfield is not attractive as Clive Newcome and Daniel Deronda are attractive. Is there any character in that story that we respect so much as Betsy Trotwood; and yet her very name suggests a person who prefers to work like a servant cleaning pots and mending clothes, rather than to employ her leisure in the higher uses of social life. If Dickens has represented a gentleman anywhere, it is Arthur Clenham in *Little Dorrit*, and he may very well pass for one; but he is rather like Scott's Waverley, a central point from which we view the circus, than a tangible person. It was a deficiency in the man himself. One could hardly imagine inviting Dickens to look at a fine picture, or to go out of his way to listen to the Prussian band. When Longfellow invited him to dinner, he walked from Boston to Cambridge, at so rapid a rate, that the college students whom he passed on the way were unable to keep up with him, though several tried to do so. His publisher, Mr. Fields, tells similar anecdotes of him in

Yesterdays with Authors, which had better have been left to private circulation.

As Thackeray went back to Fielding for his models, so Dickens returned to Scott; but in his hands the romantic novel underwent strange modifications.   It became more romantic and poetic than ever before, but also more realisitc.   *Ivanhoe* itself is not more of a romance than the adventures of *Oliver Twist;* and yet in *Oliver Twist*, if there is any ideality at all, it is expended on inanimate objects instead of human beings.   Dickens possessed a vivid imagination: he saw everything before him with terrible precision; but he saw it as if it were fixed and stereotyped.   On this account he succeeds better in describing natural objects than in representing the actions of men and women, which are not fixed, but continually fluctuating like the colors on water.   He had the heart of a poet, but his intellect did not correspond to this.   What he sees is continually at variance with what he feels, and this produces a conflict which only can be reconciled by humor.   If it were not for his humor, Dickens would be unendurable.

The intensity of his feeling cannot find an outlet in forms of beauty, for with these his intellect is not acquainted, so it takes possession of the stereotyped pictures in his mind, and exaggerates the prominent features in them.   This produces what we call caricature; which can only be properly applied to objects such as are themselves ridiculous or faulty in some respect.   By exaggerating the appearance of the fault, we make it more conspicuous and open the way for its reformation. This is the justification of *Punch* and the New York comic periodicals. If, however, these papers caricature a worthy man whom the community respects, as Carl Schurz was treated by Thomas Nast, we feel that virtue has been insulted. It is the same with any beautiful object.

The French painter, Gustave Doré, resembled Dickens strikingly. He had, for a Frenchman, a decided love for virtue, and hatred of vice; he was prolific in his designs, and drew with the same energy that Dickens wrote; but he was a born caricaturist, and the treatment of serious subjects was not suited to him. The classic grace of Dante could only be represented in form by an artist whose style possessed the same qualities,—an artist like Raphael or Fra Angelico. This has not yet been done successfully, and Doré's exaggeration of the intense seriousness of the *Inferno* only serves to make it absurd. His illustrations of *Don Quixote*, which caused Ruskin to lose his appetite for dinner, have a thin kind of humor, but it is not the genial, penetrating humor of Cervantes. It is rather a light sort of wit; whereas Dickens's humor comes from the heart and is deep-seated. There is that kind of good cheer in it, from which the phrase originated centuries ago of " merry England." It seems to say to the reader " peace on earth and good will to all men."

The mental habit of giving vitality to inanimate objects has long since been considered the true test of the poet. Was it not thus that Grecian mythology originated—at least to a large extent,—at a time when poets and prophets were one and the same. It is thus also that imaginative children people the world with inhabitants of their own making. Homer says " the dark wave roared loudly around the hollow ship," and I once heard a boy of five years say, " I know what it is that the hoe says to the gravel," and then he imitated phonetically the sound of a hoe scraping the ground. He believed that the hoe could speak; and did Homer also believe that the wave could roar of its own accord ? That is not likely; but we may feel sure that some remote ancestor of his thought so. The farmer talks to his plough, the buffalo-hunter to his rifle, and the sea-captain to his ship. They become children again, and are so much the wiser for it. Now what his gun is to the hunter, and his ship to the sailor, all external nature is to the poet: his interests are universal.

I can think of no prose writer in whom this anthropomorphic tendency is so strong as in Dickens. Hawthorne had a great deal of it. I never look at a squash blossom without recollecting the poetry he drew forth from one in his garden at the Old Manse. Hawthorne, however, was always classic, and selected his material with the greatest care. Dickens was quite the reverse: everything was grain for his hopper, and the ruder and more common an object was, the better it served his purpose. Plates on the breakfast-table smiled complacently on him; the brass head on the poker nods to him; old posts place themselves in his way, as if to beg alms of him; ships on the sea are bringing messages to him; the wind runs its fingers through his hair, and closes his blinds for him with human hands. As an instance of the heaviness of Dickens's style, I would point to the opening chapter of *Martin Chuzzlewit*, a piece of composition, equally vicious in matter and manner; but in the second chapter there is a description of a frolicsome autumn wind which is one of the best anthropomorphic passages that he ever wrote. It is too long and copious to quote more than the final paragraph:

" The scared leaves only flew the faster for all this, and a giddy chase it was ; for they got into unfrequented places where there was no outlet, and where their pursuer kept them eddying round and round at his pleasure ; and they crept under the eaves of houses and clung tightly to the sides of hay-ricks, like bats ; and tore in at open chamber windows, and cowered close to hedges ; and in short went anywhere for safety. But the oddest feat they achieved was to take advantage of the sudden opening of Mr. Pecksniff's front door, to dash wildly into his passage ; whither the wind following close upon them, and finding the backdoor open, incontinently blew out the lighted candle held by Miss Pecksniff, and slammed the front-door against Mr. Pecksniff who was at that moment entering, with such violence, that in the twinkling of an eye he lay on his back at the bottom of the steps. Being by this time weary of such trifling performances, the boisterous rover hurried away rejoicing, roaring over the moor and meadow, hill and flat, until it got out to sea, where it met with other winds similarly disposed, and made a night of it."

This is admirable, so far as the autumnal wind is concerned; but we notice that Mr. Pecksniff is overthrown in this rather exceptional manner, wholly for the amusement of the reader. The incident does not, in any way, expedite the action of the story, nor has it any moral effect on the man himself. It is doubtful if such an incident could be found in any French novel. An American walking in the streets of Rome was struck by a chain, so that he fell on his hands. There were quite a number of Italians, men and boys, standing by, and they all stared at him, but not one of them laughed. The same thing might have happened in Paris. I think amusement at the commonplace mishaps of others is a Saxon, or at the best a Germanic, peculiarity.

Dickens's poetizing faculty did not pass beyond inanimate objects, and to some extent what Goldsmith calls animated nature. Hawthorne in the *Marble Faun* represents every scene with a background graceful and atmospheric as a Claude Lorraine, and each of the four characters is a romance by itself; but Dickens's men and women are not poetic types. The best of them may be slightly romantic, and the rest are decidedly prosaic. The poetic element plays about *The Haunted Man* and a few others, but it does not emanate from them.

Though his characters seem real enough, they are nevertheless human beings whose life is based on a single idea, only one side of which is stamped—like a coin,—and which they always present to the reader. Dombey is a purse-proud capitalist whose sole object in life is to maintain the prestige of his family. He runs on this one idea, like a locomotive on its rails, pitching everything aside that comes in its way. He has no consciousness of anything else: he sees nothing, and knows nothing, of the thoughts and feelings of other people, even of those who are personally related to him. He supplies the physical wants of his family, but it never occurs to him, that there are other necessities of human existence, which it is his duty to provide. He has lost the faculty of comunicating with other minds, and is in all respects a machine man; such as are not uncommon in commercial life. His family die about him, through the lack of spiritual nourishment; but it never occurs to him, that he, Dombey, is in any way to blame for it. When a " divine serving woman," as Homer would have called her, notifies him of the fact, he is merely astonished at her impudence, and moves forward to his own destruction with as much self-confidence as ever. Murdstone and his sister are similarly self-absorbed characters, perfectly satisfied in their own minds because they follow certain fixed laws of conduct, which have become habitual with them.

Mrs. Clenham is another. She lies on her invalid bed, and rules her house with an iron rod. The only enjoyment she finds in life consists in having her will prevail,—in things great and small, but more frequently in small things. The natural affection for her son is replaced by a love of the infinitely little. It was Dickens's prime object to prove that a person might live within the bounds of the law, and also according to the conventional code of society, and yet fail to all intents and purposes of being a virtuous man or woman. " The spirit in which we act is the main thing," says the sage. And in this instance it must be admitted that Dickens performed society an incalculable service. His secondary object was, to show that those who are good at heart will always attain a moderate share of happiness, even under unfavorable circumstances. He, perhaps, considered this his duty as a Christian; but the exceptions to it, if he could have portrayed them with fidelity, would be more interesting than any of the characters that he has actually created.

Dombey, Murdstone, and others like them, are the most genuine of Dickens's creations, because only having one side to their character, and only presenting one side to the public, his method does them no injustice. Next in order come the humorous men who serve as encouragers to the weary spirits of the hero beset with difficulties, and also sometimes to encourage the reader. Traddles, Mark Tapley, Sam Weller, Captain Cuttle, and Cheryble Brothers have all a family likeness, and yet are sufficiently original to give the sense of distinct characters. Traddles, being a gentleman, is brought within the line of comedy only by the stiffness of his hair, which rises up as soon as he takes off his hat. We like him all the better on this account. A true sense of humor is always founded on humanity, and these comic people are the kindest of the kind. If we only see these two sides of them, which are parts of the same quality, it is enough.

It is not in Dickens's favor as an artist, however, that the majority of his characters have a tendency to abstract types. In *Martin Chuzzlewit* this is carried so far that we readily distinguish the qualities for which they are intended. Pecksniff represents hypocrisy; Jonas Chuzzlewit, brutality; Tom Pinch, self-distrust; Mark Tapley, cheerfulness; and Tigg Montague, mercantile knavery. The first three are very well drawn, but the other two are not so good, and are evidently not studied from life. Jonas murders Montague to escape from his clutches; but he is also supposed to have poisoned his father. The delineation of such a monster would be a rare study in human nature. Thackeray says, in the preface to *Pendennis*, that it had been a part of his plan to represent the father of Blanche Amory as a murderer, and have him removed out of Lady Clavering's way by legal process; but as he had never been acquainted with a murderer, he did not feel able to do justice to such an exceptional subject. There is nothing in the description of Jonas Chuzzlewit which might lead us to suppose that he would be capable of such a frightful crime. Brutality alone is not enough to account for it.

A party of us used to spend our summers at a hotel on the sea-shore, kept by a man who afterwards committed murder, and then failed in an attempt at suicide. He is now in the Maine penitentiary for life. This is, of course, a different case from that of Jonas, and yet something may be learned from the consideration of it. The cause which led to the act would seem to have been discouragement from several unsuccessful seasons, which had left the man heavily in debt; but there was no real need of his being discouraged. He was not a brutal person at all, but rather amiable and kindly. We heard him complained of for his laziness, and also for his mendacity,—in short he was the biggest liar in all that region. He sometimes wore a very determined expression, and he was often heard to say that he wished such or such a person was at the bottom of the sea.

In fact, Jonas Chuzzlewit is a decidedly sensational character. The description of a bogus life-insurance company also is not sufficient to give it credibility. There is need of something more than the figure of Tigg Montague installed in a large arm-chair, with a mahogany desk in front of him. It is, however, when young Martin, and Mark Tapley, come to America that we recognize the lack of study and the audacious caricature. Yet Dickens' satire on the public receptions of that time, presidential and otherwise, is rather a keen one; and quite as much so the feeling of familiarity of American travellers with the English gentry. Dickens was often nonplussed during his visit to this country, by finding that his entertainers were well acquainted with a class of English people who had never recognized him as a writer and a man of genius. On the other hand, to represent an Irish priest as a general of American militia, is drawing altogether too long a bow; and there are other statements scarcely more credible.

A book made up of such materials cannot be called

a success, and yet there is always something in Dickens's novels which atones in a measure for his faults. The midnight colloquy between Sarah Gamp and Betsey Prigg is a genuine piece of hearty vigorous humor, not of the most refined sort, it is true, but as refreshing as a glass of beer. This indeed is the general quality of his humor; whereas Thackeray's is more like a Rhine wine,—clear, quietly sparkling, delicate in flavor, and slightly acid. Whoever has acquired a sense of humor does not need to go to the theatre for entertainment, for he sees comedies continually going on about him. If the serving-man blacks boots which are not mated, and the serving-woman spreads the tablecloth on the wrong side, he laughs, and his amusement compensates for the temporary inconvenience. The conventionalities of society are a perpetual entertainment to those who perceive the unwilling manner in which poor human nature is frequently forced through their performance; or how their significance and rational purpose can be misunderstood. A young man playing cards in a railway train is tapped on the shoulder by a clergyman and informed that he is on the road to a very hot place. " Why," said he, " I supposed this train went to Indianapolis." This is the spirit in which three-fourths of the misadventures of life should be accepted. Humor reconciles antipathies, smooths over disagreements, and renders co-operation possible between people of different opinions. The expression, " to humor a man," has much in it for philosophers to reflect on. Fortunate is the family in which humor flows from he deep strata like a fountain which neither dries in summer nor congeals in winter.   A good joke often compensates for a bad dinner.

Pickwick Papers is altogether a work of humor. It has no particular plot, but consists of a series of adventures like Don Quixote's.   Pickwick himself is a quixotic person; a brave man who has no chance to prove his courage; a learned man who has no use for his knowledge; a warm-hearted man who misapplies his kindness; and a modest man, who is self-important through the veneration of his inferiors. It was Dickens's first work, and in many respects his best.   It is written in purer English than many of his novels, and besides this, it represents a fund of humor which had been accumulating for several years before he began to write.   You may open the book anywhere, and find refreshment for the weary spirit.   The notable adventure of Mr. Winkle with his horse might have been more amusing than it is, but it brings into prominence a fact well known to grooms and stable-keepers, but little thought of by others, that the horse, though among the most intelligent of animals, is also one of the most peculiar. The humor of the scene is quite as much due to this as to the inexperience of Mr. Winkle and Mr. Pickwick.   Dickens was fond of reading the court scene in the Bardell breach of promise case, and he did it most effectively.   Carlyle, who could see no wit in Sydney Smith's jokes, roared with laughter at Dickens's reading of *Pickwick*, and his imitation of the great Sergeant Buzfuz.   The name, however, is a caricature in itself, and how far such severe satire on legal procedure is justified would be an excellent subject for a debating society. Quite as much of a caricature is his description of an English parliamentary election.

One satisfaction which we enjoy in *Pickwick Papers* is, that we find no crazy people in it. The amount of eccentricity in the different characters, would, perhaps, be more than equal to one insane person; but the eccentricity is not so strongly marked in any one of them as to produce an unpleasant effect. This element, in the way Dickens uses it, borders on the sensational, and though it may be said that the interests of humanity demand that we should recognize these unfortunate persons who are sufficiently numerous in real life, and not try to hide from ourselves the fact of their existence, even this extreme view does not justify him in using one of them as the mainspring of a story, and setting Barnaby Rudge on a pedestal, like the statue of a great man, for all people to gaze at. Ruskin wrote a spirited and amusing attack on Barnaby, in which his own peculiarities were interwoven with those of his subject in a most curious manner. We do not object to the amiable Mr. Dick flying his kites, nor to Mr. F.'s aunt in *Little Dorrit*, with her crust of bread; but in the whole series there is too much of it. There is a lack of balance in Dickens's writing which gives even characters like Murdstone and Dombey a kind of stability. Strong, healthy natures like Dandie Dinmont and Henry Esmond he knew not of.

Women remember their childhood much better than men. The struggle that comes with early manhood to some, and the pleasures that come to others, obliterate the past life of a man as if it had never been. Stranded in some lonely shoal in after-life, he may be able to recollect something of it, but the larger portion is gone forever. Women, on the contrary, always preserve their relation with childhood, through their interest in children; and thus it happens that Louisa Alcott's representation of girls is more true to life than Dickens's representation of boys. Thackeray has little to say in regard to this side of human nature, but the spoiled Clavering boy in *Pendennis* could not be improved on; Dickens says a great deal, and sometimes he hits the mark, and at others he misses it. We can be grateful for the attempt that he has made, and hope that others may come hereafter to improve on it. A physician, writing in one of our magazines, has stated that Pendennis is the best account of an invalid which he knows of in fiction, and that Little Nell in the *Old Curiosity Shop* is the worst. This should not be accepted, however, as a conclusive judgment. Why should we conclude at all. Every one has peculiar likes and dislikes: let us leave our minds open continually for reconsideration.

I have been told that the same books which Carlyle made use of in studying the Revolution of 1789 served Dickens for his *Tale of Two Cities*. Dickens, wishing to write a novel on that subject, consulted Carlyle, who gave him ready assistance. The book is more remarkable for its grand prophetic background than for the direct course of the narrative. The first scene in which the cask of wine is broken in the street, and the poor, thirsty *third estate* endeavors to sop up the purple streams, and get what taste he can, is an impressive prediction of the streams of blood which were soon to flow at the bidding of an outraged people. The colloquy with the prisoner in the Bastille reappears throughout the story, like a solemnly vibrating chord in a musical composition. " ' How long have you been here ? ' —' I cannot recollect.' ' Do you wish to come out ? ' —' I do not know.' "

Dickens's politics were essentially those of the English lower-middle class, and seem to us rather peculiar, if not contradictory. He believed in Parliament and the British monarchy, but was inimical to the aristocracy. He never speaks of the nobility except in terms of ridicule. Yet he was not in the least a republican. He held our American government in very slight esteem. He went into the halls of Congress, during the debates on the repeal of the Missouri Compromise, and it seemed to him like the uproar of a school of noisy boys while the teacher is absent. As he knew nothing of our affairs, like most of his countrymen, he could not understand that one of the toughest problems of history was there under discussion; and he supposed that all the excitement was caused by the clashing of local and personal interests. A person in Dickens's position was not so much to blame for this opinion, as the peers and statesmen of the British realm might be. It was Gladstone himself, unless the reporter did

him injustice, who spoke of De Tocqueville as having written a *History of the United States;* and this
was after Von Holst's great work had been made
public to the world. It might be a good plan for
some American Arnold to visit England, and deliver a course of lectures there on universal history
and international politics.

Dickens resembles Victor Hugo more closely than
he does the novelists of his own country. He is
not grandiloquent like Hugo, and though he uses
some rhetorical devices, his diction is plain and unpretending. Otherwise their differences are chiefly
those of nationality. The morality of Dickens is
English, and Victor Hugo would probably have
criticised it as severely as he would have criticised
Victor Hugo's. They both belong to the emotional,
philanthropic class of writers, which began with
Rousseau and contains some of the most illustrious
names in the eighteenth and nineteenth centuries.
It has been represented in America by Jefferson, L.
Maria Child, Wendell Phillips, and Harriet Beecher
Stowe. However much worldlings and cynics may
scoff at these humanitarians, or more impartial critics
may complain that they sacrifice art to practical ex-
pedients, it must be admitted that they have exercised great influence, in their day and generation,
and that the most important reforms have been accomplished by their instrumentality. They have no
successors at the present time, and the tide appears
to be setting strongly in another direction.

MARIAN EVANS

THE author of the *Hans Breitman Ballads* once went to dinner, at a party, with a lady to whom he had just been introduced without catching her name (as is usual in such cases), and his first remark was, " Why is it that no woman can write a good novel ? " Soon afterward he discovered that his companion was herself a novelist of good repute, and he spent the rest of the dinner-time in making amends for this rash statement.

When the Indians gather around their camp-fires in winter, the old chiefs entertain the younger members of the community not only with tales of hunting and adventures by flood and field, but with genuine historical traditions of wars, alliances, and treaties between different tribes, which bear some resemblance to those of civilization. It is the special duty of the Indian women to remember as much as possible of these accounts, and repeat them again to the children ; and thus unwritten traditions are handed down for a century or more.

It is thus that mothers and elder sisters naturally become story-tellers, both in barbarous and civilized countries. It is an essential and important part of the home culture, and has a marked influence in the formation of family character. Does not that portion of patriotism which may be called national pride originate in this manner? But an intelligent and educated mother will not only tell her boy of Washington crossing the Delaware, and the death of Lincoln, but also of the battle of Marathon, the death of Cæsar, and of Rome pillaged by the Vandals, and thus inspire him with a desire for a liberal education, much more fruitful than the spirit of emulation which is instilled into him at school. Old family chronicles also become part of a narrative store, and if she has any inventive talent, she develops these so as to give them something of the fashion of a novelette.

So it was formerly, and, to some extent, is still in those quiet places where domestic privacy yet lingers. Women properly look at life in a conversational, rather than a logical manner. Many are called and few are chosen: there is a great deal of poor fiction written by women, and some also that ranks among the best. No account of French literature would be complete without the name of Madame de Staël; and though the descendant of Augustus of Saxony, who published under the name of George Sand, does not equal her as an artist, she has nevertheless an earnestness of thought and a tenderness of feeling which give her a kind of superiority over the more gifted daughter of M. Necker. In America as a humanitarian writer, Mrs. Stowe surpassed all others of her time, and Louisa Alcott introduced such wisdom in her stories for young people that philosophers went to them for instruction. The English Charlotte Brontë has given to the world in *Jane Eyre* an example of womanly devotion such as the world had become quite sceptical of, though we may trust Shakespeare for its possibility; and Miss Sheppard has shown in *Charles Auchester* what a profound influence fine music can have on the lives of men and women. Miss Austen, also, is a perfect artist within her own limited field.

None of these writers, however, can take rank with geniuses like Scott, Hawthorne, and Thackeray. Only two great names are known to feminine literature,—Sappho, and the writer who is generally known as George Eliot. The fragments of Sappho's poetry which remain to us fully explain the high estimate in which she was held by her contemporaries; and in depth of feeling and a thorough knowledge of human nature, Miss Evans closely approaches the great dramatic poets.

Mary Ann Evans was born at Arbury Farm in Warwickshire, on the twenty-second of November, 1819. The manager of a large farming estate in England is commonly a more responsible person than our American farmers require to be, and though the Evans family lived in a quiet and unpretending style, Mary, who was an attractive girl and indicated her superiority as soon as she began to walk, had the advantage of cultivated society, and as substantial an education as any young woman in England. The groundwork was good, and she ultimately attained a scholarship fully equal to Scott's, and better than Thackeray's. During middle life she was accustomed to read books in French, German, Italian, and Spanish, while she was as well acquainted with Latin and Greek as most of our college graduates. Then, such authors as she read; long-neglected men of genius, writers on ethics, metaphysics, politics, and sociology! Among a list of books which she gives as having spent a London winter with, there are few that any one reader of her biography would be likely to know, or even to have heard of. Their influence does not appear directly in her work, as it did evidently on Scott's prose writing, but this strongly intellectual tendency was an important factor in determining the quality of it.

She waited long to know herself and learn her own resources; writing continually letters to her friends and acquiring in that manner facility in the use of language. Her first public attempt was a review of Froude's *Nemesis of Faith*, a book now beyond the reach of purchasers, and one that ought to be republished. The influence of Francis Newman is directly traceable in it, and its influence is also traceable in *Adam Bede, Felix Holt*, and *Middlemarch*. This was in 1849, and two years later, she obtained the appointment of assistant editor to the *Westminster Review*, and for the first time found her proper element in the invigorating life of London's literary society.

Shortly after this, we find in one of her letters a reference to George H Lewes, as if he were a person constantly at her side. Lewes is not better known as the husband of George Eliot than for his biography of Goethe, concerning which Margaret Fuller had predicted some years before, that he was as unfit to write it as a coarse nature and self-conceit could make him. What attraction he had for Marian Evans has always been a mystery to her most intellectual admirers. His writings have a certain kind of brightness, like the reflection of the sun on a field of ice,—not a pleasant sort of brilliancy at all. Miss Evans recognized his peculiarities, as appears from a letter dated 16th April, 1853, in which she says: " Mr. Lewes, especially, is kind and attentive, and has quite won my regard, after having had a good deal of my vituperation. Like a few other people in the world, he is much better than he seems. A man of heart and conscience, wearing a mask of flippancy."

Lewes married early in life, and made an unfortunate selection. I have been informed that his wife deserted him; that he condoned her offence, and then she deserted him again; after which, the law could not help him. At the time of Miss Evans's marriage to Mr. Cross, a certain wise lady gave as her explanation of this, that " love was necessary to George Eliot, and I do not believe she could live without it." She had become much attached to a gentleman while staying at Geneva, who must have been interested in her, but did not realize her value. What a treasure for any man to possess, this large-hearted, sympathetic, high-minded woman ! How we all throw away our chances in life. We entertain angels and we know them not. This much at least may be said of Lewes, that he appreciated Miss

Evans better than those who had previously known her. She dedicated the manuscript of several of her books to him in a most affectionate manner, and credited him with being the chief inspiration of them.

We may suppose that he said to her something like this: " It is because I was too generous, too forgiving, and too much of a Christian with regard to my unfaithful wife, that I am not able to marry you; and now, what are we to do about it ?"; and that she replied, " I am not afraid to do anything that is honorable for the sake of the man I love." Though London society shut its cast-iron gates on her, her intimate friends all gave her cordial support, especially Mrs. Peter Taylor, one of the noblest women of that time,—and I have never yet met the person who blamed her for the course she pursued. Her own friends, and those of her husband, were society enough for her: for the babblement of tongues, and the uniforms of silk and broadcloth, which are supposed to constitute society, she never had much relish. She often went into company on the continent, and in Germany was always treated with great respect.

She was known henceforth, among her friends, as Mrs. Lewes, but to the public only as George Eliot. The publication of her novels as the works of Mrs. Cross seems like a mistake. There are no such names as Cross, Bragg, and Higgins among good writers: nature takes care of that. She was christened Mary Ann, but she claimed the privilege of changing it to Marian; and I think Marian Evans is the best name for us to remember her by.

Adam Bede was her first serious undertaking. Both she and her husband were in doubt as to the success of the enterprise, but the result astonished them and the rest of the world. It was written at between thirty-three and thirty-five, in the full strength of her maturity, and the added glow of the newly married life. Next to *Middlemarch*, it is the most powerful of her stories, and the narrative English of it is more direct, vigorous, and clear-cut than in her last two novels. The plot is substantially the same as that of *The Heart of Midlothian;* and if Scott has succeeded in giving more picturesque character to his version of the story and has enlivened it with more varied and interesting details, Miss Evans has treated the subject with deeper feeling and given to it an earnestness which goes right to the heart of every reader. Her treatment is more realistic and perhaps nearer to the truth. The ground which Scott passes over lightly, in order to avoid giving offence, is sacred ground to Miss Evans, and she dwells on it at greater length, from the very delicacy of her womanly nature. Otherwise, Dinah corresponds to Jeannie; her cousin Hettie to Effie Deans; Arthur Donnithorne to Staunton, the seducer; and Adam Bede—who is said to have been taken from Miss Evans's father, and a grand piece of realism—to the clergyman Butler who marries Jeannie Deans.

The plot is more simple than that of *Waverley*, and the action moves with the slowness and with something of the irresistible force of Greek tragedy.

Infanticide has been more common in Great Britain than in other European countries, and this has been owing to the severity of public opinion toward the mothers of illegitimate children. Whether the moral tone of society has been elevated in this way, and whether these unfortunate women ought to be looked on as sacrifices for the public good, is a debatable question. Macaulay blamed his countrymen for it, and declared boldly that the remedy was more intolerable than the disease. Thackeray, also, more than once ventured the opinion that the Engish of the eighteenth century were better than they professed, and the English of the present century seemed to be better than they were. Recent revelations certainly tend to support this view, and cases of infanticide have greatly diminished since the establishment of foundling hospitals. "The path of love is all too smooth for mortal feet to tread."

How far Marian Evans realized this, does not appear in the text. She was too good an artist to reveal herself. She did not belong to the humanitarian school; or if she sympathized with Dickens's effort for the alleviation of human misery, she nevertheless considered that more could be accomplished indirectly by high art than by rhetorical appeals. She believed that humanity would be better served by adhering to the truth, than by distorting truth in the interest of humanity. When, however, Dickens wrote to her a complimentary letter in return for a copy of *Adam Bede*,—and a highly creditable letter it was,—she replied that there was no one whose good opinion of her book could be so valuable to her. Although we may judge from this that she preferred Dickens to Thackeray, she was in no sense an imitator of his method, but kept on her own way, as independent as she was original. She is not romantic, as Scott and Dickens were romantic; that is, by carrying the hero and heroines through a series of trials to ultimate prosperity. She chose a higher method, and the goal which her finest characters arrive at is that of self-renunciation, the only reward of which is the consciousness of right. This is the keynote of *Romola, Felix Holt, Middlemarch,* and *Daniel Deronda,* and its presence may be detected as an undercurrent in all the others. It is the romance of the inner life. He who loves God, says Spinoza, must not expect to be loved in return.

Most of the conversation in *Adam Bede* is given in the English peasant dialect, which is not so interesting as Scott's native vernacular, and would be tiresome if it were not for the pith and sense which the writer has infused into it. In Miss Evans's hands, even the ordinary table-talk of workingmen, during their hour of lunch and recreation, is made to have a significance, and helps out the action of a story. She must have kept her eyes and ears well open, while living on her father's farm. She can hardly be called a humorist, though there is much wit and humor in the conversation which she has reported for us. No author who represents human nature correctly can well escape this side of it, but the humor seems to be rather in her subject than herself. She was not the first to discover a comical side to the exhortations of the Methodists and what are called religious revivals. " Oh, that blessed word Mesopotamia!" cried an excited and wild-

looking woman on the verge of an impromptu taber-
nacle.   Human nature when it goes to extremes, is
always in danger of appearing ridiculous; but the
true humorist does not seek his material so much
in the extravagances as in the follies and solecisms
of mankind.   Thackeray's account of an English
election in *The Newcomes* is witty beyond measure,
but the wit comes from Thackeray himself and depends on the point of view from which he regards it.
We are not only amused at his keen insight in penetrating the artifices, by which others are cajoled, but
we admire him for his admirable indulgence toward
all concerned.   Miss Evans has also given in *Middlemarch* a most entertaining picture of an election, but
its value consists in the truthfulness of the representation.   If she invented the scene, so much the
better.   Its humor, however, is not subjective, but
objective, and must have been based on reality in
the first place.   The author describes the methods
used as if she were in opposition to them, not as if
she had condoned the wrong, and accepted it as
part of the universe,—and of herself.   It is the
charm of Cervantes, Thackeray, and Jean Paul, that
they never seem to forget their personal share in the
weaknesses of mankind.

We feel that there is rather an effort to be witty
in *Adam Bede* and *Silas Marner*, and this is the only
sign of immaturity we find in them.   When Nancy
says to Priscilla, in the latter story, " If sisters ought
not to dress alike, I don't know who should," we
very naturally smile; but when, in the former, one
man speaks in a loud voice to another who is stone-

deaf and cannot hear a word, because he considers such a tone appropriate to the occasion, a question arises in our minds whether this would be the case. Such infelicities are usually the result of habit. Errors in *Adam Bede*, however, are the exception: artistic skill and truthfulness to nature are the rule. Mrs. Poyser, as a thrifty, practical housewife, who knows the small world about her as thoroughly as strong men of affairs understand the great world; who has the good points and the weak points of her neighbors laid away in her head like entries in a ledger, ought to last as a typical character. The manner in which simple Hetty Sorrel contrives to elude her vigilance, and to conceal her affection for young Donnithorne, is equally well contrived. Of Adam himself she says:

"A nature like Adam's with a great deal of love and reverence in it, depends for so much of its happiness on what it can believe and feel about others. And he had no ideal world of dead heroes ; he knew little of the life of men in the past ; he must find the beings to whom he could cling with loving admiration among those who came within speech of him."

This is a truth that lies at the foundation of society, and is its best safeguard against the numerical superiority of barbarism. Poor Hetty's grief, remorse, terror, and despair are depicted with an affectionate fidelity; such as Scott could not have known, or dared not to attempt.

Silas Marner and *The Mill on the Floss* contain similar episodes of common English country life, and are full of interesting scenery. Miss Evans always deals with her subject in a vigorous manner. Her designs have breadth, and the handling is masterly. Like Matthew Arnold, she always goes to the heart of her subject, and develops it from within. She is a great social leader, and draws thousands of willing followers in her train. Her sympathies are world-wide; not limited to any race or people, or, as in the case of Dickens, to a particular class. Having done full justice to English farmer life, she seeks abroad for new fields of conquest. She finds a fresh and elevating subject in the Italian novel called *Romola*, and a poem called *The Spanish Gypsy*. Then she returns to England to deal with the country gentleman in *Middlemarch*, and with the more intellectual life of London in *Daniel Deronda*. Such was her literary career.

The *Mill on the Floss* has been considered her most perfect book as a work of art,—a faultless study of the English tongue. It was selected as a text-book on English for the examination of students entering Harvard College. Perfection, however, is rather a dry attribute. When I hear of a perfect book or a perfect picture, it always leads me to think of a man of perfect behavior and a small soul. Perfection on a grand scale would seem to be unattainable. It is like the phenomena of history whose incompleteness opens the way to new phenomena. An ode of Horace may be more perfect than *Hamlet* or *King Lear;* but is it as great? Echo answers, " is it?" The *Mill on the Floss* is rather pleasanter reading than *Adam Bede*, but it is not so powerful a work.

Still, this artistic quality has a value, and indicates a certain progress in the writer, a better appreciation of form.

The kernel of the story is the same as that in Goethe's *Elective Affinities*, but the treatment of it is not as bold. Maggie Tulliver, an ardent, impetuous, and heroic nature, is one of the best drawn characters in fiction. She is exactly the opposite of Goethe's Ottilie, whose quiet, steadfast affection is equalled by such purity of nature, that all temptation flies away from her. Maggie also resists temptation at the last moment through the clearness of her intellectual perceptions. The account of her escapade in the Dutch schooner is a marvellous piece of psychological analysis. Both stories end tragically, as cases of strong magnetic attraction are likely to do. The end of the *Mill on the Floss* is, however, melodramatic, and highly improbable. Tom Tulliver might easily have escaped the floating mass of timber by rowing directly away from it. Such impracticalities are not easily avoided by feminine writers; but it is more difficult to decide how the story ought to have ended. Similar cases in real life are not always fatal. There has been an instance in the most fastidious New England society, where a married lady met a gentleman one evening for whom she experienced such an irresistible attraction that she concluded next day to desert her husband for him. This brought her, of course, into social ostracism for some years; but society finally decided to condone the offence; as did also her previous husband, who afterwards married another wife. After the temporary confusion, all parties concerned would seem to have been happier for this readjustment. It would require rare courage in an English novelist to adopt such an incident, but we should not narrow ourselves by being too moral.

To represent a man—in the *Mill on the Floss*—as saying that he married his wife, because she was dull-witted, and would not be likely to tyrannize over him at his own fireside, is truly an amusing sarcasm against the male sex. Intellectual women have been heard to make similar statements before now; but they do not consider that men of genius have quite as much difficulty in obtaining wives. What a wife Marian Evans would have made for Carlyle; and yet it is by no means certain that she would have accepted him.

Romola marked a new departure, and is a work of a higher order. The author explains in her letters in what way she prepared herself for it. She went with Mr. Lewes to Florence, and there worked day after day in the Laurentian Library, looking through books of the fifteenth century to obtain ideas of old Florentine life. When the library was closed, she walked about the city to obtain a clear notion of its topography; then rushed back to England with a full mind to begin her work. During her visit she had obtained foreign standing ground, from which to view her own country; and this was of great advantage to her, when she came again to deal with English life.

Romola has a romantic background, and the most poetic that could have been selected. Florence, the City of Flowers, and itself the flower of mediæval civilization, has a twofold background: the purple Apennines, with their olive-clad slopes and turreted foothills, as well as its own poetico-tragic history, full of all that is beautiful and inspiring. This is an ever-present idea to us in reading the book, although it is nowhere mentioned, and it is due to Miss Evans's fine taste and elevated tone that we can feel it.

I think it can be considered the most successful of historical novels. Macchiavelli, Savonarola, and others are brought back to us, not in outline drawing, like Scott's crusaders, but as veritable personages, and Florence is peopled with men and women better suited to its art and architecture than its present inhabitants are. We hear their voices; we see the morning company at the barber's shop; and are present at the discussions in the market-place. Then we are taken to the retired dwelling of the blind old scholar Bardo de' Bardi, and see him in the midst of his books and manuscripts, which his beautiful daughter is reading to him. He does not know that the Parthenon was still in existence at Athens, until Tito, the nimble young Greek, informs him of it.

I have been told that there is no such name as Romola in Italian; and that there are those who think that the character is not a real one, because no woman could be so unselfish as to take the natural children of her husband into her own home. This of course no woman would do while her husband was alive, unless she were wholly devoid of self-respect; but there is a famous precedent in history, which proves that it may be possible after his death. Octavia, the sister of Augustus, cared for the children of Antony and Cleopatra as if they were her own; and Plutarch says, that the noble behavior of Octavia, previous to Antony's death, greatly exasperated the people of Rome against him. It is more than possible that Octavia was the type which Miss Evans had in her mind, and that she chose the name of Romola as most appropriate to her. On the Via dei Quattro Fontane in Rome, there was formerly a sign, '' Baldassare, Antiquary,'' and this Miss Evans must have noticed on her previous visit to Rome, and made use of as the name of the antiquary who was victimized by Tito Melema. The latter is one of the most clear-cut characters in fiction, and is supposed to have been a study from the same adventurer who plays the villain in Winthrop's romance of *Cecil Dreme:* a man of amiable disposition, frank, healthful, and virtuous so long as it serves his purpose to be so, but not only unprincipled, but without perception of the nature of a principle. He is one of the hungry little Greeks mentioned by Horace, of whom a second edition was distributed over Europe after the capture of Constantinople by the Turks. They were equally useful and untrustworthy.

In addition to its poetic background, *Romola* has the advantage of a more lively and interesting action than an English novel of the present day possibly could have. I mean, of course, a novel taken from English life. It is like the difference between the costumes of the Middle Ages, and our modern puritanic dress, which condemns men, at least, to the gravest colors, and to the greatest possible concealment of their figures. There can be no objection to the introduction of an historical person in fiction, when treated with the natural skill of Miss Evans's Savonarola. No one has better understood the peculiar strength and the essential weakness of this Italian prophet; and the argument between him and Romola, in which the latter warns him against the course he intends to pursue, is the most brilliant passage in the book. His career was as characteristic of Italy as Luther's was of Germany, and the failure of the one is as significant as the success of the other. The attempt to repress human nature in the way Savonarola wished to do, was like trying to dam the Mississippi.

The close of the book is rather melodramatic; and the writer would seem to have lost her interest in the work after the death of Savonarola, and only to have recovered it after the death of Tito. Romola's floating down the Arno in a boat without oars, in careless desperation, is a decided fault in the plot, and not in accordance with her self-reliant character. The manner in which Tito came by his fate, and the struggle on the bridge, is well contrived, but that Baldassare should have dealt him the final blow, and then died in the effort, is too much like a tale of King Arthur's Court. At the very close the writer recovers her spirits, and the last scene between Romola and Lillo is beautiful.

Next to *Romola* the most picturesque of Miss

Evans's novels is *Felix Holt;* but it is a terrible satire on the landed gentry. She describes in it two respectable old families: that of Sir Maximus De Barry, whom she describes as belonging to the long-tailed saurian species; and the Durfey Transomes, who were in a condition of decrepitude, and only saved from extinction by the smart illegitimate son of a local lawyer. The true heir of the Transome family is an under-witted fellow, killed in a sort of riot at a parliamentary election. After this catastrophe, an heiress appears, who has been for some time hidden in the lower-middle class, but she heroically resigns her right to the property. The opening pages of scenic description are scarcely excelled in English, and seem like an effort of nature to conceal the shame of the Transome family. Otherwise the book is remarkable for a speech by the rector of Little Treby, who says, " There are two kinds of radicals,—those who never can see an object nearer than the moon, and those like my nephew here, who only see things at shooting distance." To see things at shooting distance shows the practical man.

Felix Holt was not well liked by English society, and either to atone for that, or because her powers had reached their full completeness, Miss Evans next wrote *Middlemarch*, and astonished even her warmest admirers. It has been said of the opera *Don Giovanni*, that the first note of it lifts the audience off their feet, and keeps them suspended until the curtain falls. The first sentence in *Middlemarch*, " Dorothea Brooke had that sort of beauty which is thrown into relief by poor dress,'' is a key-note which interests the reader as fine music might, and this interest is sustained throughout the book. Dorothea is the sister of Romola, but more human, more impassioned, and more like a real presence. Romola has an ideal personality and we may picture her to ourselves with the classic features and ruddy complexion of the Sistine Madonna. We imagine Dorothea of the dark Saxon type, without much color in her face but with eyes deep, lustrous, and eloquent, a voice musical and penetrating. If not herself an ideal, she is full of ideality, and at first is led astray by this, blundering badly in the most important step of a woman's life,—choosing a hus-band. She escapes the substantial but commonplace country gentleman, and falls into the snare of a desiccated pedant, whose heart is like a scroll of parchment. He is, however, an illusion to himself, as he was to her, and being disillusioned with her help,—he dies. Thus Dorothea escapes a second time, and finds her affinity at last in the generous Ladislaw, to whom she can only be united by the renunciation of her worldly goods.

Another sterling woman in this book is the sensi-ble, kind-hearted Mary Garth; who also renounces social position and worldly goods for the sake of a long-cherished schoolmate, Fred Vincy. It is a rare novel that contains two such splendid women. Rosa-mond Vincy is a brilliant contrast to both; the ex-quisitely finished beauty, with eyes of heavenly blue but with a heart of ice, who captures Dr. Lydgate and makes his life a burden to him until death relieves him from her merciless tyranny. She is the most highly individualized of all Miss Evans's creations, and enough to frighten any young man who is contemplating matrimony. Lydgate has not quite the veracity of Ladislaw, and is lacking in foresight; but his courtship of Rosamond begins with a harmless flirtation; and it may be remarked here that this is the only way in which a cold, selfish woman is likely to succeed in coming to intimate terms with a man. Beware therefore of coquetry and the voices of sirens.

The influence of Mr. Lewes's metaphysical conversation is plainly apparent in the narrative of *Middlemarch*, and still more so in the subsequent novel of *Daniel Deronda*. Miss Evans no longer writes such plain, straightforward English as in *Adam Bede*, or only writes it in detached passages. Her style has become circuitous, and her ideas are often of the hair-splitting variety: but when she makes her characters speak, she is wonderful. I do not know any book in which you hear the human voice more distinctly than in *Middlemarch;* and the variety is also remarkable. There are minor faults of plot in it ; especially where Dorothea enters Lydgate's house to find Rosamond toying with Ladislaw,—a mechanical contrivance to expedite the course of the story, and rather awkwardly introduced,—but these do not vititate the whole any more than similar errors could spoil the *Vicar of Wakefield.*

Daniel Deronda is not the peer of *Middlemarch,*

and yet it proves a certain progress in the mind of this woman who never rested on her laurels, but continued to advance so long as she lived. In *Middlemarch* we have fairly good provincial society, but in *Daniel Deronda* we are introduced to the more vigorous London life, in which the forcible collision between human beings is softened or deadened by a higher style of manners. We meet also, in the book, with a new element which points towards the future, —the evolution or moral development of character, and this is elaborated, so that we perceive the change taking place, as we see the growth of the wings in an apple moth. Again, there is a kind of splendor in the opening chapter, the splendor of highly stimulated life—the gambling-room at Baden; and there are glimpses of this here and there throughout the book. Otherwise the tissue of the novel is too analytical, and some of the speeches are so ingenious that we wonder if anyone except Miss Evans could possibly have uttered them. The action of the story does not always flow naturally, but in places seems too much forced. I have heard ladies criticise Deronda himself as being too much of a prig.

Gwendolen Harleth's conversion is the strong point of the book, but Gwendolen herself is hardly worth the trouble that she causes. She is a fine animal, but mentally and morally of ordinary calibre, and is not the material out of which a superior woman can be made. She is precisely the sort of young woman that is popularly called " superior," and this is the best possible proof that she is not so intrinsically. Her appeal to Deronda, as to one who is better than herself, is in her favor; but we fear that the dark, Semitic glance of Deronda's eye had much to do with it. She does not affiliate with Miss Arrowpoint, who is a superior woman in the true sense, and proves the fact before us in a magnificent way. She becomes a victim of the despotic Grandcourt as naturally as Lydgate became the victim of Rosamond Vincy. Grandcourt is superbly drawn: a petty Asiatic tyrant, accidentally born in England. He knows how to command, and to gain his ends, but within he is like the desert of Gobi. He would have made a good captain of cavalry, but is a burden on society. To permit such a man to be drowned is a kindness.

Is it a fault in this story, that we have glimpses in it of two characters, who are far more interesting than the leading figures? Is it not rather like real life? Do not magnificent men and glorious women appear before us like meteors, and then vanish leaving an ineffaceable impression? They were magnificent, because we saw them at their best, and knew only this of them. Looking out from a railway-train on the Lake of Geneva, I formerly beheld the castle of Chillon sharply defined in grand masses of light and shadow against the moonlit water. Twenty years have not dimmed that impression, nor could I wish to have it renewed.

Daniel Deronda is worth reading for the engagement scene between Klesmer and Miss Arrowpoint alone; for there is nothing like it anywhere else. It is curious that of the two finest male characters in this whole series of novels, one is a half-Pole, and the other a Slavonic Jew. Klesmer's portrait may have been taken from the pianist Rubinstein. Whenever we meet with him he gives a delightful sensation of strength,—of power applied in the best manner. Such characters are above the reach of the novelist, as they are above pleasure and pain. When Klesmer enters Mrs. Meyrick's little house, the room seems diminished to a nutshell before his gaze. Vast audiences are seen to be in the aspect of his face. He can not only play the piano, but talk as well; and the parliamentary hack, Mr. Bult, is confounded by his graphic sentences.

Only Miss Arrowpoint is a match for this man. She recognizes him at his true value, and seizes the critical moment, though it comes to her unexpectedly. She gives him her word, and the remonstrances of her parents cannot shake her, for she sees at once that their shots are wide of the mark. She leaves her father's house, and goes off to marry Klesmer, as calmly and quietly as if it were a call on her nearest friend. Such women are as rare as the great poets. The chapter called '' Maiden's Choosing '' is immortal.

That portion of *Daniel Deronda* which treats of the Jews is by no means so successful. Miss Evans had exceptional facilities for studying this remarkable people. Her husband was a Jew, at least by descent, and associated with Jews as well as Christians. The life-like description of the meeting of a Jewish club, and the discussion among its members, may have been taken from her husband's lips; but we had a right to expect something more concerning the only Semitic race which has kept itself abreast of civilization, and whose spirit has never been broken on the wheel of time. The result is nothing. Her delineation of the Jewish boy in a pawnbroker's shop is a bright and amusing picture; but what shall we say of the elderly brother of Deronda's pretty foundling,—the invalid with a complexion like old ivory? He has a veracious nature, but not the brain of a statesman. We close the book with some regret at the fool's errand on which he has despatched Deronda, and with a feeling of wonder as to how Deronda will finally escape from his delusion. There could not be a more impracticable notion than that of the Jews returning to Jerusalem. Even if they could be independent of the Turkish government, what employment, what industries could they find there? It is doubtful if Judea and the adjacent districts could support more than two hundred thousand of them. Indeed, the whole race ought to be grateful to Titus for having dispersed them through the western empire; for it was thus they escaped the Saracen conquest, and obtained a foothold among Christian nations.

When we read Hawthorne, we wonder why he was not the first poet of his time. It also seems natural for Scott to break forth sometimes into verse. Nor would Dickens have surprised the world by writing very good poetry. Miss Evans, however, is essentially a prose writer. It is a high order of prose, but not poetic. Even the boat scene in the *Mill on the Floss* could hardly be transformed into poetry. It is not surprising, therefore, that her attempt to tell a long story in verse should not have been considered a success. The *Spanish Gypsy* is quite as interesting as Tennyson's *Princess*, but in a different way. It would be more readable if it were not on rhythmical stilts. Marian Evans seems to have had but few intimate friends, and to have been contented with those she had. Where she obtained her extensive knowledge of human nature is a mystery; but there is a mystery of one kind or another connected with all great artists. At the same time, in spite of her genius, she does not belong with the highest class of minds. This becomes apparent in her letters in general. She goes to Rome, but she does not claim fellowship with Raphael and Michel Angelo. She admires the genius of Géorgione and Titian's *Annunciation* (which the best critics consider to have been coldly painted) and she passes by Tintoretto's *Divine Tragedy* without consideration. She stands before Michel Angelo's *Moses*, and thinks the expression must be an effort for effect. She should have read the book of Exodus before she went to the Church of " St. Peter in Prison." She finds nothing in Michel Angelo's own portrait but a very sad expression. She does not even appreciate Fielding. It is easy to perceive this from the way in which she speaks of him. His admirable essays, with which he begins the successive books of *Tom Jones,* " belong to a period when people had infinite leisure." It would be better for the present generation, perhaps, if they read more essays and fewer novels. One page of *Tom Jones* contains more than three average pages of *Adam Bede.* We miss in her writing such tributes as Goethe pays to Shakespeare, and Thackeray to Carlyle.

She insists on calling Titus a Roman brute, on account of his treatment of Berenice. Now Berenice was rather a questionable character—if her name be found among the constellations; and Suetonius speaks of Titus as we in America do of President Lincoln. He counted a day lost in which he had failed to relieve some person from distress. More true but undiscriminating was her reply to Mrs. Beecher Stowe, who wrote her a defence or apology for the magnetic table-tipping and trance-medium writing, which passes by the name of spiritualism. She wrote:

"Your view as to the cause of that great wave of spiritualism which is rushing over America—namely, that it is a sort of Rachel-cry of bereavement toward the invisible existence of the loved ones, is deeply affecting. But so far as "spiritualism" (by which I mean, of course, spirit-communication, by rapping, guidance of the pencil, etc.) has come within reach of my judgment on our side of the water, it has appeared to me either as degrading folly, imbecile in the estimate of evidence, or else as impudent imposture. So far as my observation and experience have hitherto gone, it has even seemed to me an impiety to withdraw from the more assured methods of studying the open secrets of the universe any large amount of attention to alleged manifestations which are so defiled by low adventurers, and their palpable trickeries, so hopelessly involved in all the doubtfulness of individual testimonies as to phenomena witnessed, which testimonies are no more true objectively because they are honest subjectively, than the Ptolemaic system is true because it seemed to Tycho Brahe a better explanation of the heavenly movements than the Copernican."

This is too much in the style of G. H. Lewes; but, if you would think of Marian Evans at her best, remember the scene in which Maggie Tulliver meets her mother after her escapade in the boat, " more helpful than all wisdom, is one draught of simple human pity that will not forsake us." Go out under the stars in a winter night and think of that.

17

RUSKIN

THE outward aspect of London, as an American who enters the city by the North-Western Railway first beholds it, is not an attractive one. As he leaves the station he sees before him two hotels of similar figure, in what was formerly called the Grecian style of architecture, covered with dusky brown stucco, with no ornament except a meagre conventional moulding and the iron railing in front of them; gloomy and uninviting. Between them, as the substitute for an arch, are two upright posts, and a horizontal beam with '' Euston ''on it, in bold gilt letters. If he proceeds farther, he comes to a plain stone church with a steeple divided into three nearly equal sections, the first supported by Doric columns, the second by Ionic, and the third by Corinthian. Beyond this there is no evidence of artistic skill or intellectual effort in the construction of the building.

In front of the church there is an open space or square, which formerly, at least, was inclosed by a cheap iron railing, and within is a statue of Stephenson, the engineer, in an attitude as if he were coming forward to address an audience, and with his hair as carefully brushed as if he had prepared himself for a dinner-party at Holland House. Beyond there is nearly a square mile of dwelling-houses, brick and stucco, quite devoid of anything like elegance,— smoky, economical, and monotonous. If the traveller proceeds to Waterloo Place and Trafalgar Square, he will find the same order of affairs as at Euston—on a larger scale, it is true, and with a good deal of old-fashioned English dignity; but cold and unattractive still.

This was the style of architecture which prevailed during the first half of the nineteenth century. We had it also in America at that time,—where we had anything at all,—in the Astor House at New York, a Boston custom-house, and country residences with pretentious wooden columns in front of them to keep the sunlight out of parlor windows. How different it is from the impression we receive on our entrance into Paris, Brussels, Milan, or even mediæval Nuremburg with its numerous gables and cozy balconies. Never since William I. built the Tower of London, had English taste in art and architecture been so barren, dull, and insipid.

In February, 1819, John Ruskin was born in London, a man destined by fate to smash this order of things as completely as King Olaf's strong warrior demolished the Norwegian idol. John Ruskin's father, who was originally of Scotch extraction, was an English wine merchant, and fortunately died in time to give his more gifted son an opportunity for the work which he was destined by temperament and inclination to perform. John Ruskin's biographer is no doubt an excellent person, but I

can make little from his account of the boyhood
of this genius, except that he composed verses before the age of ten, and visited Scotland where he
had cousins to play with. His parents travelled
with him on the Continent at an early age, and
his vivid imagination was strongly impressed with
the great spectacles he saw there. At the age of
seventeen he fell desperately in love with a Parisian
girl two years younger, but instead of enjoying the
happiness which often comes with such transitory
attachments, the ardor and extreme sensitiveness
of his nature showed itself in a shy and eccentric
demeanor, which gave the young woman a feeling
of repulsion toward him, and caused them both no
little discomfort.

There is no genius without intensity of feeling,
and such an early experience as this was the true in-
dication of young Ruskin's energy. We notice the
same thing in Byron's case; and Miss Evans, in
Daniel Deronda, predicts for the immature lover of
Gwendolen a distinguished career, proving her own
deep insight into human nature. Was not Shakespeare himself said to have been carried off his feet
in much the same manner ?

Ruskin's sensitiveness, however, was essential for
the work for which nature had designed him. His
literary talent was equally precocious. He began
to write and publish at sixteen—sketches of the Alps
and other small booklets, preparatory for a more serious effort; in which his wonderful faculty for description, unsurpassed in English prose, quickly gained
for him a good reputation. Meanwhile, he travelled

continually, and went through Oxford without producing any particular sensation there. In the autumn of 1842 the first volume of *Modern Painters* was ready for the publisher.

Painting.

In judging of *Modern Painters*, the tender age at which the book was written should always be considered. It was certainly a daring attempt, and it is equally surprising that it should have proved so successful. Only genius could have carried it through. The powers of observation develop themselves more rapidly than the reflective faculty, and beautiful poetry of that sort has been written at even an earlier period; but critical prose requires maturity of judgment, and what we wonder is, not that these early opinions are sometimes fallacious, but that they are worth anything at all. The work abounds with brilliant descriptive passages and keen bits of artistic insight, but also with sharp contrasts of praise and censure, ingenious partisan arguments, harsh condemnations, and not a few cobwebby notions. The faults of the book are the faults of youth, but its exceptional interest comes from the brilliant imagination of the writer. It is the outpouring of an ardent, enthusiastic nature; a freshet of pictorial ideas which carries the reader along through eddies and a tumult of waters, even against his own will. Its earnestness convinces him against his more sober judgment. If he does not find a strong character between the lines, he discovers one with noble impulses and lofty aspirations,—a soul palpitating with impressions of all that is pure, beautiful, and holy.

Charles Lamb says of his imaginary Sarah Battles, that when she spoke of games for four persons she always meant *whist;* and Ruskin's defense of modern English painters is evidently intended for a defense of Turner, who was not so well appreciated in 1840 as he is at present. In his travels on the Continent he had probably met with numerous conventional art critics and connoisseurs, who criticised Turner, and the English landscape-school, in rather a severe manner. Claude Lorraine had long been accepted as the standard of what a landscape-painter ought to be, and all differences between his work and Turner's were held to the disadvantage of the latter.

It was the oft-repeated story of conventionality against progress. Turner was judged as Tintoretto had been by the cotemporaries of Titian, and as he now is judged by German academic critics. It was the way in which Emerson was criticised by Arnold and Lowell. Byron's *English Bards and Scotch Reviewers* corresponds to Ruskin's *Modern Painters*, and represents the same spirit of independence breaking through the restraints of a hide-bound Toryism. Nothing is more exasperating to an intellectual person, than the continual reiteration that men were made for the laws, rather than laws for men. The rules for writing poetry were held by Byron in high contempt. "What was chiefly needed," he said, "was a knowledge of good society," by which I suppose he meant, human nature as we meet with it in large cities.

In regard to Turner it has been admitted that Ruskin was mainly in the right; but in the course of his argument he is often so unjust to the classical school of landscape-painting as to affect many of his readers disagreeably, and lead them to condemn his whole work on that account. Of Claude he says that he had a fine feeling for beauty of form, and his foliage is seldom ungraceful, but with regard to essential truth, his painting is only a mass of error. Cuyp, on the contrary, had little feeling for beauty, but more regard for truth. Poussin, more ignorant of truth than Claude, and with small sense of beauty, yet has more of the moral or human element than either.

There is a basis of fact in these statements, and I think he hits Cuyp pretty close to the mark, but it is not the way to dispose of such distinguished artists. Turner might also be criticised with regard to essential truth and the representation of nature, —in fact he often is so criticised. Both Turner and Claude have their peculiarities, and both rise above them; and the cork will float whether the water it is in is pure or muddy.

The charm of Claude lies chiefly in his atmosphere. It is the atmosphere of Southern France, and has a climate something more genial than our best October days. You feel its influence on approaching his canvas, and are transported mentally into the scene which he represents. Next to this he is noted for the pensive grace of his foliage, which seems to be possessed of a dreamy melancholy almost human. There is one of Claude's landscapes in the Berlin museum which may be taken as a type of the greater number of his pictures. On one side a stately edifice, half-seen, is partially shaded by symmetrical trees, in form not unlike American elms. In front, a sunny slope, on which there is a small group of men and women, leads down to a more rustic sort of scenery in the middle distance; and beyond, the lines grow fainter and fainter, and the colors continually more delicate, until both seem to fade away in the hazy horizon. Goethe said, " Such scenes as Claude represents are rare in nature, but he had all the details of a landscape at his command, and could unite them in any way he chose." This would seem to have been the manner in which he worked; and though the result is exceedingly pleasant, if all his pictures were brought together in one collection, as so many of Turner's are in London, the effect might be rather monotonous.

Gaspar Poussin had not the atmosphere of Claude Lorraine, and his coloring is comparatively cold, but there is much more variety in his work; not only in his subjects, but in his treatment of details. Claude's foliage always seems to be much the same, and some of his trees are of a species known only to himself. How far Ruskin is right in his strictures on Claude's *herbarium* it would be difficult to determine; but his chapters on the beauty of trees, clouds, and stones, show a profound study of the subject, and are among the most valuable contributions to the literature of art.

Where half a square mile of ground has to be represented on eight square feet of canvas, an amount of abbreviation has to take place which prevents us from deciding in many cases whether the truth of nature has been violated or not. In regard to the tapering trunks of Claude's trees, Ruskin would appear to be correct; for, though some trees grow in that manner, elms, maples, walnuts, oaks, and many others have nearly equilateral trunks, until they are divided into branches.

It is wonderful what clearness of perception and independence of judgment Ruskin had at twenty-three. He paid no reverence to the so-called authorities on art and literature—as if there could be such a thing on such subjects—but used his own eyes and came to his own conclusions, blinded by no great reputations, or even the prestige of centuries. He discriminates between Titian and Tintoretto in such judicious manner as this:

" Of Titian and Tintoretto I have spoken already. The latter is every way the greater master, never indulging in the exaggerated color of Titian, and attaining far more perfect light ; his grasp of Nature is more extensive, and his view of her more imaginative (incidental notices of his landscape will be found in the chapter on " Imagination Penetrative," of the second volume), but he is usually too impatient to carry his thoughts as far out, or to realize with as much substantiality as Titian."

It is perfectly true that Tintoretto's *chiaroscuro* is of a finer quality than Titian's, or than any other painter except Correggio, and that Titian's coloring is frequently too bright for a refined taste,—if you remember the two Venuses in Florence, or even the *Tribute Money*, you will recognize this,—but the statement is a severe blow to all German and Italian art criticism, which would make out Tintoretto to be the inferior artist because he was born after the grand culmination.

The difference between Claude and Turner is similar to that between Titian and Tintoretto; and it is a difference which divides the German and French schools of art in the present century, and which is like the difference between Milton and Shakespeare. It is the difference between the classic and romantic methods; the former of which permits of greater perfection, and the latter gives more freedom and variety. The varied character of Turner's work is one of its chief merits; and his brilliant flights of imagination, even where they are imperfectly expressed, are invigorating, and most refreshing to the sight. He may sometimes have repeated himself, but I do not remember an instance of it. Like Tintoretto, his mind was steeped in originality.

Dr. Lübke, in his history of art, affords Turner a rather scanty notice, in which he speaks of him as celebrated for his fine effects of light, but in his later years degenerating into a misty vagueness and loss of form. This is the Alpha and Omega of Turner, it is true, but the rest of the alphabet has been left out. Toward the close of his life he acquired a kind of chromatic mania, and the pictures he painted in this state of mind, though very interesting, are not so satisfactory as the more orderly work of his better years; but his rare effects of light continued till the close, and were even more conspicuous in his later than his earlier work.

One of the prettiest examples of this Turneresque style is the little painting in the National Gallery called *Wind, Rain, and Speed.* A railway train is approaching the station in a severe storm, almost enveloped in a whirl of rain, mist, and its own steam. Only the front of the locomotive is distinctly visible; and so far the picture is perfectly true to nature. The colors, however, which Turner has introduced into that whirling mist, are such perhaps as no other artist would have thought of. Ruskin tells us that Turner could see colors on a turbot which no one else could perceive, and this may have been true in many other cases. Whether the colors were really on the turbot is a dubious problem.

Although Turner gradually fell into this mannerism, Ruskin is mainly right in regard to his truthfulness to nature. His skies are an evidence of this. Such skies as Turner's have never been painted since the sixteenth century; and then only by a few great Venetians. They are not only atmospheric, but pellucid, and we see into them for miles. His sunsets, likewise, stand apart,—as they are indeed a part of his skies. Other painters make a warm glow above the horizon, but Turner attempted to reproduce the splendor of the twilight hour in all its magnificence. The means by which he accomplished this were peculiar to him. The setting sun in his *Decline of Carthage* is a mass of paint, built out upon the canvas nearly a quarter of an inch thick; and if you look at it long enough it will make your eyes water like the sun itself. He delighted in those long gossamer streamers which often fill the western skies in summer, and reproduced them in a most skilful manner.

One of the brightest of Ruskin's smaller publications is his *Elements of Drawing*, which is not only instructive, but as entertaining as most of his books. It includes an analysis of Turner's picture of *Coblenz on the Rhine*, and from this rather simple subject he educes rules of composition such as Leonardo da Vinci never dreamed of. His description of the *Slave Ship*, owned by Mr. Quincy Shaw's family of Boston, is rather redolent of adjectives, but I believe he hits the mark in saying that it contains the noblest sea ever painted by man; though only a person who has watched the heaving and rolling of the sea in mid-ocean after a storm would be likely to appreciate this.

Ruskin says:

" If we look at Nature carefully we shall find that her colors are in a state of perpetual confusion and indistinctness, while her forms, as told by light and shade, are invariably clear, distinct, and speaking. The stones and gravel of the bank catch green reflections from the boughs above ; the bushes receive grays and yellows from the ground ; every hairbreadth of polished surface gives a little bit of the sky or the gold of the sun, like a star upon the local color ; this local color, changeful and uncertain in itself, is again disguised and modified by the hue of light, or quenched in the gray of the shadow ; and the confusion and blending of tint is altogether so great, that were we left to find out what objects

were by their colors only, we would scarcely in places
distinguish the boughs of a tree from the air beyond
them, or the ground beneath them."

This is one out of a hundred passages in *Modern
Painters*, bright with the freshness of youth, and
keen with the clear perceptions of maturity.

Go to Italy; read the guide-books, the art histories; examine all the celebrated statues, paintings,
and churches; then return to England or America
and read Ruskin to discover how little you have
seen. The originality of his work, the extent of his
researches in fields before unthought of, is fairly
astonishing. In Verona, a city usually visited out
of respect to the memory of Romeo and Juliet, he
finds a whole storehouse of fresh material, not less
interesting to the true lover of art than Shakespeare's plays. He notices a stone griffin of the
fourteenth century supporting a column of the cathedral porch, and he compares it with a griffin
which he saw in Rome on the temple of Antoninus
and Faustina,—a griffin of the second century. He
introduces them both into his book as examples of
the true and false in composition.

This gives him also an opportunity such as he
rarely neglects, of penetrating to the intellectual
well-springs of the unknown sculptors who carved
them. His exposition of this is rather ingenious and
very amusing. In a general way he is right enough.
The Antonine griffin is made up of the body of a
lion (not very well imitated), the neck of a horse,
and the head and wings of an eagle. His right foot

rests lightly on a flower, and is twice as long as the left.   He looks as tame and peaceable as the Roman patrician under the Empire.   The Lombardic griffin is at once lion and eagle all over, and is full of life, ferocity, and energy.   His feet are so compounded that it would be difficult to say whether they most resemble claws or paws.   He is holding some kind of a reptile in them, so as to give the impression that he is a useful, rather than a harmful monster. His eyes seem to be looking into the far distance, and the aspect of his head suggests swiftness and power.   The Antonine griffin is conventional.

Conventionality is the most dangerous enemy of art; for as soon as art begins to imitate itself, and ceases to be original, it becomes like stagnant water. As the mere imitation of nature, it has only a secondary value: only thought and feeling can elevate it. The formula is: Thought *plus* nature equals art. This, in fact, was the keynote of Ruskin's teaching; and he attacked conventionality not only in art and architecture, but in the higher forms of mechanical industry.   He pointed out that so long as a man's work is honest, intelligent, and constructive, he lives and enjoys himself in a normal manner; but when he does cheap, mechanical, or fraudulent work, he will never find pleasure in its performance, and will be sure to seek abnormal enjoyment in drinking, gambling, or other vicious courses.

The freedom and fearlessness with which Ruskin advanced his views made a host of small enemies for him, and he soon became a centre of innumerable personal attacks.   He was persecuted by the English press, much as the abolitionists were, formerly, by the American press. This, however, was only so much fuel for his fire. His attack on the architecture of London Bridge almost produced a national conflagration,—no matter, his eloquence waxed fourfold. Ruskin was clad in cerulean armor, and the shafts of his assailants recoiled on themselves. When some newspaper critic asserted that art was an effeminate study, and that Ruskin himself was a sentimentalist, he replied nearly as follows:

" What we need at this hour in Great Britain is true manliness and the respect for manliness; and to take so poor an instance as my own poor life,—because I have pointed to the pictures of Turner and Luini and praised them, instead of attracting attention to anything I could do myself; and because I have always obeyed my mother, and have never treated the meanest woman but with respect, the poor wretch who pawns the dirty linen of his soul for a cigar and a glass of beer, talks about the effeminate sentimentality of Ruskin."

After this scorching rejoinder he was left in peace for a considerable time.

Together with his vindication of Turner, Ruskin wove a more discriminating criticism of Tintoretto, whose mighty works he found also lacking the appreciation they deserve—apparently because they are all collected in one city, instead of being divided among the different museums, where connoisseurs could see them conveniently and compare them with other masterpieces. Tintoretto was, in fact, an earlier and grander sort of Turner, who looked at life in an independent manner and designed his pictures to suit his own ideas instead of those of his patrons. He was complained of for not painting like Titian, as Turner was for not painting like Claude; though it would have been as fair to complain of Titian for being different from Michel Angelo. In fact Michel Angelo himself considered Titian decidedly lacking in the nobler qualities of design.

Ruskin might well be named the discoverer of Tintoretto's genius, and it is no mean honor to have done this. His descriptions of Tintoretto's pictures in *Modern Painters* are not so fine as those which he afterwards published in the appendix to the *Stones of Venice.* They have not the same cool, judicious tone. We have discussed this subject in the *Life of Tintoretto* and there is no occasion to dwell on it here. In regard to connoisseurs, Ruskin troubled himself very little. He did not wish to be called a connoisseur himself, although he was better acquainted with the technicalities of art than most of them. For that matter you will hear much less about the technicalities in Sir Joshua Reynold's lectures than in the writings of more recent critics, who are neither writers nor artists. Ruskin keeps technicalities well out of sight, and does not trouble himself whether the vehicle was thin or viscous.

Later in life he interested himself also in the genius of Luini, in whom he discovered admirable qualities not sufficiently considered hitherto. Finally he seems to have preferred the Bellini. He admired and respected the Roman school, but was more attracted personally by the Venetians. Their warm, luminous coloring evidently appealed to something in Ruskin's own nature.

Architecture.

It was in architecture that Ruskin achieved his greatest triumph. Progress and civilization may be described as a continual breaking through of conventional forms in order to reconstruct them again in a more comprehensive manner. No *one* man can do this by himself alone. It requires a popular impulse; but to the leader of the movement belongs exceptional honor, for it demands rare intelligence and courage to guide it in the right direction. Ruskin was the pioneer in a constructive movement which has made our cities interesting, and to some degree beautiful, instead of being commonplace and dreary. His instruction has borne better fruit in America than in his own country; partly because there was more building to be done here, and partly because there was less prejudice to be removed.

Thus it happens that Ruskin's writings have always an antagonistic quality. He is in the position of an advocate, who has to make an appeal for his client in an unfriendly court. Like Frederick of Prussia he was obliged to fight against a coalition, and if he sometimes had to resort to desperate arguments, and his voice became sometimes shrill and unmusical, can he fairly be blamed for it ?

His opponents may be divided into three classes.

First: such as may be called the architectural Tories; who considered the Grecian style the only

18

respectable thing, and who looked upon all other styles of architecture, as Carlyle's Scotchman considered poetry, as the productions of a semi-barbarous period.

Secondly: the disciples of John Stuart Mill's philosophy, who believed that industry and economy were the chief virtues of man, and that the true measure of civilization always should be the number of inhabitants to the square mile.

Thirdly: those who looked on wealth chiefly as a means of self-gratification; who held the fashions to be paramount to beauty, and filled their houses with expensive ornaments for the sake of ostentation.

Among these, the second class was the most formidable in its opposition; for its doctrines were as adverse to everything like elegance and ornament as the doctrines of Diogenes himself, and they were held by its proselytes with the zeal and tenacity of a religious creed.

Ruskin entrenched himself upon high ground. He fortified himself against philosophy by reference to Holy Writ, and made the words of the Psalmist, " Thy word is a lamp unto my feet," the foundation of his argument. He showed that a building erected to protect man from the elements might not be architecture at all, and, as an historical fact, true architecture only began with the consecration of buildings for religious purposes. Thus it became, like music and poetry, a divine message and means of instruction to mankind. So far as architecture fulfills this demand, it will be vital, beneficial, and beautiful; but when it fails to do this it will become lifeless and worthless. Thus, even from the standpoint of utility, some sacrifice is required to the Graces and Muses.

Ruskin's argument is always for Gothic architecture, as against French and Italian Renaissance; and the so-called American Gothic may be fairly claimed as his offspring. The value of Grecian architecture consisted in its columns and its ornamental sculpture. Their volutes and triglyphs may have had a meaning also to the Greeks; but it is now lost to us, as well as the sculpture which taught them heroism and piety from the pediments of their temples. As domestic architecture it was nothing, and as adapted to modern uses it is simply *Hamlet* without the Prince of Denmark. It is for this reason wholly uninteresting in its modern dress. We may admire the proportions of a building in the Grecian style, but there our pleasure in it ceases, for there is nothing to examine, nothing to study.

With the Romans, architecture began in its true sense; that is, according to the meaning of the word. As Christianity itself became established through the supremacy of the Roman empire, so the Roman arch and basilica served for the construction of its edifices until the twelfth century, when true Christian architecture with its pointed arch, lofty spire, and Gothic dome, came into vogue. Here was a lesson for mankind which has lasted ever since. It is doubtful if even the frescos of Michel Angelo are more impressive than the view from the central aisle of Cologne Cathedral. Man has never since constructed anything so wonderful (considering the grandeur of the whole and the perfection of its different parts, to the minutest details), and it hardly seems possible that he ever can.   The men who worked on these wonderful structures, says Ruskin, who carved the ornaments for the pinnacles and the myriad forms of animal and floral life, were fortunate compared with the modern stone-cutter, who chisels day after day in a straight line, to hollow a moulding which nobody cares to look at.   The carving on the capitols, and the stained pictures on the windows, were alike interesting to the educated and the ignorant.

Gothic, or Frankish, architecture (as it ought properly to be called) not only reflects the Christian spirit in its heaven-pointing spires and pinnacles, but also in the sincerity of its construction.   It shows on the surface what it was designed for, and the way in which it was built; so that unfaithful or fraudulent work is barely possible in it; and if possible can easily be detected.   The pointed arch permits of universal application and infinite variety.   The allegation that it is not suited to the needs of modern life, Ruskin refuted by practical experiment.   He obtained apartments in a Gothic Venetian palace, and found himself as pleasantly situated there as he ever had been in his life.   Cathedrals like Strasburg and Cologne would not serve for places of Protestant worship, it is true, but a building like the Duomo at Florence could hardly be excelled as an auditorium.

The decline in Gothic architecture was coincident with the religious decline of the fifteenth century,—

the separation of religion from morality. Then, Ruskin says, came the foul blood of the Renaissance and swept it all away. We must admit, however, that it is a mistake to condemn any particular style of architecture which has stood the test of time. The Roman Renaissance of Bramante and San Gallo has a broad simplicity—we might say, perhaps, an intelligent simplicity—which recommends it to our favor. Change is a necessity of human nature, and the palaces of the Corso are a refreshing change from the fretted architecture of Pisa and Nuremberg. It is easy to imagine how interesting any small bit of legendary sculpture would be to the common people of a city, before the invention of printing. The demand for books in the sixteenth century replaced the popular demand for pictures and images, and may have had an effect also on the external appearance of buildings.

There is no reason, however, why we should not return to the Gothic and Romanesque forms, as the great builders of the sixteenth century returned to classic forms. This, in fact, has now been done to a considerable degree. An arch is always an interesting object, whether it be the entrance to a tunnel or the door-way to a church; and no traveller who has passed over the *Tête Noir* in Switzerland ever forgets that single pointed arch, cut through the mountain flank, as the road descends into the valley of the Rhone. The only question that arises is whether, if arches were more numerous, we should become tired of the sight of them. The tendency at present seems to be to give an impartial consideration to all the different styles of architecture.   Although Ruskin carries his antagonism toward the Renaissance rather too far, he has certainly proved two cardinal points in the *Stones of Venice*, and in a most convincing manner.

First, that the best architecture in Europe arose during the lifetime of Dante, or during the last half of the thirteenth and the first half of the fourteenth centuries.   It was then that the Rouen and Cologne Cathedrals, the Duomo at Florence, and the Ducal Palace in Venice, as well as the finest English abbeys, were built.   We have no sense of disappointment on beholding these mighty structures, such as we feel in St. Peters, at Rome, but rather a feeling of exaltation.   The truly noble in architecture impresses us with a sense of awe.

Secondly, he has shown beyond a doubt that while Gothic architecture * had a gradual rise of more than a century and a half, and almost as gradual a decline, the best Renaissance architecture in France and Italy came at first, and it has been gradually declining in elegance and beauty ever since.   The palaces designed by Bramante and San Gallo are certainly superior in every way to the Rococo churches of the eighteenth century; and so is the Louvre built by Francis I. and Henry II. more chaste at least than the palaces of Louis XIV., or the Opera House of Louis Napoleon.   The best English Renaissance belongs of course to the time of Sir

* A Boston gentleman, inspired by Ruskin's writing, built a Gothic porch to his front door on Columbus Avenue, and it is really the one attractive piece of architecture in the street.

Christopher Wren, since which there has been a steady decline till the middle of the present century. It seems time that a new style of architecture was evolved: but whence can it come ? Society is weak because there is no agreement of opinion. New languages grow out of ignorance, and before we can have a really original architecture in America we must forget all that we know of Europe.

The *Seven Lamps of Architecture* is an exposition of what may be called the transcendental principles of building. Many architects have confessed to me their indebtedness to this little book. Each chapter in it is a *lamp*, as bright and sparkling with spirituality as one of Emerson's essays. In the *Lamp of Power* he analyzes those forms of construction which make the strongest impression on us; in the *Lamp of Beauty*, those which give us the most agreeable sensations; and in the *Lamp of Life* he treats those mental conditions which give vigor and vitality to inanimate forms.

The *Stones of Venice* is Ruskin's finest work, surpassing *Modern Painters* in greatness of design, clearness of statement, and maturity of thought. The first volume is occupied with a discussion of architectural principles and is consequently as interesting and dry as the higher mathematics. I think few people who read for information (as distinguished from knowledge) ever get through with it. The second and third volumes belong to English literature, and they are written in a style of such grace and flexibility as is rare enough in any language. Ruskin's narrative has a tender pathos, and his argument a persuasive coquetry which is like the pleading of an affectionate woman. The introductory chapter on Venice itself is a wonderful piece of description, and a refutation to those who assert that pictures cannot be painted with a pen. It is in prose what *Childe Harold* is in poetry; for in it the smallest details and most delicate impressions are thrown into relief and given vitality. The early Venetians, he said, had no stone quarries to draw from, but they could obtain clay for bricks, and their ships brought beautiful marbles from other countries, with which they gave their dwellings a coating of enamel as the mollusks do their shells.

With all this poetry he makes a thorough and practical investigation of Venetian architecture from the earliest times. He goes first to the old church at Torcello, seven miles away—a church dating perhaps from the seventh century—and finds in it the invigorating influence of the Gothic occupation, which changed the Italian language and laid the foundation for Mediæval Italy. In the old Romanesque church at Murano he also discovered marvellous things; the floor one great mosaic, " dyed like the neck of a dove," and pieces of rare marble inserted under the windows of the apse, like jewels in a diadem. He identifies six distinct styles of Venetian architecture: the Romanesque, the Byzantine, the Gothic, the Roman Renaissance, the Byzantine Renaissance, and the grotesque Renaissance ; besides which the Doge's palace, the noblest building in the city, is a composite of Byzantine, Gothic, and Roman Renaissance. The tendency of transition types however is to die out, as Darwin shows us in animal life.

All of these forms except the grotesque Renaissance are to be seen side by side on the Grand Canal, and though there are some fine Renaissance palaces there, the general verdict is that they are excelled by the Gothic, and that the old Byzantine palace, now called the *Fondaco dei Turchi* is the most interesting of them all. The *Palāzzo del Camello*, where Tintoretto lived, is one of the finest examples of Italian Gothic in the city; while the *Casa d'oro*, which is always pointed out to travellers, is a showy building and badly designed.

Ruskin points out that the greatest architects of Venice are now unknown even to the Venetians, and that Palladio, with whose name we are all familiar (perhaps on account of its pleasant sound), was in truth very little of an architect. His chief work, the church of *San Georgio Maggiore*, has a commanding position, certainly, and an imposing appearance; but who cares to look at it twice ? If it attracts attention from the *Hotel Anglais* it is for the bad proportion between its four great columns and the portico above it,—a huge, gaunt, unedifying building. And here let us observe the one important omission which Ruskin makes is, that the quality of architecture depends much less on the style, than on the sense of beauty in the architect. That is something for which no rule can be given. A fine sense of proportion is necessary for a good general effect, and a refined taste for the selection of ornament; but even these two united will not always produce a satisfactory result. I believe the best architecture in Harvard University is Holden Chapel, the oldest and smallest building on the grounds; and yet it belongs to the later English Renaissance, closely resembling Roman Rococo. How many fruitless attempts have been made to engraft Egyptian architecture on modern life; and yet the New York jail called " the Tombs " is perhaps the most impressive building in that city.

The Venetians became weary of their pompous, palatial Palladio in the seventeenth century, and reverted to Byzantine types, with which they formed a mixture called the Byzantine Romanesque; and it extended itself over a large portion of Southern Europe, even to the Azores, and is often improperly called Moorish. It has neither the dignity of Roman Renaissance nor the originality and vigor of the true Byzantine. After its day was over came the grotesque Renaissance, the most degraded style of architecture of which there is any record.

Refined taste always accompanies a high standard of morality, and bad taste the reverse.* The formula is: first, excellence; then, weakness; and finally, degradation. We read of the decline and fall of the Roman Empire and do not yet feel certain of the causes which produced it. There was quite as decided a decline of civilization in Catholic Europe from the fifteenth to the eighteenth centuries. At the time that Napoleon put an end to the Venetian state it was little better than a clan of

* The early Puritan church architecture of New England was in much finer taste than that of the first half of the present century.

barbarians, doing nothing, producing nothing, and without skill or virtue in its individual members. If we investigate the causes of this more recent decline, we shall perhaps understand better the character of the preceding one.

Ruskin's investigation of the Venetian funereal monuments is invaluable to the historian, and comes to the same result. Who has entered the Church of the Templars at London, and seen those old warriors of the Cross resting in their coats of mail, without feeling a deeper sense of the earnestness of life. Those are the noblest monuments in Europe, and if the sculpture is somewhat rude, it is none the less suitable for those grim heroes in their eternal silence. From the thirteenth to the sixteenth centuries the monuments of the dead declined in seriousness, but increased in artistic skill: from the sixteenth to the nineteenth centuries they declined in both. Nothing is more disgusting than the least touch of ostentation or vanity about the grave; and there are some sad examples of it in the Venetian churches. I recollect in one of them the group of a Doge and two ladies, all attired in the highest kind of French millinery, their hair dressed as if for a dancing party, and with a simper on their faces as if they were at that moment entering the ball-room. This was to ornament the Doge's own sepulchre. The sarcophagi in the Roman churches adorned with variegated marbles are sufficiently showy, but this Doge and his ladies are beyond expression in respectable English.

Miscellaneous Work.

After architecture Ruskin turned to sculpture, but did not succeed so well. In 1873, I purchased in London the most beautiful book that I have ever seen, called *Aratra Pentelici*, or the Quarrying of Pentelicus. A fine name, and a still finer book, bound in plum-colored calf, (evidently Ruskin's own design,) with matchless illustrations, mostly taken from ancient coins; but the reading matter was not so interesting.

Ruskin tells a pretty anecdote in the book, of a little beggar-girl who was brought into his kitchen, and amused herself by modelling cats and mice out of scraps of pastry.

This he declares to be the origin of sculpture; but in saying so, he contradicts his previous statements in regard to architecture. The mere imitation of natural objects in wood or stone may have led to sculpture, as the erection of a hut led to the building of a temple; but in order to become sculpture it requires the addition of *ideality*, either in the form of an elevated purpose like an Egyptian deity, or of superior excellence as in the *Wild Boar* at Florence. An Egyptian idol may be considered a work of art, in spite of its stiffness and crudeness, because it is a definite attempt to represent an idea; whereas a Malay idol only represents a hideous confusion.

Ruskin had an essentially pictorial mind. In *Aratra Pentelici* he deals chiefly with coins and relief-work, which approach most nearly in treatment to the art of painting. His criticism of the sculptured ornaments on architecture is also interesting, but when he reverts to the masterpieces of classic sculpture his remarks are not always pertinent. He does not like the *St. George* of Donatello, or the *Night*, and *Moses*, of Michel Angelo. He may be correct in supposing that the face of the *Venus of Milo* is not exceptionally beautiful, and that the statue owes its pre-eminence to the expression which the sculptor has given it.

Ruskin's later writings correspond to Carlyle's latter-day pamphlets, and also resembled Turner's later work; being characterized by vagueness, impatience, and also a slight eccentricity. Brilliant passages may be found in them; but they are like roses choked among weeds. Inconsiderate people have judged him by this, instead of his earlier and better sort of industry. He published a number of small volumes in the same exquisite style as *Aratra Pentelici.* One was called the *Eagle's Nest, or Hints to Young Housewives;* another, *Sesame and Lilies*, containing two admirable lectures on education for the sake of education,—instead of education for mercenary purposes, or for the sake of distinction. If he had gone to Germany he could have found thousands of well-equipped scholars, who have studied devotedly without the slightest hoped of distinction; but Ruskin always had a prejudice about Germany. He disliked German painting, and condemned German philosophy, of which he had imbibed much himself through Carlyle, without studying it. He never learned that a writer should confine

himself to those subjects with which he is best acquainted.

His political economy is pretty mad stuff; yet he
half consciously made a satire of it on that arrogant
young science, which is still in its school-boy days.
His fundamental principle, that the true wealth of
a nation consists rather in superior men and women
than in gold and silver—that we should subsidize
character and talent rather than steamship lines, and
not leave them to the mercy of Darwinian evolution
—is something that our legislators would do well to
consider.   His literary criticism (published only in
magazines) was interesting, but decidedly erratic.
He liked Byron for his mental breadth, and disliked
Wordsworth, who was after all the Fra Angelico of
poets.   He admired Scott, and railed against
Dickens.

I have said nothing of Ruskin's Oxford lectures,
which aroused such enthusiasm among the students,
instead of chilling the blood in their veins; nor of his
philanthropy, which was enough of itself to adorn
and distinguish him.   Nearly at the close of his life
he performed a graceful act of kindness, by interesting himself in an American artist, Miss Frances
Alexander, living in Florence.   With one word he
made her famous.   This was partly because she had
carried to perfection the principles he elaborated
long since in his *Elements of Drawing;* but it was
also' well deserved.   He edited her *Story of Ida,*
which has become an American classic; and her
simple but interesting tales of Tuscan life.   About
the same time he published a small book called

Mornings in Florence, which contains some of his purest and most delicate art-criticism.

We feel the highest obligation to seers like Goethe and Carlyle, who point out the way for us to a better future; and next to them we are indebted to those who recall the mighty past, to check the arrogance and self-sufficiency of the present time. This was Ruskin's privilege in life, and he felt it to be a privilege. He taught most emphatically the lesson, that the progress of a people in civilization does not depend so much on their institutions, as on their being animated by the right mental tone. This it is on which the permanence or improvement of all institutions will depend.

F. MAX MÜLLER

FICTION, written by a man or woman of genius, will contain more valuable truth than those facts of nature which we collect for the purposes of generalization and which we could collect again if the dog Diamond, or a servant-girl, should destroy them for us; but there is no romance yet written so stimulating to the imagination as the story of the migration of the Aryan races from their primeval home in Central Asia. How they started from a small community, perhaps from a single family, multiplied and increased through the wisdom which destiny had given them as a birthright, until now they have inherited the whole globe, with the exception of China, Turkey, and Farther India. The Aryan, or ploughing races, began by cultivating the soil, and afterwards proceeded to cultivate themselves; and this application of the word both in a physical and spiritual sense, is thoroughly characteristic of their history. It is through language alone, and their respect for language, that we are able to learn the course of their development and their migrations. Otherwise, it would never have been suspected that the light-haired English were related to the dark-skinned inhabitants of India.

If we return to Asia, however, to find the ancient domicile of our distant ancestors, we are disappointed. The house is no longer standing. We like to think that they came from the vale of Cashmir, the most beautiful spot of ground in Asia, if not in the world; but there is no certainty of it. Neither have we discovered the parent tongue of which Sanskrit, Zend, Greek, Roman, and all European languages are the progeny. We can approximate it closely, but cannot say decisively what it was. We cannot conjugate *to be* or *to have* in ancient Aryan. We see the oak-tree that has grown up and spread its branches to the sky, but if we uncover its roots we find no trace of the acorn from which it sprang. Even the Greeks, who were among the last of the many offshoots from the parent stem, and the first to become intelligent in the modern sense, remembered nothing, and had no tradition of their original birthplace. It is only through comparative philology that we are able to make out something of these prehistoric movements, and can determine nearly the degree of relationship which one branch in this large family bears to another. We know, for instance, that we Anglo-Saxons are more nearly related to the Greeks and Romans than we are to the Russians, or, perhaps, to the French and Spaniards.

These grand results of comparative philology, as determined by Oriental societies, were known, in a general way, before the publication of Max Müller's work on the *Science of Language*, in 1861; but the

19

honor belongs to him of being the first to give a definite and elaborate form to this subject, and to develop from it a literature similar to that which Ruskin founded on art.

Max Müller, as he is universally called, was born at Dessau, in 1822, and graduated at Leipzig in 1843—an early age for a German university. From his earliest years he showed rare facility in the acquisition of knowledge, and became so thoroughly versed in philosophy, history, and literature, that he might soon have obtained a professorship in either of those branches. This universality of acquirements lasted him through life, and is a distinguishing feature of his career as a scholar and man of letters. German universities are admitted to be the best in the world, but Müller was a cosmopolitan by nature. He accordingly went to Paris to learn the best that was to be had there and soon fell under the influence of Eugène Burnouf, the Nestor of oriental scholarship. He made such progress in the study of Sanskrit, that, depending on his splendid constitution, he determined to attempt a complete translation of the *Rig-Veda*, a gigantic work, such as man has rarely attempted without assistance. In order to do this he was obliged to change his nationality once more, for the only complete manuscripts of the Vedas were in the Bodleian Library. He became professor of modern languages at Oxford in 1854, and the chair of comparative philology was tardily bestowed in 1868. He has, however, remained a German at heart, as appeared from his patriotic feeling for his native country during the Franco-German war.

He is probably the most distinguished scholar living, and one of the most famous of the century. That he is an honorary member of the French Academy, and associate of some forty other learned societies, may be taken for what it is worth. No man's celebrity is increased by such honors. The true honor consists in deserving them without receiving them. But Müller is not only a scholar; he is also an excellent writer. His English is not studied, but rather careless, and the great number of his publications would indicate that he wrote without taking much pains to revise his manuscript. We like him the better for this, for it shows that he is aiming at the exposition of his subject rather than for literary reputation. We much prefer such a style to the elaborate periods of Macaulay, for it leaves the reader more free to form his own impressions. He is as fluent as Cardinal Newman, and at the same time more frank and manly. Standing almost alone among Englishmen in regard to some of his opinions, he has always expressed them in a fearless and candid manner. It is remarkable how perfectly at home he has made himself in a foreign tongue. Although he deals with the most marvellous subject since the discovery of the planetary system, he never loses himself in the marvellous, but is always cool-headed and self-contained. At the same time he has a pleasant enthusiasm for his subject, which he communicates to the reader.

Müller's sense of fine literature, which is not so very common, even among the educated, has three distinct advantages,—one for him, one for his subject, and one for his audience. It has made an important difference, whether our knowledge of the Vedic Hymns, *Zend-Avesta*, and of the Buddhist sacred writings, came to us through the medium of a liberally cultivated mind, or from the hands of a narrow and intolerant pedant. It is not only scholars who wish to know about them; they profoundly interest the general public, especially clergymen, and other serious thinkers. A great religious revolution has been taking place in the nineteenth century, only surpassed by that of the sixteenth. It has been a quiet revolution, but none the less deep-seated and radical. Even the Catholic Church felt it, and has remodelled itself somewhat in consequence. Fortunately, the religious toleration which we learned of our ancestors has prevented it from being as bloody as the political revolutions which have taken place during the same period. This may be owing to indifference as well as toleration; but moderate indifference is better than that kind of religious devotion which leads a man to sacrifice his life for the sake of small distinctions in creed. The liberal movement has had its martyrs, however, none the less devoted because their torture has been slow and gradual. Men have starved and finally died for it, without attracting public attention in a considerable degree.

It should be noticed that all established forms of Christianity, have been based, not on the teachings of Christ, but on their interpretation by synods or councils of ecclesiastics. This was found necessary as soon as the new faith had acquired the ascendancy over paganism; because where every man was allowed to make his own interpretation, such wide differences of opinion arose that the Christian church was in danger of being disintegrated and swamped by them. With the progress of knowledge, and scientific inquiry, as the world became more enlightened, continual revision of the proceedings of the councils was required. Thus there has been constant change from one century to another, until a great division came in the sixteenth century, which ultimately reformed the Catholic Church, as well as those sects which had seceded from it. Now comes the nineteenth century with its formidable array of scientific facts, which the stoutest believers are unable to ignore. They may explain passages in the Bible allegorically or poetically, but their consciences are not satisfied. So we have Unitarianism, Transcendentalism, and Andover Heresy; and in Europe an undertone of radical distrust threatens to break forth at any moment, in revolt against established usages.

The breaking down of so many old beliefs and traditions, has brought with it a desire to reconsider the whole subject and to find out not only where Christianity stands to-day in its relation to the present needs of humanity, but also to learn what is its relation to other important religions. The idea gains ground continually, that, as the human race constitutes one great body, whose interests are identical, and from which no one part can effectually separate itself, so that, (as President Lincoln said in his Proclamation), by giving freedom to the black man, we insure its preservation to the white,—thus, likewise, do all the religions of the earth form a complete whole, a code of sacred laws, in which one part bears a distinct relation to every other, and in which not even the most degraded creed can properly be treated with contempt. When Christianity was struggling for existence, the case was different; but we have recovered from the notion that all men are condemned to hell-fire who have not been baptized in the name of Jesus; and in the day of their supremacy Christians can well afford to look with impartial eye on other forms of faith. Has not even the rude fetich of the South African a representative character by which it is closely allied to words like *spirit, understanding, perdition*, which from a material significance have passed to a spiritual one ? Max Müller says in his lecture on the Vedas:

"In the study of mankind there can hardly be a subject more deeply interesting than the study of the different forms of religion ; and much as I value the Science of Language for the aid which it lends us in unravelling some of the most complicated tissues of the human intellect, I confess that to my mind there is no study more absorbing than that of the Religions of the World,—the study, if I may so call it, of the various languages in which man has spoken to his Maker, and of that language in which his Maker " at sundry times and in divers manners " speaks to man.

" One religion, Mohammedanism, is so well known to us that we may almost say we have seen it rise and progress with our own eyes. It is the latest of all the important religious faiths, and the most aggressive. As a creed it has noble qualities ; as Hegel says : 'Modern Europe has produced no grander personalities than some of the Saracen monarchs ; but the literature of Mohammedanism is confined to a set of rules of conduct and a record of religious observances ; and for that reason, we suspect, is incapable of progress.' Brahmanism however, has an extensive literature ; probably the oldest records of human thought and feeling in existence. When we read *Homer* we realize that we have a very old book before us. If we next go to the Book of Genesis, we feel that to be still older. It is like the speech of a man of ninety ; but the hymns of the Vedas have the vagueness and nebulosity of thought that has been crystallized into speech gradually, and for the first time. As a record of the earliest spiritual consciousness of the human race, they are invaluable. Portions of Genesis may be as old or even older ; but the Vedas represented to the Hindoo mind what Exodus and the Psalms meant to the Hebrews. Buddhism and the Persian Sun-worship also have a literature, less extensive than Brahmanism, and more limited than the Hebrew ; but still no honest person can study them without admiration and wonder. The five commandments of Buddha correspond, with some limitations, to the Ten Commandments of Moses. The story of his life is a religious romance of the highest order."

Thus Max Müller became not only the translator of these sacred texts, but their commentator, and brought their significance within the reach of all intelligent English-speaking persons. The Zend-Avesta, it is true, had already been translated, but he has given us the most impartial and penetrating criticism of it,—unless a more elaborate is to be found in Samuel Johnson's *Oriental Religions.* An English reviewer says, " Max Müller is always a little bit of a preacher, and ready to let his arguments stray into broad theology, a fact which endears him to those who are seeking a safe channel between the Scylla, of Newman, and the Charybdis, of Huxley." There is sufficient truth in this, and the reason for it is, that he brought with him to England the philosophy of his native country. It is the transcendental philosophy which forms the basis of Max Müller's critical work, and has made him what he is as a writer.

This is not the place to open a discussion on the merits of German philosophy, but in the very first consideration of the subject we are met by a curious anomaly. It is the only notable school of metaphysics in the nineteenth century, which has not extended itself over France, England, and America. It has gained a foothold in Edinburgh and Dublin; it has been taught at Harvard College; but, I believe, never at Oxford or Cambridge, in England. In England and America it has been treated with ridicule, contempt, and something like abhorrence. Yet it has proved the one source of mental inspiration of the century. In America, Longfellow, Lowell, Emerson, and Channing have all depended on it; and so have Carlyle, Byron, Coleridge, Wordsworth, Matthew Arnold, and Tennyson, in England. Horace Mann was a transcendentalist ; and so is William T. Harris, the chief of our national bureau of education at Washington. Many have felt its influence who never heard its name; and in proof of this general assertion I will summon a single witness whose orthodoxy is beyond question and whose name carries with it the profound respect of millions of admirers. William E. Gladstone says in his Romanes Lecture:

" As the German philosophy has in recent times largely dominated the thought of the world, it is matter of interest for us all to look back to its fountain heads. In a work of authority by Zant, on the amount of influence brought to bear on that philosophy during the eighteenth century by English writers, from Bacon onwards, that influence is stated to have largely exceeded any that was drawn from other foreign sources. Further, we learn that the power exercised by Locke, and familiarly known to have been extensive in France, went far beyond that of any other British writer, and, indeed, reached such a height in Germany also, and in America, as well as in England, that it can only be compared with the dominion of Aristotle over the middle age, or that of Kant over the German writers of the present century."

Two points are conspicuous in this statement: first, that the influence of German philosophy is considered proven; second, that German metaphysics have also been largely influenced by the earlier English philosophers, from Bacon to Locke and Hume. The two taken together prove that Kant and his successors hold an established position in the history of philosophy, which no student in that field can safely disregard.

Why is it that the English critic speaks of Müller as offering a safe deliverance between Newman and Huxley,—between blindly following in the footsteps of tradition, and falling back on the absolutism of physical science ? The reason is, that German philosophy is the only school which recognizes spirit or mind, as an entity. " There is one mind," said Emerson, " common to all individual men." " I know only two things," said Wasson, " mind and matter; and it is the mind in the Universe which makes it go." Mind is the master and matter is the slave. The positivist affirms the opposite of this. He goes outside of himself, and takes his stand on *terra-firma*. He classifies all things as either animate or inanimate; but both to him are physical.   He cannot understand what constitutes the difference between these two, because he has gone out from himself, and left *spirit* behind him. He is like a man looking for his hat while it is on his head.

> " Thou seekest Him through globes and fires ?
> He is the essence that inquires."

The English utilitarian recognizes the existence of spirit, but treats the subject objectively, instead of subjectively, and by his doctrine of usefulness, a doctrine which cannot be carried to the length of self-renunciation, gives the dominion to physical causes.

The sentence which we have seen so often on the *Journal of Speculative Philosophy*, a saying of Novalis, " Philosophy can bake no bread, but it will give us God, freedom, and immortality," sounds the key-note of German metaphysics. It is based, as all constructive philosophy must be based, on the validity of consciousness. We know the world is real, and that life is not an empty dream, because we are conscious of its reality. We know that we possess freedom of choice and action, because we are concious of free-will. We believe that the soul is immortal, because we are conscious of ourselves as spiritual entities; and in like manner we are conscious of a central spiritual power, which we denominate God. As soon as we commence to doubt this, everything becomes unreal and the world goes to pieces before our eyes. A fact of consciousness can never be proved like a scientific fact. Endless discussions on the subject come to no result. We must either believe or disbelieve, as we do in religion.

Thus German metaphysics became the religious philosophy of the nineteenth century, as Platonism was the religious philosophy of the Greeks. Even Cardinal Newman is ready to admit the influence of Greek philosophy, and especially Platonism, on the first centuries of Christianity. This faith in the spiritual unseen, may not have an equal value with absolute truth, but it stands next to it; and there are many who will always believe that it has a greater value. There can be no doubt, for instance, that the influence of a belief in hell-fire on the barbarous Franks and Goths, when first converted to the Roman Church, was favorable and beneficial. The relation between Transcendentalism and Platonism is a very close one,—Emerson probably knew more of Plato than he did of Kant,—and if we go back two thousand years, we find in the

Vedas a religious philosophy of the same general character. Hegel says, " Since vastness of imagination is the true measure of poetry, if the form of these hymns were equal to the content, they would be the greatest of poems." Their grandeur is beyond question, though, as in all poetry, it requires imagination to appreciate this; but they are vague, cloudy, and almost incoherent to our modern sense. Dark and indefinite as they are in expression, here and there the light breaks through them, with such clear-shining intelligence that we seem to penetrate to the very *arcana* of creation. There are glorious vistas in them. The passage which has been rendered into modern verse, with the title of *Brahma*, still remains the noblest description of divine power in all ages. There is nothing in Dante or Milton to be compared with it for philosophic depth and pictorial grandeur. The rays of morning light which the Greeks called the arrows of Phœbus (shafts of intelligence slaying the monsters of darkness,—a figure which Carlyle makes use of) were a perpetual object of veneration with the Vedic poets, though they were not worshipped literally,—or at least not till the later traditional age,—but in their representative character. They are symbolized as the " fast-running hounds " and by other metaphors which seem to us curious enough. The disappearance of the sun in the west, and its re-appearance in the east, was a constant source of wonder to these primeval sages; as it well might be to any one who reflected on the subject, and was at the same time ignorant of physical causes. The fables by which they accounted for this are among the strangest and most monstrous in all mythology; but the fact evidently signified to them the conflict and triumph of the powers of light over darkness, or, carried a step further, of intelligence over ignorance and dullness. The Sanskrit *Devi*, which was collateral with *deus*, from which we derive *deity*, is derived from a root meaning bright or shining.

Nor does the fact appear improbable. The less the primitive man knew of natural causes, the nearer he would feel to the supreme power (if he once recognized it) which presides over nature, and which appeared to him in the lightning and the storm, the beneficent rain, and the deadly bite of the serpent. As these phenomena came gradually to have a physical aspect, and their action appeared more intelligible, he would lose that sense of deity, with which they were at first connected, until the undevout master of sciences ceases to find a deity anywhere in the universe. The philosopher, however, perceives in the correlation and conservation of forces that there must be an originating rationality at the other end of the chain; a mental power, immeasurable, but still like his own; and he returns at a single leap to the same point from which the Hindoo seer started in the dawn of civilization. Let us not forget, however, the words of the Psalmist, '' If I take unto myself the wings of the morning, and fly to the uttermost parts of the earth, lo! Thou art there ''; an apostrophe unequalled and unsurpassable.

Max Müller's various essays on Brahmanism and

the worship of Zoroaster form a *literature*, that might almost be called sacred literature, so pure are they in thought and expression, so comprehensive and impartial. The Orientals themselves might well feel grateful to have found so candid an interpreter of their creeds and rites. Not long since a venerable clergyman said to me, " Prof. Müller is not only an interesting writer, but he gives an elevated character to whatever topic he touches." In fact, he shows the finest qualities of a Christian.

One of his most valuable publications is the volume called *Science of Religion*, which also contains a treatise on Buddhism, and a translation of the Dhammapada, or Buddhist path of virtue. Traditional theologians were much disgusted at the title of the volume, but I never heard that they succeeded in discovering any flagrant heresy in it. Taking the religions of the world as an organic whole, even if we divide them into the primitive or natural, the idolatrous, and the revealed, certain underlying principles are discovered in them, which correspond to the principles which Müller has established in the *Science of Language ;* not that there is any correspondence between different languages and different religions, but as Müller makes out, the same process of generalization may be applied to both. This is his theory, and the natural result of taking so broad a survey of the subject; for the reflective mind will always seek points of similarity from which to deduce general laws. It is thus that the most important discoveries have been made.

If we look at the civilizations of Egypt, Palestine,

and Greece, and compare them with those of India, Persia, and China, the former have the same relation to the latter that a man's right hand bears to his left. We improve with our right hands continually, but the left always remain subordinate, and rarely attains an equal dexterity in any respect. The Egyptians, like the Brahmans, were polytheists, but the Persians were monotheists, though their religion had not the same elevation as that of the Jews, whose deity could not be expressed in outward form, or by a natural symbol. The Persians despised the polytheism of the Greeks, as monotheists always despise it. The correspondence between Buddhism and Christianity, even to the doctrine of the Immaculate Conception, is almost startling. It is, however, a negative correspondence, like the wrong side of a carpet, teaching a submissive goodness instead of active, energetic virtue. *Nirvana* is a negative heaven; the inactive goal of all human activity. Buddhism was the protest and reaction against the iron-bound traditionalism of the Hindoos; and like Christianity, it was cast out from the people among whom it originated, and adopted by alien races. While, however, the converts to Christianity were, if anything, superior to the Hebrews, the converts to Buddhism were decidedly inferior to the Aryan race from which it sprang. Whether its lack of progress is due to this fact, or is inherent in the character of the faith, it is not easy to decide. As Samuel Johnson says, "Modern European civilization is compounded of Christianity, the Roman Law, the Grecian art, and German manliness," while the

Buddhist races have only the advantage of a pure, but limited religious faith. The Dhammapada is an elevated gospel, so far as it goes, and contains much practical wisdom. It says, " Run not after the pleasures of love; in contemplation there is sufficient joy "; and those who have had experience can testify that there is no pleasure like reflection,—of thinking on elevated subjects.

We have not yet exhausted Plato and Aristotle. The idea contained in Plato's *forms*—that the form of an object, like a cup, for instance, is as real as the material of which it is made—is a lesson that ought to be taught to every school-boy. Aristotle believed that the ultimate reality is *self-activity;* and this is the problem which scientific men are now attempting to solve—the difference between animate and inanimate. The most powerful microscope, however, does not bring them any nearer to it than the naked eye; and it is safe to predict that it never will. Quite as deep a chasm exists between self-conscious and unconscious life. Of all the distinctions between man and brute, this is the primary and all-including. Only through self-consciousness could language become possible, and the origin of both language and consciousness is the most important problem that philosophers have now to deal with. It is the intellectual correlative of the Darwinian theory. I understand Prof. Müller's opinion to be, that language forms a barrier between man and brute that the latter, as such, will never be able to cross. This seems like an opposition to Darwinian evolution, and has brought him into conflict with the school of Huxley and Darwin, who wished to explain everything in nature by physical causes. At the same time Müller does not deny the probability of the human race being descended from even the ichthyosaurus. The distinction is a puzzling one, and to those who do not recognize Aristotle's *self-activity*, it seems like a contradiction.

J. K. Paine affirms that there is no music in nature; that the songs of birds are melodious, but they are not melody. When we think of it, it seems difficult to decide whether the song of a mocking-bird is music or not; but real music has a definite form and arrangement, to which the songs of birds do not correspond. The songs of mankind are not derived from birds, and they require a high degree of civilization. One is the result of nature and the other of art. There is a gap between the two of a hundred thousand years. Both kinds of singing are produced in the same manner, however; and so are the words of men and the cries of brutes. But the latter do not subserve the purpose of language in the smallest degree, for they are not intended for communication. This is the important point.

One of Emerson's fanciful notions was, that the time might come when we could communicate with birds and beasts as we do with one another. I think we already communicate with them, much more than they do with one another. The cries of animals express affection, pleasure, fear, and rage, and they are uttered simply as interjections. There is evidently more communication between an intelligent horse and his groom, than between two horses in the same pasture. If a calf is alarmed, it runs to the cow; not the cow to the calf. There are mice too shrewd and cunning to enter a trap, but they do not know how to prevent their own offspring from doing it. The instinct of animals is a wonderful thing, and among them all there is nothing more remarkable than the regulation in a hive of bees. Yet we can hardly suppose it owing to reason; and it is to be feared that many of the anecdotes illustrating the sagacity of animals, which Darwin collected, have an *ex parte* character.

If we take it for granted, or as already proven, that man is descended from the gorilla, the origin of consciousness and the origin of language still remain to be explained. Neither do I believe they can be explained by physical phenomena. To say that they are the natural concomitant of the physical change, might be called *stealing* the question. The gorilla still roams through the forests of Africa, without any need, and apparently without any desire, for a change in his condition. Do we not perceive in our own lives that the mental change always precedes the physical ? A young man finds that his arms are weak, and entertains an ambition for good muscular development. Nothing is easier than to obtain this if he is assiduous and persevering. Such is the history of civilization; but where does the impulse come from ? It is like the impulse of the poet or hero, and when it attains universal importance, we call it inspiration. It is easy to imagine that the first word was spoken from the urgent desire of a father to warn his family of approaching danger; or it may have been from the feeling of awe at some exceptional convulsion of nature. Whether the inspiration came from without, or was concealed in the germ of the earliest protoplasm, or earliest monad, it certainly was not a physical impulse. The voice of man is not like the sound of a hollow tree. If language originated, as Max Müller thinks, out of such cries as workmen make use of to one another, yet these cries are wholly different from the exclamations of animals. They have a deliberate *intention*, which the cries of animals never have. Children, and men under excitement, think aloud, and we may infer from this that in the beginning, thought and language came simultaneously. As it is now we do not wholly think in words, nor are we able to think without them.

This may seem like a digression, but it was necessary in order to make the character of Prof. Müller's work intelligible, and to explain his position in the intellectual life of the century. Although he has excited strong opposition, standing almost alone among academic men, his influence has been second to that of few. The number of sermons that have been constructed from his *Chips from a German Workshop* would be almost beyond estimate—and so much the better. Thus his ideas and rare information have been scattered broadcast over the Anglo-Saxon world. He has been looked upon as a dangerous Radical by some, and by others he has been considered the enemy of progress; but he has held his course consistently to his own thought and belief, for forty years, without swerving from the ideal of high-minded scholarship, which he set for himself in the beginning.   Like Froude he has considered that his business in life was to extend the knowledge of mankind, and not to waste time in fruitless controversies.   When he has found occasion to answer his opponents, his replies have been spirited and entertaining.   His final retort to Prof. W. D. Whitney caused amusement, even at Yale University, where public opinion was naturally in favor of its own *savant*.   As the venerable clergyman said, " Whitney and Müller did not disagree so much, as Prof. Whitney supposed." *

If we were to quarrel with Max Müller on any one point, it would be on his opinion that nationality is the result of a common language.   This is so near the truth, that we have to admit that nationality is impossible without a common language; but if we look at it from the other side, we see that it is nationality, and that only, which gives language a definite form, merging a number of similar dialects into a common vernacular.   The two are inseparable, though it is true that a language may survive after its nationality has become extinct.   A common descent, however, and community of interests, also have their share in constituting nationality. The French have many of the same traits now, which Cæsar describes as belonging to the Gauls, and yet the Gallic race has changed its language twice since that time.   The Irish race in Great Britain, America,

* However, as an English reviewer noticed, we should always remember the priority of Professor Müller's work.

and Australia constitute a nationality of their own. They have a language of their own, but comparatively few of them speak it. In this country they do not consider themselves Americans, and though they take an interest in national affairs it is only for the benefit of their own race. There is something in the nature of language which defies analysis It is the most ingenious of human inventions, and yet it seems like a natural growth.

Professor Müller is now engaged upon a large work on mythology, but he doubts if his time will be extended until he can finish it. " I have spent my life," he says, " in quarrying a big stone—the translation of *The Vedas;* but it has made a slave of me and cost me dear. Now I want to say a few things, but I fear it is too late.

" I have always remained a German; but I have never regretted pitching my tent in England. I have lived here till over seventy without being interfered with. I consider England a *sine qua non* of Europe."

MATTHEW ARNOLD

WHEN we were boys at school in Concord we read, at Emerson's suggestion, a book by Thomas Hughes, called *School Days at Rugby ;* much the best book of its kind that has yet appeared in English. In it there was a character different from all the rest, a boy named Arthur, of a poetic nature, and superior to his companions in sincerity and purity of manners. When the sequel to *School Days at Rugby* was published, we missed Arthur in its *dramatis personæ*, and regretted that he had disappeared from our view. I have long supposed that this high-minded youth, who assisted Dr. Arnold in reforming Tom Brown, was intended for Dr. Arnold's own son, who must have been at school at about the same time with Thomas Hughes.

Very few of the external facts of Matthew Arnold's life have yet been made public. In the necrology of the London *Times* for 1888, his name appears as the most distinguished of that year. We only learn that he was born in 1822; that he studied at Laleham and Rugby; that he was chosen a Fellow of Oriel at Oxford; that he served the Marquis of Lansdowne for a time as private secretary; was appointed on a commission to examine the systems of education in France and Germany; and suddenly fell dead in the streets of Liverpool on the 15th of April. The *Times* did not notice the fact that Arnold had been professor of poetry at Oxford for nearly twenty years; a position comparable to that held by James Russell Lowell at Harvard University. Perhaps it was more than comparable; for while Lowell only delivered a few lectures on literature to the students during the spring term, Arnold's duties extended during the whole academic year.

He belonged to the same class of minds as Lowell and David A. Wasson, and it is difficult to say which of the two he most nearly resembled. He was more like Lowell in his poetry and like Wasson in his prose, without being as witty as Lowell or as profound as Wasson. He also resembled Emerson in his earnestness and his practical adaptation to the needs of his time. While he united in himself the best qualities of these three, he scarcely equalled them in their several excellencies. He certainly had not the moral power of Emerson, or the contemplative depth of Wasson.

He began life as a critical poet and ended it as a poetical critic. We are reminded of this by his statement that poetry is at heart a criticism of life. It was the freshness and beauty of his early poems that first gave him distinction. He called them new poems; and certainly they are new, fresh, and original. They contained no hackneyed phraseology—there is nothing in them about the oak and the ivy, or the canker in the rose, or like Byron's " thy dear hands still clasped in mine." Exceptional words are introduced it is true, but always in just the right manner. They are simple and yet intellectual. What they lack is eloquence; and it is remarkable that without this they should have become popular. If there is an exception it is *Sohrab and Rustum*—a battle-piece with its tragic termination, which has something of the grandeur and elevation of Milton. His *Tristram and Iseult* is also a most interesting treatment of that oft-repeated tale; full of tenderness and brilliant glimpses of mediæval life. None of his poems, however, make an impression like Coleridge's *Ancient Mariner*, or Emerson's *Problem*.

Now the manner in which Matthew Arnold made use of his popularity and influence gives the key-note of his character and his writing. In his essay on a *French Eton*, he praises Father Lacordaire for absenting himself from France at the height of his celebrity, and devoting himself to missionary work in other countries. This is what Arnold did himself, with an improvement on his predecessor. He discontinued writing poetry, considering, like Carlyle, that there was more important work to be done; and he became a self-appointed censor of public morals, than which nothing was more likely to stir up public animosity against him. Yet he went about this in such an intrepid manner, with such amiability, and in so impartial a spirit, that where he lost his admirers by it he gained substantial friends. The true strength of England resides not in her wealth, nor in her control of the sea, so much as in the national respect for manliness and character; and Matthew Arnold received full credit for his moral fearlessness. When, in 1886, a London paper made the experiment of a trial vote for members of an English Academy, based on the principles of the French Academy, Matthew Arnold's name stood third upon the list; Gladstone being first, and Tennyson second. Nevertheless he continued on the unpopular side, and never retreated from his independent position.

He constructed his platform on a broad basis—on the basis of impartiality. He would not criticise from any one standpoint, but looked at a subject from all standpoints. He would even run the risk of being unpatriotic in order to be just. This was the ideal method which Matthew Arnold has unfolded to us in his essay on the function of criticism; and though he finally fell somewhat short of this, it cannot be denied that he made a brave effort to realize his plan. When employed on the educational commission, he perceived that the system of education in Germany was, as a whole, superior to that in England, and that there were points in French education which might be considered to advantage by both nations. On his return he stated these facts, with suitable arguments, frankly and boldly, in a report which has become an historical document. So he laid down the rule that a literary critic who is only acquainted with the literature of his own country may almost be said to be acquainted with none. If he is an Englishman he should also know French and German literature, and if possible

Italian and Spanish. The danger always is, that he will take his own time and country as a measure for all things. He should go to the best classic periods; nor even accept these as absolute. In fact, it is only by avoiding everything like dogmatism that the critic's work can become of service to his time and generation. The poet, the orator, and the statesman may be partisan and prejudiced; but the critic who does not rise above party passion fails from the start. He must try to divest himself even of hereditary tendencies. He must separate himself from his surroundings, and regard them from an external point of view; as one who is departing on a sea voyage looks back on the country he has left. This gives his vocation a noble and elevated character. The true critic thus comes to be the equal of poets and orators, by rising above them in this one respect. We are not troubled by Shakespeare's injustice to Joan of Arc, or Hawthorne's contempt for John Brown, as we should if Lowell or Matthew Arnold had expressed such opinions.

It is very difficult to maintain this perfect equilibrium of thought and feeling, and it necessitates a life of constant self-denial. Matthew Arnold says, that he who would see things as they are in themselves, will soon find himself one of a very small company. Those who have attempted this can bear witness to it; but if their associates are few, and they separate themselves in a manner from the sympathy of mankind, their intellectual horizon is widened immensely. He who has attained the intellectual centre of the universe finds the world greatly changed for him,

Burdens are lifted from his shoulders, animosities and antagonisms vanish into thin air; what seemed before ugly and deformed, becomes, if not beautiful, at least interesting; he finds peace and repose where there was strife and vexation. There is no escape from disappointments; there will be disappointments in the future but like those of the past: but it is a breaking of false idols, and an escape from delusions.

Matthew Arnold defines the function of criticism as " an effort to discover and celebrate the best that is thought and known in the world." This lifts the profession at once above all carping and small fault-finding. The genuine critic is a truth-seeker quite as much as the devotee of science is. Among the enormous quantity of chaff which is thrown upon the public, he should be always on the watch to detect anything of real value, and to distinguish it from that which is cheap and commonplace. He should also remember Lessing's suggestion of a review for forgotten books, and on fit occasions endeavor to revive an interest in them. It is not always the stars of the first magnitude which are most interesting to astronomers: those which have no popular names are sometimes quite as important as Rigel or Arcturus. Critics are the proper guardians of literature, and they should never cease to call attention to that in the past which is positively great; for otherwise it is too likely to be forgotten; and they should be equally persistent in demanding that the future shall improve upon the present.

Nothing is more interesting than good literary

criticism, and yet how little there is of it. After we have visited a foreign country we read with eagerness anything that will recall its customs, scenery, or art. After we have studied *Faust* or the *Inferno* we wish to know how such mighty works have impressed the minds of others; but where can we find vitally appreciative commentaries on either ? None such are at least accessible to the English-speaking public. We like to read criticisms on works of art, as we do to hear the praises of an absent friend.

Such then are the cardinal points in his essay on the *Function of Criticism;* and he illustrates them by a number of essays in the same volume on French, German, and even Latin authors. This is the best book that Matthew Arnold ever published, and it were well if more heed were given to it than now is or has been. Like his poetry, his prose (though there are beautiful passages in it) never quite reaches eloquence, but he atones for this by his clear-sighted penetration. If he does not always touch bottom, he at least swims in pretty deep water. His earnestness and sincerity are everywhere conspicuous: above all his friendliness to his subject. He does not write such clear English as Froude, but his style is pleasant, and encourages the reader to turn over fresh pages. It is true he has something of Macaulay's habit of repetition, but he makes a better use of it; not to produce a cumulative rhetorical effect, but to impress the reader with some particular statement which he considers of exceptional value.

In regard to exceptional writers of slender fame, Matthew Arnold says :

" Now in literature, besides the eminent men of genius, who have had their deserts in the way of fame, besides the eminent men of ability who have often had far more than their deserts in the way of fame, there are a certain number of personages who have been really men of genius,—by which I mean, that they have had a genuine gift for what is true and excellent, and are therefore capable of emitting a life-giving stimulus,—but who, for some reason or other, in most cases for very valid reasons, have remained obscure, nay, beyond a narrow circle in their own country, unknown. It is salutary from time to time to come across a genius of this kind, and to extract his honey."

When we read this in the light of Matthew Arnold's popularity, the lines become illuminated, and we perceive between them an earnest desire to celebrate those whose merit has escaped the caprice of popular attention. The love of justice is the noblest quality in man, and the best argument of his immortality. It is also the parent and fountain-head of earnestness, from which we derive immortality on earth. Was it not the foundation originally of the Roman Law and the Roman Empire ?

Perhaps the finest of these lay sermons is the one on Marcus Aurelius, of whom Arnold writes in the true vein of a poet '' who loves another's song more than his own singing.'' The nature of this remarkable man, of whom it has been admitted that he was the one person fit to rule the world, and combined in himself the finest qualities of the saint and the statesman, was particularly attractive to Matthew Arnold. He quotes from his contemplations again

and again, until the measure of his essay is full, preferring to let the hero-sage speak for himself, rather
than to be his interpreter.   Finally he concludes:

" In general, the action he prescribes is action which
every sound nature must recognize as right, and the motives he assigns are motives which every clear reason
must recognize as valid. . . . Yet no, it is not on
this account that noble souls love him most ; it is rather
because of the emotion which gives to his voice so touch-
ing an accent ; it is because he, too, yearns as they do, for
something unattained by him. What an affinity for
Christianity had this persecutor of the Christians ! What
would he have said to the Sermon on the Mount and the
twenty-sixth chapter of St. Matthew ? Vain question !
Yet the greatest charm of Marcus Aurelius is that he
makes us ask it. We see him wise, just, self-governed,
tender, thankful, blameless ; yet, with this, agitated,
stretching out his arms for something beyond."

Arnold makes a mistake, however, when he blames
Aurelius for not having greater influence over his
son, and moulding him to better purposes. It is
part of the irony of nature that high-minded men
should beget base children; and it was chiefly because Aurelius was so far above Commodus that he
had so little influence over him.

We notice his opinion (or Joubert's) of Madame
de Staël, that she had more vehemence than truth,
and more heat than light.   Schiller wrote to Goethe,
'' what we call poetry does not exist for Madame de
Staël.''

The chapter on translating Homer does not properly belong with *Essays in Criticism*, and was omitted from a subsequent edition. This may have happened from the complaints that were made that Matthew Arnold, after declaiming against English Philistines, had proved himself in his argument against Francis Newman's translation to be also something of a Philistine. For Newman himself, Arnold had felt always a filial respect; but he believed that his translation of the *Iliad* was grounded on erroneous principles, and he did not hesitate to expose this. In truth, he carried the matter to an extreme, and does not appear like a considerate friend. His enemies exaggerated this small fault, and never ceased to harp on it; so that even now if Matthew Arnold's name is mentioned in any small company, some one will be likely to say, " I think he was a good deal of a Philistine himself "; the real objection in the mind of that person being something else.

Whether Matthew Arnold's theory in regard to translating Homer in English hexameters can be made to hold water, is yet to be proved. To judge by the extracts of his own which he has left to us it is much to be regretted that he did not attempt the work himself. Chapman's translation of the *Iliad* is thus far the most poetic, but it suffers from the involved phraseology of the Elizabethan period; Pope's is equally spirited, and more readable, but lacks gracefulness, and repose; Lord Derby's comes more closely to the original sense, but it is not poetic. The passages Matthew Arnold has translated for us, are, however, free from those objections; and I have always felt that they were the only adequate rendering of Homer's language and style to be met with in English.   They possess the particular merit of being more like Homer than they are like Matthew Arnold; whereas, with Chapman, Pope, Newman, and Derby it is just the reverse.   Consider this piece of scenic description, in which Homer compares the fires of the Trojans to the stars in the sky.   Matthew Arnold considered the first portion of this passage too difficult for him, but he has rendered the last six lines with Homer's beautiful plainness:

" So shone forth, in front of Troy, by the bed of the Xanthus.
  Between that and the ships, the Trojans' numerous fires.
  In the plain there were kindled a thousand fires : by each one
  There sat fifty men, in the ruddy light of the fire :
  By their chariots stood the steeds and champed the white barley,
  While their masters sat by the fire and waited for Morning."

This is pleasant to the ear, and stimulating to the imagination; which are the two prerequisites of good poetry.   An English critic, Joseph Jacobs, doubts if there exists such a metre as English hexametre.   Could he have been oblivious to Longfellow's *Evangeline*; if this short passage did not satisfy him ?

Emerson's essays are interesting from the freshness of his thought, but Matthew Arnold's from the fulness of his scholarship.   The former stimulate like mountain air, and the latter are as refreshing as a sea-breeze in August.   A first-rate scholar may be the most interesting or the most tiresome of men, according to the character of his studies, and the spirit in which he deals with them. Matthew Arnold was a born investigator; he wished to know what the world is made of. So long as he lived he continued to read, study, and inquire. He subscribed to French and German newspapers such as were otherwise unknown in England; he read foreign periodicals of all kinds, and mixed with all classes of people, continually trying to learn what their intellectual life might be, and what were the tendencies of their thoughts and wishes. Like the Caliph of Bagdad, he likéd to travel in a disguise which any man may assume in our time, the disguise of an amiable gentleman, and to talk with people who could not know of his celebrity.

For his enthusiastic admirers he had small indulgence, and social entertainments easily wearied him. The Longfellow party met Matthew Arnold wandering about Italy in 1869, and found little satisfaction in him; but some time afterward two American clergymen, voyaging up the Rhine, made the acquaintance of a gentleman from London, with whom they talked over social and political problems of the time, and spent a very pleasant day with him. As he was about to take leave of them he remarked, " About a month ago I was in Switzerland and spent an evening at Lucerne with a gentleman who held nearly the same ideas on these subjects that you do. I did not know who he was at the time, but next day the people informed me that it was Matthew Arnold."

There appears to have been a gradual change in Matthew Arnold from poetry to literary prose, and from that to politics and sociology. He wrote constantly for the magazines, but published few books. His volume of *Mixed Essays* appeared about twelve years after the *Essays in Criticism*, and as literature it indicated a slight falling off, both in style and temper. The book is a mixture of literary and political discussions. It is the inevitable fate of a critic to become with years more fastidious, more suspicious of excellence, and ever more difficult to please. The essay on " Democracy," with which this later series begins, is one of the fairest, most impartial reviews of that political doctrine that has ever been published; but what he calls French criticism of Goethe is equally narrow and unsympathetic.

We all have our individual tastes in arts and poetry, but it seems as if much of Matthew Arnold's later criticism was capricious, if not prejudiced. We in America think of Whittier's pretty school-mate rather as the friendly spectre of his verses, and Matthew Arnold's Boston audience smiled at his judgment that Whittier's *School Days* was worth the whole body of Emerson's verse. This was a *non sequitur* which did not require Doctor Holmes's cutting exposure to make it plain to us. Of similar tone was Arnold's unfavorable commentary on Shelley, published soon afterward in an English magazine. Shelley was not the greatest poet of the century, but he is worth his reputation, and here and there in his verses there are touches of true grandeur. Why not let him flourish, and permit his fond admirers to enjoy his poetry unmolested ?

In his *Mixed Essays* Matthew Arnold has apparently joined hands with a French critic, M. Scherer, in an ill-disguised attack on Milton and Goethe. We do not find Scherer to be a profound or luminous writer, but rather ingenious and superficial. What value can we place on a criticism which condemns *Hermann and Dorothea*, the world's finest pastoral, as a cold, eclectic work ? Neither does he speak more favorably of *Tasso* and *Iphigenia*, which for pure classic beauty are at least the rivals of *Samson Agonistes*. He says of the autobiography, '' when Goethe goes in for being tiresome he does it with a vengeance.'' It is to be feared that the battle of Sedan had much to do with this unfavorable judgment; and if Matthew Arnold did not approve of it he should have made a suitable protest at the time. It is with regret that we meet him in such company.

In his *Discourses in America*, Matthew Arnold appears again in a more favorable light, and as it were renews the vigor and freshness of his earlier work. He is not as careful of his English as he might have been, and each of these essays has some special point of weakness; but they are replete with passages of lofty thought and fine discrimination. Even the lecture on Emerson, which is the least satisfactory, opens with an intellectual vista rarely beautiful and significant. There was a discussion going on at that time in regard to the respective value of classical and scientific study, and into this he entered with all the ardor of a young debater. '' The final value of all study,'' he said, '' must be its effect on *character*"; a proposition which, although used in the interest of the classics, may be said to have a scientific value. An equally valuable statement is his distinction, in the lecture on *Numbers*, between true and false patriotism, though he does not give us credit for the political organization which makes great numbers possible.

The little volume named *Friendship's Garland* might have been called the Book of Philistines, and though rather sensitive in places, contains some keen political satire; especially his presentation of Dr. Russell of the London *Times*, formerly known in America as " Bull Run " Russell, whom Matthew Arnold boldly describes mounting his war-horse with the assistance of the German Emperor, while Bismarck holds the bridle and the Crown Prince is patting the animal on the flank. Such a caricature is rather startling, even when well deserved. Matthew Arnold's modern Arminius would make the London *Times* and *Telegraph* responsible in part for the Franco-Prussian war; but I have never encountered a Prussian so blunt and slashing as Arminius is represented. They are a frank people, but prudent in speech.

The purity of motive, which is essential to a poet, often enables him to see more clearly into public affairs than those who make politics their business. Matthew Arnold was remarkable for this. His writings on political subjects have not only an elevated tone, but they show a clear comprehension of the case before him. [He appears to have always been on the right side. He did not follow Gladstone in eulogizing Jefferson Davis in 1861, but, like John Bright and a few others, gave his moral support to the Union cause. ⸣ In 1886 he perceived at once that Gladstone's scheme for the settlement of the Irish question was one which could bring no lasting good to that country, and was such a measure as a majority of the English people would never support. His own proposition, that Ireland should be divided into states, such as we have in America, each with a legislature of its own and representatives in Parliament, commends itself to every prudent and sensible mind.   At that time the same writers here who advocated free-trade for America were clamoring for protection for Ireland.   What Matthew Arnold said of Gladstone, that he had no foresight because he lacked insight, was generally true.

The dangers which he foresaw from Democracy are such as appertain rather to the present French government, which is more highly centralized than any European government except the Russian, and in which public opinion acts too rapidly and violently, than to a government of checks and balances like our own.   The more serious danger, which he finds applicable to all popular governments, is the difficulty in maintaining a high national ideal.

" Nations are not truly great," he says, " because the individuals composing them are numerous, free, and active ; but they are great when these numbers, this freedom, and this activity, are employed in the service of an ideal higher than that of an ordinary man, taken by himself. Our society is probably destined to become much more democratic. Who or what will give a high tone to the nation then ? That is the grave question."

Arnold's critical essays on civilization in America present a curious discrepancy, which illustrates how large a share the personal element sometimes claimed in his opinions. His first essay on this country was in a measure contradicted by the second, and that in turn by the third.

Lowell was so often disappointed in his hope of finding an Englishman who could understand America, that he finally concluded that it was no use for them to try to understand us. The reason for this, however, is not remote. We have a class of people in New York and Boston not to be met with in other countries, who spend every alternate year in Europe, and who naturally lose much of their affection for, and interest in, their native land. An English traveller of note coming to the United States inevitably falls into their hands. His banker belongs to this class of people, and very likely he has been acquainted with others in Europe. So he is handed about from one to another, and after some months returns to England without seeing anything of genuine American life. When Prof. Tyndall came to Boston it was some weeks before he could discover where his friends and admirers were to be found; and Thomas Hughes complained that the people he met in America did not appreciate Lowell's poetry. Matthew Arnold's first essay on America was incautiously based on the statements of the New York *Nation*, an English paper with a foreign editor transplanted to American soil, for the benefit of this half-foreign population.

The first essay on America, therefore, was what might have been expected, considering the sources from which it came. Matthew Arnold culled from the *Nation* the following statement, which he used as the major premise for a lengthy argument:

" In America, scarcely any man who can afford it likes to refuse his son a college education if the boy wants it ; but probably not one boy in a thousand can say five years after graduating, that he has been helped by his college education in making his start in life. It may have been never so useful to him as a means of moral and intellectual culture, but it has not helped to adapt him to the environment in which he has to live and work ; or, in other words, to a world in which not one man in a hundred thousand has either the manners or cultivation of a gentleman, or changes his shirt more than once a week, or eats with a fork."

Now " world " in this connection must be intended for the United States, for otherwise the passage would have no sense, and it was so that Matthew Arnold understood it. We may not like to hold an editor responsible for everything that appears in his columns; but this looks too much like a libel on a sober and cleanly people. The true cause of the difficulty is that too many of our young men go to college without considering sufficiently what they will do next.

Matthew Arnold was not the man to be tied down by letters of introduction. As soon as he arrived in

America he began to look around for himself, and to make his own investigations. The results he obtained were in marked contrast to the opinions he had previously formed of us. He discovered that the people of the United States were at least an ingenious, frank, manly, and generous race. He saw that our government had been framed with great skill, and was suited to the conditions of the country; and that we felt free and unconstrained in our social and political life. He saw, also, that the Anglo-Saxon race, in crossing the Atlantic, had escaped from a large encumbrance of mediæval conditions, which still fetter the activity of European nations. He considered it a decided advantage, that the distinctions of classes in America are neither arbitrary nor stereotyped. Americans, he says, think straight to their object, and see it clearly.

In a second visit to this country he was not so fortunate. His health was bad, and he knew that his time on earth was limited. This, perhaps, gave his thoughts a gloomy caste, and the antagonism of the newspapers to his views in regard to Ireland, irritated him. As he had previously represented the bright side, so now he dwelt more earnestly on the unfavorable side of American life,—for there is an unfavorable side in all times and countries. The essay, however, was hypercritical, and of a despondent tone. Many of his complaints were in respect to matters of trifling importance. It is true that great quantities of unripe fruit are sold in America, but the reason is that the laboring classes in this country can afford to purchase fruit, which they are not able to do in Europe; and Matthew Arnold was mistaken in supposing that peaches raised under glass are better than those which ripen in the open air. I have heard other Englishmen express this opinion, but there is no comparison so far as flavor is concerned.

In what he said of our newspapers, however, there was only too much truth. He does not appear to have read our best periodicals. The New York *Times* is better than the London *Times*, and the New York *Tribune* will compare favorably with the London *Daily News;* the Boston *Transcript*, the Providence *Journal*, and the Philadelphia *Ledger* are excellent newspapers; and there are others also which deserve respect; but there are a multitude of cheap, licentious, rowdy papers published here, such as are not to be met with in France, Germany, or England. They are a disgrace to the country, debilitating the minds of our young men, and vulgarizing our women, with unspeakable trash. Since the Roman amphitheatre there has been no such engine of public demoralization as the Sunday newspaper. It replaces religious worship and serious reading with the most frivolous of conceivable entertainments. If we are to take our choice between the Sunday newspaper and the prize-ring, by all means let prize-fighting flourish.

Immediately after Matthew Arnold's death, all the living poets in Great Britain, with the exception of Tennyson, met together and united in a request that he should have a monument in Westminster Abbey. We all feel that he deserved this. He was the apostle of intellectual culture, as distinguished from mere scholarship and erudition.   He belonged to the simple and refined civilization of the future; and his writings will continue valuable, until the slowly gravitating world has come round to his position.

APPENDIX

A

It is remarkable that a scholarly gentleman, who has given us such fine poetry as James Russell Lowell, should not have written more graceful and elegant prose ; as his friend Cranch remarked, his style is labored, his sentences frequently long-winded, and his choice of words not such as would seem to indicate an artistic discrimination. Such expressions as, " The preacher up of sincerity " and, " The oddity becomes odder," would certainly suffer correction at the hands of a professor of English in a college theme. Nor is this the whole of it. As a literary critic he was perhaps without a superior, but he was often tempted to deal with subjects of which he knew too little to do them moderate justice. His essay on Lincoln and his criticism of Carlyle's *Frederick* are instances in point.

Frederick deserved the admiration of his age, and we should not think less of him because he was born on a throne. He was a king not only by hereditary but natural right,—if there be such a thing. Lowell says that " he looked on Prussia as his patrimony, of which not even his subjects had the right to dispossess him " ; but, to judge from his actions, Frederick did not consider the kingdom of Prussia as so much property that he could dispose of as he pleased. He treated it rather after the fashion of the good servant who was entrusted with the ten talents of gold, and who gained with them other ten talents. He called himself "the humble servant of the state," a title quite equal to that of Webster's "servant of the people." The population of Prussia was quadrupled in his lifetime.

"He was not so great a soldier as Napoleon," said Minister Bancroft, "but a much better statesman." At the close of the second Silesian war, when he had defeated Austria and Saxony in four brilliant engagements, and was applied to for terms of peace, Frederick replied, "I want nothing of you but peace." It would have been better for Napoleon perhaps if he had sometimes made the same conditions. Lowell thinks Frederick was a better general than Wellington but not equal to Turenne, and that "he succeeded chiefly from the weakness of his adversaries"; that to compare him with Cæsar and Alexander was ridiculous; and that "the fact that one of his intimate friends called him an 'old tyrant,' is worth considering."

It is not customary to compare modern generals with ancient, since the discovery of gunpowder has so completely changed the art of war; but it is customary among writers on military affairs to place Frederick next to Napoleon, on account of the number of his campaigns, the novelty of his tactics, and the decisiveness of his victories. For six years he was obliged to contend against forces three or four times greater than his own, well trained and disciplined, and commanded, if not by *the* greatest generals, yet by officers of no mean ability. Count Daun was the Fabius of Austria, and General Loudon might well be compared with Lee or Sheridan. Such a long stretch of camp life necessarily had a brutalizing effect on Frederick (and Napoleon also suffered from it), but he remained to the last an indefatigable worker, and lover of justice.

Lowell considers Frederick's preference for French literature, and contempt for German writers of his time, superficial and unpatriotic ; but Goethe thinks that he accomplished by this a great deal of good, calling the attention of his countrymen to a class of virtues as different as possible from their own. The writings of Frederick himself, especially his poetry, have little enough value, but his interest in literature and in the advancement of science will always be a credit to him.

APPENDIX

B

Froude's American Critics.

The Irish take a natural pride in the fact that Roman civilization survived in Ireland during the dark ages, after it had been crushed out in Britain and Gaul. They did not like, therefore, Froude's picture of mediæval Ireland, and while he was lecturing in America an Irish priest named Burke attacked him with a series of articles in newspapers and magazines; while Wendell Phillips, who was irritated by Froude's animadversions on O'Connell, joined in the conflict. The hotel waiters also mutinied and refused to serve Mr. Froude.

Burke's criticism was finally published in a book, and is now chiefly valuable for its evidence in favor of Froude's theory of the Irish character. His argument is heated and blustering, and the following extract is a fair specimen of it :

" Mr. Froude says : ' I hold the Catholic Church accountable for all the blood that the Duke of Alva shed in the Netherlands ' ; and I say to Mr. Froude I deny it. Alva fought in the Netherlands against the subjects that rebelled against Spain. Alva fought in the Netherlands against a people, the first principle of whose new religion seemed to be an uprising against the authority of the state. With Alva

335

or his state questions the Catholic Church had nothing to do; and if Alva shed the blood of rebels, and if those who rebelled happened to be Protestants, that is no reason to father the shedding of that blood upon the Catholic Church."

We wonder what Father Burke would say to the Thirty Years' War : whether he would say *that* was caused by the opposition of the German states to the authority of the emperor. While Froude was fighting Burke and Phillips he was assailed in the rear by a more dangerous enemy, the editor of the *Nation*, who was not generally known to be an Irishman, and whose statements, therefore, escaped from the suspicion of party prejudice. The *Nation* summed up its review with the defiant assertion that Father Burke had not left Froude a leg to stand on ; and educated people, supposing the editor was an Englishman, looked on this as good authority.

E. A. Freeman.

In an obituary notice of James A. Froude, published in the London *Times* of October 22, 1894, I find the following statement :

" The feeling which these men, and others, entertained for Froude was one of the most pronounced hostility, and in Freeman's case it continued till his death, some five-and-thirty years after the appearance of the first volumes of the *History*. For years and years at regular intervals, the columns of the *Saturday Review* contained Freeman's attack upon Froude, in which his blunders of fact were castigated as if they had been offences against the fundamental laws of morals. Freeman, indeed, always maintained that they were ; and that Froude either did not know the difference between truth and falsehood, or wilfully ignored it."

This reminds us of the Müller and Whitney controversy, which was carried on about the same time and in a similar manner, in which Professor Whitney played the same part as Mr. Freeman. People do not like such obstinate reiteration, and Mr. Freeman would have done better to have adopted different tactics.

When Henry Adams was professor of English at Harvard University, he gave his class Freeman's text-book on early English history, with a sort of apology for it that it was the only one to be had. His students, looking up subjects at the college library, discovered a number of errors or misstatements that Mr. Freeman had made; while the professor himself was only too well pleased to expose the unpractical character of Mr. Freeman's political ideas. It would seem doubtful if Freeman were more accurate than Froude.

The letters on historical subjects written by Mr. Freeman for the Boston *Transcript* in 1888 were of the same illogical and inexperienced character. Mr. Freeman's researches will always have a substantial value, but, so far as the understanding of history is concerned, he is, compared with Froude, merely an undergraduate. The character of Froude's opponents is as significant as the intellectual quality of his friends, Carlyle, Max Müller, and Mathew Arnold.

Mr. Freeman is reported to have given an opinion that the proper cure for the political troubles in the United States, would be for every Irishman to kill a negro and be hung for it. As Professor Adams used to say, "I make no comment."

INDEX.

www.ingramcontent.com/pod-product-compliance
Lightning Source LLC
Chambersburg PA
CBHW021748110726
47902CB00006B/1441